THE MAIN CAGES

By the same author

A FAR COUNTRY: TRAVELS IN ETHIOPIA
THE CROSSING PLACE: A JOURNEY AMONG
THE ARMENIANS
THE BRONSKI HOUSE
THE SPIRIT-WRESTLERS: AND OTHER SURVIVORS
OF THE RUSSIAN CENTURY

THE MAIN CAGES

PHILIP MARSDEN

Flamingo

An Imprint of HarperCollins*Publishers*

Flamingo
An Imprint of HarperCollins*Publishers*
77–85 Fulham Palace Road,
Hammersmith, London W6 8JB

The HarperCollins website address is
www.**fire**and**water**.co.uk

Published by Flamingo 2002

A catalogue record for this book
is available from the British Library

ISBN 0 00 713639 0

Set in Stempel Garamond by
Rowland Phototypesetting Limted,
Bury St Edmunds, Suffolk

Printed and bound in Great Britain by
Clays Ltd, St Ives plc

For my grandfather
JG Le NK
and
Zofia Ilińska

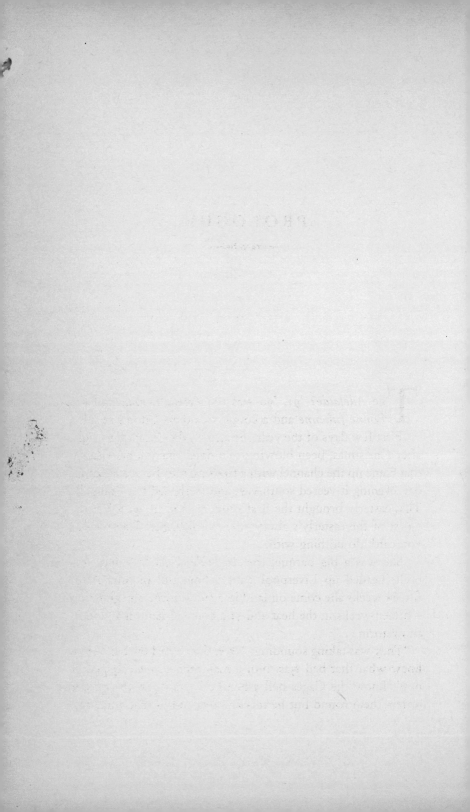

PROLOGUE

'The *Adelaide*? '91. '90 was the *Prima Donna* and the *Bonne Julienne* and a couple of others I don't recall.

'First few days of the year she struck, they dead days right after Christmas, been blowing two days straight, an easterly that come up the channel with a freezing mist before it. Saturday evening it veered south-east and freshened to a full gale. That easterly brought the first snow we had in years but the worst of the easterly's always the run it brings. Damn swell you can't do nothing with.

'She was a big barque, the *Adelaide*. Steel hull and new built, headed up Liverpool with a hold full of jute. After fifteen weeks she come on land in a snowstorm. Imagine that – fifteen weeks in the heat and you come to land in a bloody snowstorm . . .

'They was taking soundings when they heard the bell. They knew what that bell was. Not a man who's sailed this coast don't know the Cages bell when he hears it. So the master orders them round but he misses stays and in that wind and they seas he didn't stand a chance of getting free. Just out from Hemlock Cove, they struck the edge of the reef square on.

'We was all down at the hall that night, Freeman Rooms, listening to a speaker. Colonel'd been staying up Dormullion but the weather was so bad he couldn't get back and he was telling us about Africa or someplace. Anyway that's where we was when the maroons went up. No one spoke a word. We're off like long dogs to the station and of course the whole bloody audience follow us and that poor wretched colonel's left talking to an empty hall.

'In they days the boat was the *Eliza Jane* – pulling she was, just paddles and a pair of great heavy drop keels. Couple of the launch crew heaved open the doors and the noise hit us with the wind. I never heard such a noise. The sea against the piles of the slipway and some bloody howling easterly and a biting wind with thick snow in it. The crew was picked and we checked the gear and got on board, ten of we oarsmen and the cox and a couple of others and still none of us saying a word. So we're sitting there and each of us takes hold of the gunwale and there's snow all around and we're sitting waiting for the launch.

'Cox was Sam Tyler and he was standing in the stern looking out over us and listening to the wind and trying to get the seas and it's still not too late for him to stop. But we saw him nod to Joshua Ball and take his seat at the helm.

'That time the slip was new, roller-slip built just six months, and Joshua Ball was on the hard below us. He took away the strops and looked down at the surf. Once he's knocked that pin out the chain drops and there's nothing you can do. That's the moment you dread – once you're gone you're gone but it's the waiting that gets to you and it's his decision when to launch. Someone asks where the service's to and Tyler says in from the Cages and we're all thinking what'd that be like in an easterly like this.

'Josh knocks out the pin and the boat starts on her rollers, slow at first and then faster and all of we waiting for the bows to strike. We faced astern and that night I could see old Josh at the top of the slip getting smaller, with his hammer and the chain on the ground by his feet. He had the face of the hangman watching us go out in that.

'Well we hit the water and pulled like hell. Got through the short seas into deeper water. Wasn't too bad in the bay. There was great big swells but long and they weren't breaking and we soon forgot the cold pulling as we were. Once out of the bay we hit the wind full on and the seas right above us. The very first one of they seas pushed up our bows and we was looking down on the cox, then the next he was up above us like we was on a bloody seesaw.

'At night in a sea you never know the one that'll break and swamp you. You don't see it – but you can hear it. At first he's distant – then he comes full and heavy above the noise of the wind and you can hear the size of him in the sound. Then one astern, and one abeam and you never know which one'll get you. We got one going out, broke just as we came into it, steepened up ahead of us and then the noise of the crest breaking right above us and we knew he was a big one. We lost the bows and would have gone over if the starboard crew hadn't backed their oars. Wave washed clear over us and no one stopped pulling but the cold afterwards – you could feel every inch of yourself that was wet and our fingers locked tight around the oars so we couldn't let go even if we wanted – and we just thought of the seamen and the ship on the rocks and we pulled harder.

'By the time we got to the ship the snow'd stopped and there was a moon. She was already well down by the stern, and with her stern under, the seas was breaking against her mizzen and washing up the decks. One of the deckhouses was breaking up and her bowsprit pointing up towards the cliffs and up there was the land crew come from Porth, but it was too far and in that wind their rockets were a bloody waste of time.

3

'We looked around for survivors but there was no one on the decks. There was already timbers and bales of jute and debris and the Lord alone knows what swilling about in the water. Wasn't a soul on deck or in the water and we thought, they've all gone already we're too late and all that pulling for nothing. Then someone pointed up and we saw them – clinging to the mast and the yards and hanging on to the halyards.

'She'd struck with her starboard bow and we had to get in leeward of her. We came in under their stern and along midships and one of their crew came down and you could see him waiting on the ladder 'til he could get across the decks between waves – the decks was awash one minute and then they was clear. We came in alongside and threw a line and it dropped on the deck and he jumped down but the next wave came and he had to get up in the rigging. We threw the rope again and this time he got a hold of it but the whip fouled and he had to leave it. Then we dropped in a deep swell and for a moment we lost her and went round abeam, thought we was about to broach but we got her round and dropped in again. We got three aboard that time, each coming down on deck and jumping and two of our crew hauling their weight. The tide was dropping and the deck was clearing and we had two more off no difficulty and each was so cold they could hardly speak when they came aboard.

'Then we heard a noise, a groaning noise from in her hull and we knew she was starting to break up. Every time one of they waves pulled back it sucked more out of her hold.

'First crack frightened the hell out of us. Like a gun. Then there was another crack and soon it was like a bloody battlefield. We didn't know what it was and some of us was ducking and the cox was shouting, Keep her up, for Chrissake! Then one of their crew pipes up it was her rivets he says and we all knew then she hadn't long to go.

'Cox sent Giles Penna aboard, see 'em down out of the rigging and they came down one by one with each of we at our stations and watching them come hand over hand and

4

slow with the cold and the seas rising and falling below. And we was each saying to ourselves – come on now, boy, one step now. The noise was terrible – the surf on the rocks, the cracking of they damned rivets and then the cries of the poor beggars still in the rigging. The bowman was shouting out, trying to get us to hold her steady and then a wave picked us up and we lost the bows again.

'We was struggling to get back in when the first of the topmasts went – four of them in the rigging and the topmast goes and they hung on until it was half down and then they fell, away over the stern.

'Could do nothing for them and there was another dozen or so in the for'ard masts so we went back in and one came down and we got him on board and Penna shouted up to the others to come down. He was shouting but on the wind they couldn't hear. We was finding it difficult keeping steady. The snow was starting again and we could see they last ones up there clinging to the yards. The ship was going. Her back was broken and she was sliding off the ledge into deep water. We was all shouting to them and trying to stop them being afraid and they was too terrified to move. Then one of the survivors on board he took Tyler's arm and says: "You won't get them down now, my friend, they're frozen to the shrouds." '

Thomas Treneer in conversation with Jack Sweeney,
Polmayne, 1935

The following unsourced passages, describing Polmayne and the Main Cages rocks, appear at the beginning of a notebook which belonged to Jack Sweeney. The covers of the notebook are of black oilcloth, and on subsequent pages are entries beneath the general heading of 'Fishing Diary'.

'Polmen is a pretty towne and rich, much abundant in fish and flesh and in it be a meatly strong pile but the roves there be sore defacid and woren. Few men be glad to inhabite this town for al the plenty, for robbers cam from sea that take their catail by force. The robbers be Frenchmen and Spaniards. Ther be one rocke there cawled Man Cayge yn which the sea boil sore with fishes but yf ship or punt go thyther they be devored. The town was desolated in recenti hominum memoria. The whole number of householdes that were yn this town cam to a marriage or fest and going homewarde were al drowned upon that Cayge rocke . . .'

'Beautiful in the bright sunlight, wild and terrific in tempest, ever chafed and burrowed by the ceaseless wave, the effect on the imagination of the Main Cages rocks is truly sublime. Looked at from the nearby headland of Pendhu, at the lowest ebb of the tide, they form a jagged line of silhouettes against the sea, spreading eastwards in tooth-like rows from the largest one, the twin summits of Maen Mor. At the far eastern end, and only seen at low water is a rock known as the Curate, from a fancied resemblance to the nose of a cleric who at one time assisted in the parish of Polmayne.'

'**Main Cages** – *main*, from maen, Cornish for "rock"; *cages*, possibly from Cornish kegys – "hemlock" (on the coast east of Pendhu Point is a Hemlock Cove); or perhaps from cagal, Late Cornish for "the dung of sheep, goats or rodents", and also denoting "clotted or spattered filth on the coats of beasts", which, in certain lights, the rocks are said to resemble.'

'The Main Cages.

'From the little town of Polmayne it is not possible to see those natural assets which have in many ways proved to be both her greatest adversary and her greatest provider. Walk out beyond the lifeboat station and you can see them; better still, take a ferry across the Glaze River, amble on up through Priory Creek and you will see them coming into view beyond the grassy top, rising against a vast sparkling panorama of sea. But from the town itself they are tucked away, out of sight, hidden behind the granite knuckles of Pendhu Point.

'It is sometimes said that Polmayne would not be half the town it is were it not for the rocks of the Main Cages. Not only do the waters around them provide some of the most profitable fishing in the south-west but the rocks' deadly and destructive effects have yielded regular dividends of their own. From unfortunate ships have been salved the teak beams for the cottages of Cooper's Yard, the mahogany joists for numerous potting sheds, the lintel of the Fountain Inn, one of the brass bells that hangs in St Cuby's church tower and the Tyler family, descended as it is from a single Irish sailor who stumbled ashore in 1822 from the wreck of the *Fortune*. In the cupboards of certain houses you can still find a few plates and cups unbroken from the SS *Coventry*. The Antalya Hotel is named after an opulent ship of the White Star line which was stranded on Pendhu Point in 1912.

'Look back in the Parish records and you will discover that several of the town's daughters were christened Martha in 1857 after an elegant schooner of the same name was stuck for two days on the rocks. In 1882, a baulk timber from the Dutch ship *Beatrix* was salvaged and set into the wall of Polmayne's Town Quay. It has become known as Parliament

Bench, where on sunny days old men gather to lament the passing of better times.

'Of all the hundreds of years of wrecks perhaps the worst period of all was during the 1860s. In no more than a decade nineteen ships struck the Cages and in particular one brigantine in 1867 which went down with five of her crew and three of Polmayne's lifeboatmen. Such was the feeling locally that Jacob Freeman, a gentleman of great energy and enterprise who had amassed a fortune in the guano trade, stepped forward and said he would finance a lighthouse to mark the Main Cages. Being a man of vision, Mr Freeman proposed another one too. A twin beacon! On that twin Celtic shore, the far-off Breton coast! The two lights would be dedicated to the telescope-explorers, Adams and Leverrier, who had discovered the planet Neptune. Thereby, proposed Freeman, the Western Approaches would be marked by sentinel lights "acknowledging with luminous nods the dominant claims of commerce and the brotherhood of nations".

'The plan came to nothing. Mr Freeman is here remembered for his gift of the Freeman Reading Rooms which have in a small way fulfilled his vision by being illuminated with Polmayne's first electric light. By the time of his death in 1902 all that marked the Main Cages, on their seaward side, was a buoy in which a vast bell, recovered from the wreck of the *Elsie K*, swings with the seas, clanging its warning against the bars of an iron cage.'

I

1934

CHAPTER I

W̲hen Jack Sweeney arrived in Polmayne in May 1934, he brought with him several bundles of letters, his mother's diamond ring and a small, oak-framed painting of a bird of paradise. He was twenty-eight.

Behind him was a farm in Dorset which had been owned by Sweeneys for three hundred years and probably a lot more. He himself would never have needed to farm if his elder brother had survived the shrapnel shard which sent him face-first into the Flanders mud. Nor would he have been left in charge so young if his father had not succumbed to pleurisy in the winter of 1925. And he may have come to keep the farm, to make it prosper, even perhaps to love it, had he made some provision for the upheavals that took place in the early 1930s.

But in truth farming had never appealed to him. As a child he resisted a practice which made narrow enclosures from the land and planted each one with a single species of plant. Nor could he feel a part of anything that made such a mockery of the beasts – the lumbering cattle, the confused sheep, the swollen pigs. He had already built his own pantheon from the world and its virtues were diversity, rarity, independence; the farm seemed opposed to all three. He bred rare hawk-moths, collected birds' eggs. He had a habit of making remarkable finds. He was a dreamy child, they said, a natural.

He had been to Polmayne once before, in May 1913. The winter before had been a fug of bronchitis and come spring his mother took him to the Antalya Hotel. He loved the town. He loved its hugger-mugger houses, the strange sea creatures that came up in baskets from the boats, the constant harbourside shouting. Within two days he had seen a peregrine falcon, a pair of seals and a group of basking sharks. On Pendhu Point, a smudge of orange wings sped past him and he cried: 'Mother, look! A milkweed!'

That autumn his mother became ill. By Christmas she was dead. Jack could not understand what it was that changed her so quickly, that sucked away all the flesh and reduced her voice to a whisper. But when the farm collapsed, twenty-one years later, and his father's cousin offered him a job in a forestry project, and everyone else was surrounding him with their platitudes and promises, all he could think about was how to get away. He remembered Polmayne. He put the sale of the farm in the hands of solicitors, bundled up a few possessions and took the train to Cornwall.

In Polmayne he rented a room from a Mrs Cuffe. It was a loft room. It had its own staircase, its own entrance and two dormer windows which looked down over the sea wall, over the bay and out to Pendhu Point. At one end was a slate mantelpiece and there he propped his bird of paradise.

He never intended to stay. Polmayne was a stopgap, a stepping stone, a place in which to sit back and look around before starting afresh. But the weeks passed and the mantelpiece filled with assorted top-shells and pebbles, with rounded shards of pottery and ceramics and a piece of surf-polished driftwood that resembled the torso of an erotic dancer. Soon the bird of paradise was hidden by a foot-long blade of a ship's propeller prised from the mud of Pritchard's Beach.

That summer the threads that bound him to the earth thinned and frayed. He took his meals alone in Mrs Cuffe's dining room. He listened to the alien murmur of the other guests. The only person he spoke to was Whaler, the almost blind husband of Mrs Cuffe.

Whaler Cuffe had spent his working life as bosun and mate on a succession of ships. He had never served on whalers but had once told a story about a whale and after that everyone called him Whaler. In the summer months he lived across the yard in a lean-to shed while Mrs Cuffe rented out their bedroom to visitors. Most of the day he sat outside the shed with his hands propped on his cane while the sun glowed against his sightless eyes. He told stories to anyone who listened and mainly it was strangers as no one in Polmayne believed him. On Parliament Bench, his stories were a byword for fantasy: 'Tall'n a bloody tree, Whaler's yarns.'

It was from Whaler that Jack first heard about the Main Cages. He reeled off the names of the ships that had been lost there as if they were the dead from some age-old campaign – the *Carlisle*, the *Athens*, the *Prince Henry*, the *Adelaide*. He told Jack about the *Phoenix* whose cargo of sugar turned to syrup as she sank, drowning the crew; and the *Constance*, loaded with rice which swelled as she filled and burst the hull open like a pea-pod. On the seabed below the rocks, he explained, there are thousands and thousands of barrels, locked there by the cement that spilled from them and hardened; the cement was on its way to San Francisco to assist in rebuilding the city after the 1906 earthquake. In gales, Whaler continued, you can hear in the pine trees the moans of 'all the poor beggars who perished on the Cages'. He told Jack that they used to leave pirates on the rocks sealed inside an iron cage.

'And that's why,' said Whaler with a vague waving of his cane in the direction of the sea, 'we call the rocks as we do.'

Jack found a copy of Tom Bowling's *Book of Knots* and spent the mornings working his way through it, sitting on his steps with a ball of whipping line and various lengths of lanyard. Beside him was a pump with a cow's-tail handle and it was this pump that gave the cobbled yard the name of Bethesda. Each morning Mrs Cuffe come into the yard to draw water.

'Still tying they knots, Mr Swee?'

'Still tying, Mrs Cuffe.'

'Well, one day you'll knot your own fingers together and starve yourself to death . . .'

In early July, he woke on a cloudless morning and found he could not move his head. He lay staring at the ceiling. Veins of sunlight reflected off the sea and flickered on the rafters. An hour later he had managed to reach his stool in the yard. When Mrs Cuffe came to the pump she told him he looked 'stiff as a scarecrow'.

Bending to pick up her pails, she told him: 'I seen others like you, Mr Swee. You get out on the water, have a bit of a row-round.'

He did just that. He went down to the harbour and hired a boat, twelve feet of clinker-built dinghy with long, heavy paddles. On that first day he could barely move them. The following day he managed to push out through the Gaps and across the bay. The next morning he reached the entrance to the Glaze River and by the fourth, when he hauled the boat over the sand and into the water the last of the stiffness had gone.

It was a day of no wind. The sea stretched flat and featureless into a pale haze. The dinghy surged forward with each stroke, splitting the water. The only sound was the rowlocks working back and forth in their sockets: *cler-clunk . . . cler-clunk . . .*

He pointed the bows of the boat out of the bay. Pendhu Point slipped astern. A slight swell rose from the east. In the bright midday, the heat fell on his back and bounced off the sea and he shipped the paddles and uncorked his water bottle.

He looked back towards Polmayne. In the haze was the white blot of buildings around the quays. He raised the bottle to his lips and drank deeply, then he pressed in the cork and rowed on. He rowed south-east. Some time later he stopped again and pulled in the paddles and drank some more, and as he drank and wiped the last trickle of it from his chin, he heard from the direction of the open sea the very faint sound of a bell.

There was nothing at all for several seconds but then it came again. Three loud clangs and a softer one – then a silence and two soft clangs and some louder ones, and he realised that it was not a mechanical bell but one rung by the irregular motion of the sea.

Jack raised one hand to his brow, shielding the sun. He squinted towards the sound. In the flood of light he made out three or four shapes of rocks. He took up the paddles and headed out towards them. As he rowed closer so there came from them the noise of surf. Even with no sea to speak of and the tide almost slack, he saw how uneven the rocks made the water. It ran smoothly among their low summits, made eddies over those that remained just below the surface. The long swells rose and fell against them.

He drifted in among the rocks and came to the place where a channel ran between the two parts of the largest one, Maenmor. With each swell, the water sluiced through the gap and Jack held the boat off for a moment. The gap at its narrowest was about six feet wide, perhaps thirty feet long. He looked at it a long time, holding the boat still against the tide. It was dark between the rocks and he squinted to see in. He then spun the boat round, took two swift strokes and shipped the paddles. The bows shot into the gap. They did not swing but with the weight of the boat kept true. The sun was blotted out by the high rock above and the air was suddenly cool. The boat slowed and he felt the brush of weed against the hull. Then the bows started to swing and the stern nudged the rocks. He leaned over and his hand came up against the wall and he pushed off and all at once was out again, into the sun and the warmth and the still water.

He started to row again. He spotted a smooth patch in the water and shipped his paddles again and leaned over the side. The sun's rays haloed his head and he could see down into the water, through the dust-motes of plankton, to the shadowy form of a rock. Oarweed flopped about beside it, swaying as the swells passed over it – back and forth, back and forth. And that is the image that remained with him from his early days in Polmayne – of his own lone figure suspended over the side of a boat, staring down into the water, while from below rose the half-hidden shape of a rock.

That August Jack Sweeney bought his own boat. He sold his mother's diamond ring, gave Mrs Cuffe four months' rent and walked up the Glaze River to Penpraze's yard. He had already discovered the place on his wanderings. Just beyond the church was a pair of black tarred sheds and on the larger one a sign: 'P. PENPRAZE, SHIP, YACHT & BOAT BUILDER, BLOCK & SPAR-MAKER & SHIPSMITH'.

Inside, years of sawdust and paint-chippings had been trodden down to form an uneven, hard-packed floor. The roof was hung with wrights' moulds and assorted spars rested on the beams. Peter Penpraze blew the dust from a varnished half-model and told him: 'Fourteen foot six, grown oak frames, timbers of pitch pine, oak garboards, elm keel. Whatever thwarts you like, Mister, and a good locker astern. Lovely little boat, steady as a rock in a blow, pound a foot.'

Three weeks later, on a cloudless afternoon, Jack rowed between the Gaps and moored his boat in the inner harbour for the first time. That evening Whaler tap-tapped his way along the Town Quay and Mrs Cuffe drained a bottle of stout over the boat's stem, saying: 'Blessed be this craft, and blessed be all her crafty tasks.'

Over the coming days Jack brought out the lines he had been preparing – the eye-spliced painter, the stern-line, the rope fender, and a few he had made up for good measure. He bought a small galvanised grapnel and spliced that on too.

He began potting. Whaler put him onto Benny Stone, a cousin of sorts, and a man half-crippled from twenty years of crabbing. From Benny Stone, Jack acquired a set of inkwell pots – 'Woven from best Penpraze withies, Mr Swee, three seasons' use' – and a great deal of advice: 'Haul at low water ... use shore crabs to catch the wrasse, use the wrasse for the lobster ... put out your old pots March-time, save the new for better weather ... find a pitch round the Cages and ee'll not go wrong.'

Rights to the potting grounds were divided up along complicated lines of allegiance, decided either by ties of blood or by any one of a dozen tacit fraternities. Jack rowed around the grounds and on an old Admiralty chart shaded in where he saw other pots. He ringed the other places marked 'R' (rocks) and 'ST' (stones) and on fine days took out a greased lead and plumbed the water, recording where sand was stuck to the grease, and where it came up clean.

But his early potting was not a success. He experimented with different sites – west of Kidda Head, down towards Porth, east of Hemlock Cove. In three weeks his efforts yielded little more than spider crabs, velvets, devils, a few small lobsters and a number of conger. He lost a third of his pots in a gale, and another string from leaving too short a head-rope at springs. When he rowed back through the Gaps the men on Parliament Bench watched him with their cold, omniscient stares.

In late October the weather came in and he stored his pots and kicked his heels around the town. On Armistice Day he saw the luggers leave Polmayne for Plymouth and one afternoon on the East Quay he met a young woman from Devon called Alice. She had red-brown hair the colour of fallen leaves and was working in the kitchens of the Antalya. He took her out rowing and she showed him the slate grotto of St Pinnock's holy well. Alice said the waters were known in the town to cure barren women. In bed she would sing softly as he held her, and her eyes fill with tears.

In the middle of December, Polmayne's luggers returned from Plymouth; they loaded the herring nets and went back east for several more weeks. Jack found a note under his door: 'Dear Jack, it's lonely here even though you're kind. I gone back home to my people. Goodbye, Alice.'

That Christmas Jack accepted an invitation from his great-aunt Bess to spend the week in Bridport. He passed a few days in her hot and over-decorated rooms. On the third night he went into town and got drunk and fell asleep fully clothed. In the morning mud stains covered the foot of the counterpane and he told his aunt Bess he was leaving. She said Cornwall was not the place for him. 'You're a Sweeney, Jack, this is where you belong.'

January swept in over Polmayne with its two-day gales and its grey, restless seas. Squalls dashed around Pendhu Point, driving the water in the coves into chest-deep scuds of foam. Along the front, shop signs swung and squeaked in the wind. Jack brought his boat into Bethesda, upturned it on two sawn-off barrels and rubbed it and primed it and re-glossed its clinker hull. He went to see Benny Stone with an armful of withies. His first pots looked less like inkwells than doughnuts but in time he produced something serviceable. He counted off the days until March. He was running short of money.

One morning in late January he was walking on Pritchard's Beach. It was a bright morning and the beach was scattered with the detritus of another storm. Squinting into the sun he spotted a figure pushing a wheelbarrow up the strand. The man was struggling to keep it going through the shingle. Jack recognised his black smock and the sand-coloured beret – it was Mrs Cuffe's nephew, Croyden Treneer.

Setting the barrow down, Croyden caught his breath. 'That's some bloody heavy beast!' He bent to light a cigarette and tossed away the match.

'What is it?'

Croyden pulled aside the weed on top of the barrow and Jack glimpsed beneath it a stretch of leathery skin. And he smelt it. He put a sleeve to his nose.

'Dolphin. Put him in under my potatoes and they'll come up lovely.'

Croyden leaned on the front of the barrow and shuffled the pebbles with his boot. 'Started potting yet?' he asked.

'Not yet.'

Croyden said nothing but stood for some time smoking in silence. Then he flicked away his cigarette, picked up the barrow and said, 'You won't get nowhere with it! I was you, I'd go back to England.'

CHAPTER 2

C royden Treneer had once been a fisherman but now he
worked ashore. He picked up jobs on building sites.
He grew vegetables on his 'piece', one of the dozen or so
allotments cut out from the gorse-cleared slopes above the
town. He also had two pigs which he kept in an old quarry
behind his house in Rope Walk. The pigs ate barley flour and
scraps and lived beneath the upturned halves of a sawn-in-half
dinghy. Their names were Three and Five. One and Two had
been killed in previous years but in the autumn of 1934, when
it had come to killing Three, Croyden couldn't do it. He was
still a fisherman at heart and killing Three was bound to bring
him bad luck. He killed Four instead.

The Treneer family had always been in Polmayne. They
had been boat-builders, ropemakers and sail-cutters, huers,
blowsers and triggers. They had gone to sea in drift-netters,
long-liners, crabbers and shrimpers. Some had dispersed to
Plymouth, America, London, taken jobs on ships and sailed
to Odessa, Genoa, Bombay, Panama. They had made new

homes in Canada, Australia and New Zealand, lost their lives in the Bay of Bengal, the Menai Straits, Mount's Bay. Three Treneers had been Coxswain of Polmayne's lifeboat. The most recent was Tommy Treneer who was not yet Cox but crew when the *Adelaide* foundered in the winter of 1891.

Croyden was his second son. The eldest had gone to buy a pony at Bodmin Fair in 1913 but couldn't see one he liked, so he went to America instead. When he failed to return, Tommy marched down to the board school and took Croyden away. 'What he don't know now,' he told the headmaster, 'he don't need to know.' He was twelve.

Croyden worked with his father on the *Good Heart* seine and took to long-lining and potting when the pilchards weren't running. At eighteen he became the youngest-ever member of the Polmayne lifeboat crew. Though small in stature, he developed enormous strength and agility. He could pull a four-foot conger from a crab pot without flinching. He could bait up a boulter line at an astonishing speed. He knew the sea bottom, the underwater valleys and peaks, the sandy plains and rocky outcrops, as if he could see it all with his own eyes. He acquired the useful faculty, when fishing, of being able to wake in his bunk precisely at the turn of the tide.

But whatever his skills as a former fisherman, Croyden had always set much greater store by a set of well-moulded rituals and beliefs. He would mutter blessings as the nets went out, always eat a fish from tail to head, not let a priest near the boat, and refuse to load gear on a Friday. Above all he would never utter the word 'rabbit' either on board or ashore – and if he heard anyone say it at sea, he would be forced to head for home. If he needed to talk about rabbits he called them sheep.

Croyden's ability at sea was not matched on land. As soon as he came ashore and left the quays, he was lost. People used to say: 'Really there's two Croydens, like they's twins or something.'

Even as Croyden began with the *Good Heart*, the days of seining were reaching an end. The pilchard shoals did not come as they once had and in 1918 the *Good Heart* was laid up for good. Croyden was offered a place on the *Blucher*, a drift-netter in Newlyn. He was given a sixth share in the catch and returned to Polmayne sporadically – either out of pocket or flush after a good splat of fish. To Tommy Treneer, Croyden's position was a betrayal. It was the drift-nets alone that he blamed for robbing the coast of pilchards. 'The devil's own nets,' he called them and refused to address a word to his son.

But the *Blucher* did well. One moonlit night in December 1924, some ten miles south of Mount's Bay, they struck a shoal of herring with such perfect timing that at once a total of 114 cran of fish caught their gills in the mesh. It took seven hours to haul the nets. While the others tired, Croyden found that the deeper the fish lay about his ankles the more vigorously he could haul. His share of the catch earned him more than £52. On board that evening, he leaned back on the *Blucher*'s frosty deck and felt he could stretch out his cutch-stained hands and rearrange the stars. Such dazzling high spirits lasted long enough to catch the eye of Maggie North whose mother ran Newlyn's quayside tobacconist. Croyden returned that summer, in a borrowed boat, and after the wedding took his bride away from a harbour lined with waving well-wishers, back across Mount's Bay and around the Lizard where, as they picked up an easterly swell, Mrs Croyden Treneer scattered the nibblings of her wedding lunch into the long arc of the boat's wash.

In the coming years Maggie grew to hate the sea and all it represented. In the early thirties both prices and shoals became ever more unpredictable. Expecting her fourth child, she said she could no longer tolerate his feast-or-famine work.

'Fishing's a gambler's life, Croyden Treneer, and all you seem to do is lose.'

Croyden came ashore. He bought his first pig. He worked

his piece, planting potatoes and brassicas and using an old tuck-net to keep out the birds. He found a job on the roads – laying the first tarmac on Polmayne's only approach road. When that came to an end, he spent a winter building one of the bungalows that were beginning to ring the town and every day he was reminded that he would rather be at sea. Working on solid ground to a clock and not to the tides, dealing with straight lines and right-angles, all contributed to a faint nausea. The truth was that labouring on land made Croyden seasick.

Then under the Housing Act of 1930 a compulsory purchase order was placed on Cooper's Yard and a dozen old cottages around it – 'unfit for habitation ... prone to flooding ...'. A large site was excavated for new homes above the church. Before they were even completed these houses became known as the Crates. Suddenly in Polmayne there was work for all and Croyden found he was earning more than he ever had on the drift-netter.

His father, Tommy, still refused to speak to him. He lived in Cooper's Yard and now he was told he must leave. He had been born there. Croyden had been born there. Treneers had always been born there. Drift-netting was one thing, said Tommy, but at least it was fishing.

'We was always seiners,' he growled, 'and now look at him – putting up bloody Crates so they can pack we away.'

In early March 1935, Jack Sweeney spent a couple of days plumbing out at the Main Cages. There he stumbled on a small unclaimed area of rough ground. It ran for about fifty yards just south of the gap between Maenmor's two peaks – the tunnel that he'd shot in his punt the summer before. It would be hard to work in any kind of a sea, but in the middle of the month came a spell of settled weather.

On his first haul, he pulled seven good-sized crabs. Two days later he had five crabs and two lobsters. Within a week he had caught more than he had in the entire two months the year before. He began to make money – and on Parliament Bench they took to nodding at him as he came in. Once a week he gave part of his catch to Mrs Cuffe. Whaler told him about the lobsters he had seen the size of dogs and a crab in the tropics that would scamper up the palm trees and happily pick dates with his claws.

One evening at the end of March a freshening westerly began to flick at the wave-tops of the bay. *Put out your old pots March-time* . . . Jack had put out the lot. He cursed himself as he pulled on his boots and ran out through the yard.

Tommy Treneer shouted from the Bench as he passed: 'Should take better bloody care o' your gear!'

At the Main Cages the seas were already large. He rowed round into the lee of Maenmor. His marker buoys were rising and falling on a long swell. He hauled the first string quickly. It was mid-tide and flooding. The line was heavy. It jammed tight against the gunwale as he pulled and the boat dipped with each tug. Then came the bump of the first pot against the boat and he hauled it in. He extracted a good hen from inside. From that first line of pots he had three crabs. He rowed over to the others.

On the other side of Maenmor he could hear the seas breaking hard against the rock but for the time being he was sheltered. Through the tunnel came the roar of surf, and sudden white surges of water.

The other string was even heavier. The first pot had a spider crab and he threw it back. The pots were mounting in the bows and the boat's roll was growing wider. He knew he'd lose some pots now; he'd never be able to row them all back in such a sea. As the third pot came in, the boat slipped off the top of a wave and Jack fell. The line slid back over the side and he found himself eye to eye with a cock crab on the bottom boards. He tried again. As the pot came up, still beneath the surface, he could see the dark form of a lobster. It was a vast lobster. Unable to fit in the pot it had its thorax wrapped around the outside. Its claw was so big that it was that that had jammed in the spout. Jack balanced the pot on the gunwale. With one hand he flicked a series of running hitches around both pot and lobster, lashing to the withies the starry sky of the creature's back, the boxer's forearm of its one free claw. He then cut the rope and abandoned the rest to the storm.

By the time he reached the quays, the water in the boat was slopping at his ankles. Within half an hour, a crowd had gathered to view the giant lobster. It was measured at 29¼ inches tail to claw and even Whaler, who came down to the quay and ran his fingers over its full length, admitted it was 'a beauty'.

'In Australia,' he said, 'I saw one like him, only –'

'He was ten feet long, eh Whaler?' teased Toper Walsh.

'And wore spectacles,' suggested Tommy Treneer.

'Came up on our anchor chain and we measured him claw to tail at just over . . .'

But no one was listening to Whaler. They were all looking at the lobster. Two weeks later it was mounted on a wooden board in the saloon bar of the Antalya.

In the coming weeks, Jack's luck continued. When he came in to the Town Quay, Tommy Treneer and the others would wander over from the Bench to see what he had. They never tired of hearing how he caught the big one – was it gurnard that got him, Mr Swee? Parlour pot or inkwell? Where d'ee say 'ee had him, near which of the rocks? Show us again how he was caught, how he was twisted round the pot and which was the claw he had hisself with, Mr Swee?

Then all at once, the catches stopped. During the middle two weeks of April, while others were reporting good hauls, Jack pulled nothing but empty pots. He set the strings at different angles. He replaced the wrasse with gurnard and then the gurnard with mackerel. He tried a piece of shark but it made no difference.

One morning Croyden Treneer came into Bethesda. Jack was sitting on the steps with his knots and Croyden came over and leaned against the wall beside him. He lit a cigarette. 'You been having trouble with your pots.'

It was a statement, not a question. Jack waited for the 'I told you so.' But instead Croyden pushed up his sand-coloured beret, scratched his forehead and said: 'Perhaps 'ee'd let me take a look.'

'I'm going out tomorrow –'

Croyden shook his head. 'Tonight. Meet me on the Town Quay ten this evening.'

CHAPTER 3

The moon rose plum-red behind Pendhu Point. The tides were working up to springs. Jack and Croyden rowed round to the darkness of Hemlock Cove and beached the boat. They climbed over the rocks until the shapes of the Main Cages appeared against the moon-bright sea. A light wind blew from the west. They sat down to wait.

It was two hours before they heard the sound of paddles. A small boat appeared underneath the point and headed out to the rocks. They could see the silhouettes of two men on board. The boat worked Jack's pots and replaced them. The men had passed beneath them, had gone round the point before Croyden hissed: 'Bloody Pig. Might a' guessed it'd be the Garretts.'

Jimmy Garrett and Tacker Garrett were two brothers who lived together in a room above the East Quay. They kept apart from the rest of the town. To visitors they were well-known characters as in summer they ran the pleasure steamer, the *Polmayne Queen*. Tacker was the younger and many in the

27

town thought him simple. Visitors never noticed because he was so adept on the *Polmayne Queen* and because he had a singing voice to break hearts. On summer evenings, returning home from Porth or St Mawes or Mevagissey, Tacker would stand in the stern and sing 'The Streams of Lovely Nancy' or 'The Cushion Dance' or 'Three Sisters' and bring tears to the eyes of grown men – but without his brother Jimmy, he was lost.

Jimmy was taciturn, bull-necked and bald-headed. He rarely came out of the *Queen*'s wheelhouse. He wore a constant frown as he was always calculating – tides and times and winds, or fuel costs and fares.

The Garretts had arrived in Polmayne as teenagers, without family or connections, and in the early days before the war Jimmy supported the two of them in a number of ways. One way was to go to wrestling matches in Truro or Bodmin where he invariably picked up the £5 prize. There was something rough and untamed about Jimmy but in those days he was more mischief than malice. One summer he took to wearing a pig's trotter around his neck, and he knew that all he had to do was to open his shirt and people would back away from him. That was how he became known as 'Pig' Garrett. Others, who saw none of that, remembered a certain gentle charm and the endearing way he looked after his younger brother.

Jimmy went to war in 1915 and the following summer was reported Missing in Action. Tacker was found half-starved in their room beside the Fountain Inn and Mrs Kliskey took him on to help in Dormullion's gardens. Three months later Jimmy returned from the dead. He had been wounded in the thigh and lain for thirty-six hours in no-man's land. When he limped off the bus in Polmayne he went straight to see his fiancée Rose Shaw. Her mother told him she was in Penzance. Three days later he received a letter from her: *'Dear Jim, You was missing a month so I married another. Rose.'*

Those who had known Jimmy before the war said he came

back a changed man. He was bitter, and more withdrawn than ever. Before, he had never fought in anger but now he got into scrapes and when he broke the arm of a Camborne man in the Fountain Inn, he was convicted of assault.

'Tell me why' – he said quietly from the dock – 'I fight for King and country for a year and get a wound for thanks but when I fight for myself for a couple of minutes I get fined?'

Jimmy gradually ceased to have any real contact with anyone but his brother.

Instead he worked. In the post-war collapse in fishing he bought a crabber, converted it to a petrol engine and sold it when the market picked up again. From then on he became an inveterate boat-dealer, a habit he preferred to keep secret by indulging it in other towns. He was spectacularly mean. By 1926, he had amassed a sizeable cushion of money but because he still lived with Tacker in one room, and because he continued to go long-lining and crabbing, and put out nets and haggle up the jouster to the brink of anger, it was assumed he relied on his catch to live, just like everyone else.

Then on the last day of March 1931, a forty-five-foot converted steamer named *Queen of the Dart* pulled in through the Gaps. From the bows of the boat Tacker leapt onto the Town Quay and secured her fore and aft.

'Where'd 'ee steal that to, Tack?' called Tommy Treneer from the Bench.

'The future's in pleasure craft!' said Tacker, parroting the words of his brother.

'Nonsense. Even Pig knows visitors have no money now'days.'

But day-trips on the *Queen of the Dart* – renamed the *Polmayne Queen* – proved popular. It was the winters that were long for the Garretts. Rumours that they pulled others' pots had been circulating for some time but until Croyden and Jack saw them that night, no one was quite sure.

When Jack Sweeney drew his pots the following day he

did not replace the gurnard baits. Instead he stuck pigs' trotters onto the stakes of the first two pots. He left the pots out for two days then reverted to gurnard. Within a week he was beginning to catch again, and his catches were good and he said to himself for the first time: perhaps this way of life really is possible.

Towards the end of April he received a letter from his solicitors in Bridport. The final lot of the farm had been sold, but a sum of £236.3s.6d remained outstanding. So that was it. He didn't have that sort of money, nor could he earn it pulling a few strings of crab pots. Only when he read the letter a third time did he realise that the money was not owed *by* him but *to* him.

Two days later he started to look into the possibility of buying a bigger boat.

'What?'

Maggie Treneer was lying in bed. Her two-week-old daughter lay beside her. Croyden was standing in the doorway and he was telling her that Jack Sweeney was buying a boat and was offering him a crew's share. He was going with him, he was going back to sea.

Maggie looked at him not with anger but with a calm hatred. 'What makes you think you can do any better this time?'

Croyden was holding his beret, toying with it.

'What's happened to you, Croyden?'

He shrugged and looked away. 'Nothing.'

'You yourself said this man Sweeney knows nothing of fishing.'

Croyden looked at her again and said, 'You wouldn't understand.'

'Understand what?'

'He's lucky.'

First they went to Mevagissey. They found an old friend

of Croyden's called Sydney Bunt who offered them a black-hulled tosher that was much too small for their purposes. 'There's plenty more selling,' he pointed along the harbour. 'Try the *Howard*.' But the *Howard* was in very poor condition.

Two days later Jack and Croyden took the train down to St Erth and from St Erth to St Ives where they saw a suitable-looking driver going for a good price. The man selling leaned back against the bulwarks and watched them as they inspected his boat. 'From Polmayne, is 'ee? You'd know the man I bought her from. Jimmy Garrett?'

They thanked him and left and went to see a very talkative man named Edgar Pearce who owned a lugger named the *New Delight*. They looked at her closely and afterwards they stood on the sand and Croyden said: 'Seems sound enough.'

Edgar Pearce shook his head. 'She might look all right to you, but she's no good.'

In her early days, he explained, she had been worked with a full lug-sail and a mizzen but in 1910 they'd put a steam engine in her and of course that meant drilling a hole there, out through the stern for the propeller but not central, on account of the deadwood bolts, and then so that the propeller spun free the rudder had to have a bit of a cut in her and then the stern-tube forced the crew's quarters up for'ard and that meant the mainmast had to be restepped and that made the hold hard to get at, and then he'd put in a petrol-paraffin engine, and there was a knock she'd had the previous summer –

'Wait,' interrupted Jack. 'Why are you telling us all this? Don't you want to sell?'

He looked at them sheepishly. 'Don't believe I do.'

In Mousehole they met an elderly man with a Mount's Bay driver that had been in his family thirty years (too big). In Porthleven the boat they came to see had just been bought by a Helston doctor as a pleasure 'steamer'. In Falmouth, they

31

looked at a drifter that was going cheap because she had been in a collision and 'her handling'd gone strange'.

In the end they found the *Maria V* back in Mevagissey where they'd first looked. She was a high-bowed, thirty-seven-foot drifter with tabernacled mainmast and a mizzen astern. She'd been built in 1925 by Dick Pill of Gorran Haven and had been fitted more recently with a Kelvin engine. Maria V herself was Maria Varcoe, who had left the money to her great-nephew, the Gorran man who had originally commissioned the boat.

Beneath a sky of grey-brown cloud, Jack and Croyden motored the *Maria V* back around Pendhu Point and into the bay. Then came a week of strong northerlies and the *Maria V* remained on her moorings, tugging at the chain.

On 6 May the last of the winds blew itself out, the seas settled and the Cox of the old lifeboat died. Samuel Tyler was eighty-three and he died in his bed. He had been Cox in 1891 when the *Adelaide* struck the Main Cages. The following year he lost three fingers fishing and handed over the command to Tommy Treneer. In his years as lifeboatman Samuel Tyler had helped save a total of 233 lives.

At eleven o'clock that Saturday the cortège gathered at the lifeboat station. The RNLI flag flew at half-mast. The same flag lay wrapped around the coffin, its insignia uppermost. Tyler's cork lifejacket and a yellow sou'wester rested on top.

The procession was led by two black cobs and Ivor Dawkins of Crowdy Farm. He wore a khaki coat and Wellington boots and carried a switch of hazel. Dawkins did not share the town's reverence for the sea, nor did he have much time for those who risked their lives upon it. He was keen to get his horses back to work and was leading the cortège at something rather quicker than a funereal pace.

Funerals were as popular in Polmayne as lifeboat Cox-swains, and almost the whole town turned out to line the route. Jack Sweeney stood with Mrs Cuffe outside Bethesda. Whaler leaned on his stick, staring over the procession to the glow of sun above the bay. On the Town Quay they set down the coffin and for the first of several times sang 'Crossing the Bar':

> *Sunset and evening star, and one clear call for me;*
> *And let there be no moaning at the bar*
> *when I put out to sea ...*

Beside the coffin stood the six pall-bearers in their red dress-hats: the current Cox, Edwin Tyler; his lineman, Dee Walsh; Red and Joseph Stephens; and Croyden and Charlie Treneer.

In front of them all, struggling to keep up with the coffin as it left the quay, was Tommy Treneer. He was hunched and shuffling. His black jacket was too large for him. But the others dropped back to give him space. From his lapel dangled, one above the other, three RNLI service medals. He was now Polmayne's senior retired Cox.

CHAPTER 4

The following week the town gathered together again, this time for the Jubilee of King George V. On a breezy afternoon, they made their way to the recreation ground. At one end of the field was a low stage, topped by bunting and flanked by a pair of poles. On each of the poles was a trumpet-shaped speaker through which a Broadcasting Apparatus, loaned by Mr Bradley, relayed a crackling version of the ceremony in London.

Major Franks stood on the stage and began by addressing the town's children. 'My dear little friends! You have more opportunities for enjoying yourselves than any generation before you. You are living in a wonderful age, you must always endeavour to make the most of this privilege . . .'

That afternoon's endeavour was sports. Not a child over two was denied the joys of competition. Each one was placed on the starting line and instructed to run, skip or hop towards a flickering white tape. They were given eggs and spoons and sacks. They had their knees tied together for three-legged races, were upended for wheelbarrow races. They were arranged into relay teams and given a stick. There were chariot races, sprints, sixty-yard slow cycling and a snake race.

All afternoon the cheers rose from the recreation ground. Spirits were high. It was that brief moment between the beginning of fine weather and the coming of the visitors.

Mrs Kliskey of Dormullion was there in her bath chair to hand out the prizes. Two spaniels sat at her feet, their collars wrapped in red, white and blue ribbon. Jack had brought Whaler Cuffe. At three o'clock various people assembled on the stage and the elderly Reverend Winchester was helped to his feet by Mrs Winchester.

'What's happening now, Jack?' asked Whaler.

'Speech,' he whispered.

'Good! Who is it?' Whaler enjoyed speeches.

'Winchester.'

'Oh.'

'On this auspicious day,' mumbled Winchester, 'we thank God for our King's service to the Empire. We ourselves should never be ashamed of being his servants. For service never degrades. All honest, useful work is a means of glorifying God –'

'Piff!' grunted Whaler.

'Time was when artisans were proud to hang the implements of their craft on the walls of cathedrals. Some foolish people used to be ashamed of certain kinds of manual work, but to the true Christian, work brings dignity –'

'What does he know of work?' hissed Whaler. A murmur of conversation began to rise from the crowd.

'Our King is a devout man who recognises full well his dependence on God. He has been an example of reverent and unaffected devotion. There is in him nor in his Queen no cant or hypocrisy, which is an enemy to the cause of true religion. Loyalty is an easy thing when such a king is on the throne and when . . .'

The Reverend Winchester turned the page. But it was the

35

wrong one. He turned the next page, and the next. Major Franks took the chance to nod to Mr Bradley and once again Polmayne's celebrations were bolstered by sounds from London's streets. Already the crowd was moving away from the stage to a row of trestle tables where several tea-urns had been set up by the ladies of the Jubilee Committee. The Reverend Winchester looked confused. Mrs Winchester took his arm and said: 'Come along, dear. Tea.'

The following day, the Garrett brothers brought the freshly-painted *Polmayne Queen* into Polmayne's inner harbour. Her funnel was painted custard yellow, her topsides strawberry red, and like a stick of angelica a cove-line of green ran along her side. On the Bench they said, 'Looks more like a bloody fairground ride 'n a boat.'

At Penpraze's yard they were preparing the Petrels. One by one they brought the pencil-thin yachts into the shed. Their canvas covers were peeled back to reveal the honey-coloured varnish of their combing, their gently raked decks, the immaculate curves of their hulls. A team of three men rubbed down the top-sides and filled every tiny blemish. Then they closed the big shed doors, damped down the dusty floor and in absolute silence applied coat after coat of gloss paint until it shone like enamel.

On the third Saturday in May the first visitors arrived. Whaler took his chiming clock and cane and crossed the yard to his lean-to. Mrs Cuffe and the other landladies gathered outside the Antalya Hotel to wait for the arrival of their paying guests. Shortly after four, the rumble of an engine came from the direction of Pritchard's Beach and Harris's Station Bus rolled to a halt. Soon two dozen people were spilling from it, stretching their shoulders in the sun, collecting their bags and turning their faces to the south for the first real smell of the sea.

It was shortly before dawn, mid-May. Croyden Treneer leaned on the *Maria V*'s gunwale, watching the dan buoy.

Charlie Treneer, his younger brother, was holding a T-hook aft of him. Bran Johns was between them. Jack Sweeney was half in and half out of the wheelhouse. The fishing lights were strung above the deck. Pushing up his beret, Croyden scratched his forehead and nodded to Jack: 'Knock her in!'

The bows edged forward. Croyden leaned over to make a grab for the buoy. Pulling it aboard, they flicked on the motor jenny and started to haul the line. Fishing aboard the *Maria V* had begun.

In the first week they caught over a thousand stone of fish – ray, ling, conger and skate. They threw back a good deal of small conger but in all they grossed £146. For the next three weeks they fished ground to the south of the Lizard. The bait was patchy at times, and in late May they lost almost a week to the weather, but when they did go out they never came back with less than a couple of hundred stone.

Jack himself settled into the rhythm of long-lining – the chug of the Kelvin as they headed south to the grounds, the softer note as they paid out the line, the netting, the hauling, the baiting, the relentless wear on gear and boat. He was constantly tired. He woke tired, rowed tired to the *Maria V*, motored out of the bay tired, felt morning drag him from the night's swamp still dripping with fatigue and drop him back there before they were home. When the weather came in the *Maria V* stayed on her moorings and Jack filled the time splicing spare warps, making monkeys' fists, doing odd jobs on board. He learned that if there was anything more tiring than fishing, it was idleness.

But the catches when they did go out were good. Croyden directed the fishing, decided where to go and when. Bran and Charlie followed their given roles and, so long as the fish were there, all was well on board the *Maria V*.

Regular summer visitors to Polmayne spent their first day or so checking the town for damage – as though they themselves had lent it out for the winter. In May of 1935 they saw the newly-occupied properties of the Crates; they counted the five new villas above the church, the group of half-built bungalows above the Antalya Hotel. They recorded the gap left by various toppled trees and the thatch replaced by slate on the roof of Major Franks's harbourside house. 'It'll be ruined!' they said that May as every May. 'They'll wreck the town.' (The mysterious trenches that had appeared did not worry them as they were told that these were for 'something ornamental', probably beds of Jubilee flowers.)

But after a few days the visitors tended to forget all about the changes and settle instead into the indolence that arose from the far greater number of things that had not changed: the granite curve of the twin quays, the smell of escallonia in the mid-morning sun and the swish of evening waves on the pebbles of Pritchard's Beach.

The trenches, it turned out, were not for flowers. On the last day of the month, a public meeting was convened in the Freeman Reading Rooms. A Mr Perkins was going to explain all about the wonders of electricity. For years there had been generators in Polmayne – Dormullion had one, so did Pendhu Lodge and the Reading Rooms – but now mains electricity was coming, and for many it was not a moment too soon. Not that the electric itself held much attraction; it was just that in Porth the cables were already laid, and no one in Polmayne could accept that Porth might get it first.

There were those however who saw only ill in the invention: 'I'll not have that damned spark in my house. Supposing he spills out night-time and burns 'ee?'

Whaler Cuffe asked Jack to get him to the meeting good and early. They were the first to arrive. Whaler unbuttoned his coat and told Jack a story about a holy man he'd met in China who had shown him a perpetual candle made from the tallow of a pregnant yak.

Major Franks and Mrs Franks arrived and sat in the front row. They were joined by Mrs Kliskey, Dr and Mrs White and the Winchesters. Before them was a table covered in green baize and behind it Mr Perkins.

Mr Perkins was from Redruth. He had a well-clipped moustache and a heavy green suit of Harris tweed. On the table before him were a lightbulb, two smoked-glass lampshades (orange and brown), a plug and a length of flex.

Major Franks checked his watch and signalled to Mr Perkins to start. Rising to his feet, Mr Perkins pushed each object on the table forward an inch, and looked up.

'Ladies and gentlemen, I would like to thank you all for coming out on such an evening to hear what I hope will be an – er – illuminating experience.' Sunlight seeped in behind the curtains of the hall. Mr Perkins was used to making his speech in the winter.

'I have here before me a number of objects with which many of you will be familiar. Others may look at them and say to themselves: *"My goodness me, what manner of device have we here then?"* But I can assure you that in years to come these articles will become as indispensable to you and your daily life as the very roof over your heads.

'And I am offering them to you now free of charge. They are free to all those who decide to welcome the miracle of mains electricity into their homes.' Mr Perkins gripped one of his lapels. He fixed his gaze on the rafters two-thirds of the way down the room.

'A great tide is sweeping the county, ladies and gentlemen – a tide which now laps at the fringes of Polmayne. We who live at this time should count ourselves lucky to witness such glad improvements.'

'Hear, hear,' whispered Whaler.

'I myself have no doubt that when history looks back at our century it will be amazed. It will say to itself: how did they manage to live then? It will look to the moment when life for all classes was immeasurably improved by this' – he held up the length of flex – 'the advent of electric current.'

Tentative applause spread back from the front row. The

39

Reverend Winchester stood and pulled out the unused section of his Jubilee speech.

'Light, ladies and gentlemen, is symbolical of knowledge and guidance and hope. As we survey the years to 1910 we thank God for –'

Major Franks stood and started clapping. 'I'm sure you'll agree that Mr Perkins has made a most convincing case for electric current. If you'd like to come up, I believe Mr Perkins will be happy to answer your questions.'

Mr Winchester sat down.

One or two people stepped up and looked at the props on the table. They asked Mr Perkins: 'How's it made?' and 'What's it look like?' Jack signed up for Bethesda and on Whaler's instructions collected a brown shade.

Later that evening, with the careful placing of several slates, Dee Walsh managed to divert the stream below the holy well. The water crossed the road and poured into the cable trench in Chapel Street. He kicked over the hazard fences, threw in some rocks and pissed over the whole lot. He had nothing against electricity. But the trenches were being dug by Truro men and if there were trenches to be dug in Polmayne it should be Polmayne men that dug them. It put the work back by a few days and the corporation agreed to recruit a number of local men for the job. Walsh was not among them.

CHAPTER 5

One evening in early June a giant anvil of white cloud rose into the sky beyond Pendhu Point. The light sharpened. Every grass-tussock glowed on the headland. In each of the town's barometers, the mercury dipped, then dipped further.

The next day dawned muddy yellow. The wind blew hard from the south-west and shafts of sunlight broke low out of the running clouds. The sea was very disturbed. Two warning cones were hoisted on the East Quay and in the inner harbour the punts twisted and tugged at their warps. No boats went out.

Throughout the morning the wind freshened. Shreds of thatch were torn from the roofs and spiralled up into the gloom. Along the front, one or two figures passed each other in silence, bent against the wind, clutching their collars together. No one was sitting on the Bench, but Toper Walsh was on the Town Quay, telling whoever was around that the weather had 'gone a bit dirty'.

At two o'clock Croyden Treneer opened Jack's door and called up the stairs: 'Mizzen's loose, Jack!'

Jack cursed. He pulled on his coat and his boots and ran out along the Town Quay. Even Toper had now gone home. Shielding his eyes, he looked across to the *Maria V* and could see the boom swinging back and forth in the gale. Dammit! It was only a matter of time before it did some damage.

The wind was on his beam as he rowed and he had to follow a long arc out across the bay. He reached the boat and secured the boom. The timber was scarred and the lacing at one point had worn through. He made it all fast and checked the halyards and the stays and the bolt on the wheelhouse door and went up in the bows to look at the mooring.

It was now blowing very hard. The water ahead was streaked with spume. The mooring buoy was jerking at the chain, but secure. From the slopes ashore came the roaring of the wind in the pines. He stood blinking into the rain, then turned his back to it and looked astern. He felt safe with the force of the weather and everything stowed and fastened and his boat braced against the gale. The gusts howled in the rigging. It was difficult now to look into the wind. He would not attempt to row back to the quays. He would drop down on the wind and leave his boat in the quiet of the river.

As he pulled in his punt, he became aware of two figures on the rocks several hundred yards downwind. They were a man and a woman. The man was wearing a big double-breasted jacket and carrying a small box on a string. With his other hand he was waving his hat. They were both soaked.

Jack rowed down to them and they climbed aboard. 'Thank God!' The man had to shout over the noise of the wind. 'No ferry! Thought we'd be spending the night there!'

The woman was wearing a sky-blue headscarf. Her hair kept spilling from it and eventually she gave up, pulling off the scarf. 'I don't know – how does it blow so quickly?' The rain ran down her cheeks and dripped from her chin. But she was laughing.

Three, four, five ... Tommy Treneer was sitting in Cooper's Yard. He had been sitting there for half a day now and he was counting the rows of cobbles between him and the rising water. That one stopped seven short of his feet and pulled back. Through the arch he could see the inner harbour and each wave coming through the Gaps and spreading out inside and up onto the road. There was still more than an hour until high water.

The first of the boats had long since risen into view and he had been watching the rogue seas among them. He knew the yard would flood because it was just three days since new moon and now this south-westerly would drive the spring tides in even higher. Knowing the yard was going to flood gave Tommy a satisfaction of sorts when it did, when he looked through the arch and saw the first waves rise and flop their water onto the road.

The others had all left. The cottages around Cooper's Yard were empty. It was now some days since the Stephenses and Mrs Moyle and the other Treneers had gone 'up the Crates'. For weeks before they had been packing up, but Tommy would have no part of it. He spent the time on Parliament Bench, or wandering the town, or in the lifeboat station. Sometimes he sat on his stool outside the cottage and showed a contemptuous indifference to all the activity around him. 'Sorry about Tom,' Mrs Treneer apologised for him. 'Just he's gone back-along.'

She herself spent those days going through the cottage room by room, packing the trunk with the clothes she no longer wore, the lace and embroidery she had been given for her trousseau, her Bible wrapped in untouched silk and her well-used copy of Old Moore's Almanack. She took down the framed picture in their bedroom of Moses viewing the

Promised Land. Croyden and Charlie came to collect the bed, the wardrobe and the boxes and they too took no notice of their father as he sat and scowled in the yard.

Mrs Treneer had now been a week at the Crates and she liked it. She liked the flat's new smell and the blood-red linoleum floors and the sunlight it received for most of the day. She tried to convince Tommy to join her. 'It's lovely up there, Tom. We got a tap.'

'I'd sooner die here,' he told her.

Now they had all gone and he sat on his stool in the gale. Dusk had come early. He did not look at the empty buildings above him; he ignored their lampless windows. He saw only the grey-black shape of the water that formed a channel beneath the arch. He looked beyond it to the flooded road and out into the inner harbour and through the Gaps to the open sea. All his life he had been gazing at the sea and now it was here and he was alone with it. It had reached his boots and crept in under the door behind. The yard was submerged. He sat there muttering and scratching his forearm and scowling and still there was another half-hour until high water.

In the morning, small clouds drifted in the pale blue sky. The sun sparkled on the water. A barnacled bottle crate, stamped with 'ST AUSTELL BREWERY' and containing the snapped-off leg of a china doll was jammed in under the steps of Eliza Tucker's general store. In the churchyard the roots of an old Monterey pine had prised open a newly-dug grave as it fell. The Reverend Winchester stood over it, horrified.

The good news was that a large section of sea-wall had collapsed beyond Pritchard's Beach and it would keep four men busy for at least a month.

In Cooper's Yard a thin layer of sediment lay over the cobbles. Pools of water remained on the slate flags inside; a brown line three inches up the wall marked the height of the flood. There was the soft smell of sewage.

Croyden found his father in the old kitchen. He was sitting on his stool, scratching his forearm. He looked up at Croyden with watery eyes. He stood slowly, and without a word brushed past his son and made his way up the hill to the Crates.

'*Maria Five*!'

Jack and Croyden were bringing the *Maria V* in through the Gaps, and on the end of the East Quay Jack recognised the man he had rescued from the rocks. He was waving.

'Ahoy there! *Maria Five*!'

Beside him was the woman in the sky-blue headscarf. Jack nudged the boat in against the quay wall, and as Croyden took a line ashore the man came up and thrust his hand over the gunwale towards Jack.

'Abraham,' he said. 'Maurice Abraham. And my wife, Anna.' He looked up and down the boat's length. 'Look, Mr er –'

'Jack Sweeney.'

'Mr Sweeney. I was wondering, could you take me out next time you go? I wouldn't get in your way – just need a corner to sketch. I'm an artist, you see.'

Jack told him to be there tomorrow morning at five-thirty.

Croyden watched them both go, merging back into the quayside crowd. He shook his head. 'Damn boxies.'

CHAPTER 6

Above Penpraze's yard and above the withy beds, the Glaze River narrowed and there was the old crossing-point for the ferry. In years gone by, the ferry allowed smallholders to get over the river and take the twice-weekly boat to Truro market from Polmayne's quays. Porth's sea-captains, en route to ships in Falmouth, also relied on it. Until some years before 1914 a man named Crimea Trestain ran the ferry in a boat which, every Easter, he lovingly upturned on the shingle bar outside his cottage and painted pale pink.

'Colour 'a maid's ass,' he explained. 'Room aboard for eight men, six women, three sows – or a parson.'

No one knew how old Crimea was. It was not clear whether he'd been born on the day the Crimean War broke out or the day it ended, or some other day entirely. Nor in the end could anyone remember whether it was him that gave out first or the boat, but by the Great War a new ferry – much less regular – had replaced it downstream. Crimea and Mrs Trestain disappeared up 'Bodmin way', the boat was laid up in Gooth Creek and the lease of Ferryman's Cottage was bought by an artist from London. The artist was Preston Connors.

Through Connors, the town of Polmayne and Ferryman's Cottage began to acquire a certain status among painters and writers in London. A new strain of incomers sought out lodgings there. They spent their days perched on clifftops or sauntering thoughtfully through the creekside woods. In the evenings they crammed into the main room of Ferryman's Cottage or gathered on the shingle beach outside. They had *al fresco* meals and made impromptu music. They talked. All were stirred by the remoteness of the place, and by the immanent beauty of the river and the woods above it. After his first stay in Polmayne the watercolourist Russell Flower wrote to his host: 'You have found a wonderful place, dear Connors. The mystical buttress of Pendhu Point opens up mineshafts of perception in man...'

It was at about this time that the first of Polmayne's net lofts was converted to an artist's studio. The people of Polmayne became used to coming across semi-circles of easels on the quays or around the holy well. The painters became known as 'boxies' for the wooden cases they carried. In the summers before the war, many of the town's young men, including Croyden Treneer and his brother Charlie, learned that they could earn sixpence for stripping off and cavorting in the coves around Pendhu while L.J. Price – in velveteen coat, hobnailed boots and cravat – sat on the rocks and painted them.

After the war, Preston Connors and Mrs Connors, now in their late fifties, moved up to Wicca House. The cottage continued as a haunt for artists. Throughout the twenties, an ever more colourful group beat a path to it. The sculptor Denton Sykes rode up the river at low tide on his Royal Enfield. Edeth St John, the surrealist painter and mystic poet, spent a winter in Ferryman's, composing her haunting book *The Dances of Still Things*. In the Introduction she wrote:

'Sometimes I listen to the wood-spirits sing above the Glaze River, and sometimes I listen to them weep . . .'

It was in a loft near Cooper's Yard that the Russian émigré Nikolai Bukovsky experimented with his famous mathematical paintings, where he wrote *The Furious Manifesto*, and where, one morning in 1929, he was found hanging from a beam.

Bukovsky's suicide cast a shadow over Polmayne's small colony of artists although in truth, by the summer of 1930, the group had already begun to dissipate. The art market had collapsed. Some went to St Ives or Lamorna, others returned to London, a few went abroad. Preston Connors entered the first stages of senility.

In June 1934, Maurice Abraham made a pilgrimage to Ferryman's with his wife Anna. Distressed to see the cottage abandoned, he applied to the Connorses for the lease.

At that time, Maurice Abraham was an accomplished if not particularly innovative painter. For all the precision of the portraits, the evocative power of the Scottish canvases and the moodiness of the seascapes, his work had always been overshadowed by his own physical beauty. The sculptor Brenda Fielding said: 'One would rather wish that Maurice was a statue so as to be able to stare at him at length without having to talk to him.'

Photographs show his girlish beauty. His two or three self-portraits do not, but reveal instead an oddly blank expression.

Maurice and Anna Abraham lived in a four-storey house in Hampstead inherited from Maurice's father. In June of 1934 they closed it up and came to Polmayne for several months. They had the roof re-thatched. They pulled off the ivy and re-rendered the walls. They replaced the rotting stairs. Preston Connors, who understood less and less of the world around him, applauded their efforts. 'Fine place for partridges, Ferryman's . . .'

In May 1935, having spent several months of the winter in

South America, Maurice came back to Polmayne with Anna. They planned to spend the summer there. As the weeks passed Maurice found himself transported by the atmosphere at Ferryman's – not so much by the river or the woods but by the great names who had preceded him – Sykes, Bukovsky, Connors, St John.

'Here in the darkness,' he wrote to the poet Max Stein in Germany, 'one feels the echo of a thousand unspoken conversations, the presence of a thousand unworked canvases, and the whisper of a thousand yet-to-be-written poems.'

'Marvellous light!'

Maurice Abraham took a deep breath of morning air. He was wearing his double-breasted jacket and a floppy trilby that shadowed his face. He was standing in the wheelhouse of the *Maria V* with Jack. As they motored out of the bay, he lit a pipe and began to talk.

What had occupied him over the last couple of years, he explained, was 'man and work'. 'In our machine age, work has become more and more mercenary, something done for money rather than something that is fulfilling in itself. Work should be a noble thing, Jack. Instead we see it as a chore. Mind if I call you Jack?'

Jack shook his head. He was thinking about the tides. Springs had eased a little but were still strong. If they didn't reach the grounds within two hours, the ebb would make fishing impossible. They should have left earlier. He opened the throttle to full.

Maurice sucked on his pipe and raised his voice. 'This winter I spent some time hopping up the Amazon, place to place, painting. The further up the river I went the more of a stranger I was. But you know what struck me most of all?'

Jack leaned out of the wheelhouse and called out to Croyden, 'We're going to be pushed!' Croyden and Bran hauled out two maunds and hurriedly finished the baiting up.

'It was this. The difference between those who hunted and those who had abandoned hunting for agriculture. Something was lost, Jack. Hard to put your finger on what. That's why this is so interesting.'

'What?'

'This!' Maurice gestured out to the deck with his pipe. 'You fishermen are neither cultivators nor pastoralists. You do not control the stock you depend on. Essentially you are hunter-gatherers – perhaps the last in all Europe to make a living like this. Do you see?'

They were coming round under Pendhu. 'Well . . .' Jack was only half-listening. He was watching the open sea as it came into view. On the horizon he could see a line of low serrations; it was going to be lumpy. He picked a course of 170 and the boat began to pitch in a long swell.

Maurice dipped a match in his pipe and puffed on it twice. 'Mind if I start?'

Outside he began to sketch Croyden and Bran as they slipped the pilchard fillets over each hook. He worked with great application for a few minutes, alternating pipe and pencil in a well-practised rhythm. He swayed a little with the motion of the boat, but lodged in under the bulwarks it did not affect his drawing. Then he put away the pipe. Ten minutes later he put aside his pencil and looked at the pad. Then he put aside the pad, stepped over to the side, and vomited. Croyden glanced at him, finished baiting up and joined Jack in the wheelhouse. Within a few minutes Maurice appeared at the door.

'Take me back . . .' Maurice groaned.

Croyden shook his head.

'I'll pay. How much do you want?'

They were passing the Main Cages and Croyden pointed to the lee of Maenmor. The rock shielded the sun and despite the swell outside, the sea was quiet in there. Slowly, Maurice realised what was happening. 'You can't – you can't put me there.'

Croyden leaned close to him and said, 'We're not losing a day's fishing on account of you, Mister. We put you ashore here or you carry on aboard. Up to you.'

Maurice looked up at the hulk of the rock.

Croyden stood by the gunwale. 'Hurry! We got work to do.'

They reached the grounds in time and the fishing was good. When the *Maria V* returned to the Main Cages that afternoon, Maurice climbed back on board in silence. In Polmayne he mumbled his thanks to Jack and hurried off along the East Quay without a backwards glance.

On Saturday afternoon, Jack returned home from fishing to find a note pushed under his door:

Beach Supper – Ferryman's Cottage 7 p.m. – do come!
Maurice and Anna Abraham.

He rowed there. After a day of broken cloud, the sky had cleared and left the bay wrapped in silky evening light. There wasn't a breath of wind. Jack passed the *Maria V*, motionless at her mooring. He passed the other working boats and the three rotting schooners in the mud, and the Petrels near Green's Rock with the sunlight flickering on their glassy sides. Beyond Penpraze's yard the river curved inland and there were no more boats. Nothing but the boughs of scrub oak brushing the top of the tide. He heard the cry of a curlew and he leaned on the paddles and let the boat drift on in silence. He gazed at the woods and their reflection in the water and felt the last of the sun on his back. Then he caught the faint smell of woodsmoke and the sound of voices. He dipped his paddles again and rowed on around the corner.

As soon as he arrived at Ferryman's Cottage, Jack wished he had not come. About a dozen people were sitting outside. He let the boat slide in to the beach and he climbed out and hauled it up. One of the men was standing, telling a story in a succession of different voices. 'In the back was a darkened room and he told them . . .'

Maurice saw Jack and came over. In a hushed voice he explained who everyone was. The story-teller was the 'poet and distinguished Communist' Max Stein. There were several painters from London, St Ives, Lamorna. Jack recognised Preston and Dorothy Connors. There was a sculptress called Peter, a 'radical', an 'anarchist' and several others. Everyone had an epithet. Everyone was listening to Max Stein: '. . . and he says – there's only two of us but the woman's for free!'

Laughter rang out around the creek.

Max spotted Jack. 'Ah, Maurice – your fisherman!' He came over and looked Jack up and down. 'Are you *un vrai pecheur*?'

'Hardly . . .' muttered Jack.

'Know how to tell a true fisherman?' Max turned to the others.

'You ask him,' said the woman called Peter.

'He catches fish,' said the anarchist.

'The smell!' Max made a show of sniffing Jack's shoulder. 'Sea-salt . . . damp . . . soap . . .'

Anna Abraham came out of the cottage, wiping her hands on her apron. Her sky-blue scarf was tied peasant-style behind her neck. She said quietly to Jack: 'Please – I need your help.' She had a crisp, rounded accent: Icelandic, according to Mrs Moyle, whose late husband had spent five years fishing up there and had come back speaking exactly like Mrs Abraham.

He followed her inside. On the slate floor of the kitchen were four hen crabs. One of them was slowly snapping a paintbrush in its claw. Anna lunged for it but it scuttled away. Jack removed the brush himself. He captured each of the crabs and put them in a large bucket. Anna Abraham boiled water on the range and Jack dropped the crabs in one by one. When the crabs were cooked Jack smashed the claws with a scale-weight. He showed Anna how to open the carapace and extract the good meat with her fingers.

'What a strange fruit the crab is!' Her hands were smeared with crab meat. 'Maurice said he had a very interesting time fishing with you.'

'He told you about the rock?'

'What rock?'

Jack told her about Maurice's day spent on Maenmor.

'Poor Maurice!' Anna was still laughing as they took the plates of dressed crab outside.

When Jack rowed back, it was nearly dark. A thin moon had risen over Pendhu and its light glittered and spread across the water. He rowed on into the middle of the bay, filled with an elation that he could not quite explain.

CHAPTER 7

The following afternoon Anna Abraham came to call on Jack. She brought him a bag of cherries. When he opened his door, she made a mock bow. 'You must accept my thanks, Mr Sweeney – twice.' And she made another little bow.

'Twice?'

'One – for explaining to me the crab. Two – for saving our lives in the storm.'

She was not wearing her headscarf. Without it, she looked different. The hem of a fawn raincoat reached down to the top of her Wellington boots and she said: 'I am out for a walk. Will you come?'

So they walked along the front eating cherries. The sky was a deep blue and there was little wind. They followed the path to the end of the houses and up out of town. At the top of the hill they caught their breath and looked back over the roofs to Pendhu Point. The dark tops of the Main Cages were just visible beyond it, ruffed with white surf. In one corner of Dalvin's field were the first of the visitors' white tents.

Anna said, 'They look like mushrooms.' At the lifeboat station, she stood on tiptoe to peer in at the boat and was amazed how ugly it was. 'A bull in a barn!'

There was a small beach below the station. Anna pulled off her boots and paddled in the water. She splashed through the shallows and then they sat on the rocks and she laid her bare feet on the weed and looked at him askance. 'You have bird's feet, Mr Sweeney, here beside the eyes. We say that's a happy sign.'

'In Iceland?'

'Iceland?'

'You *are* from Iceland, Mrs Abraham?'

She laughed and shook her head. 'I'm not even sure where Iceland is. I come from Russia!' And she jumped down from the rocks and ran back to the water.

Two days later Jack rowed up the river to Ferryman's Cottage. He had brought the Abrahams a turbot. Finding no one there, he wrote a note thanking them for supper. He put it on the table under the fish, then changed his mind: he rolled up the note and jammed it into the fish's mouth.

One afternoon in late July a red, snub-nosed lorry drew up on the Town Quay and Jack and Croyden stepped away from the wall to meet it. On the side of the lorry was written 'Hounsells of Bridport' and in it were twenty brand-new pilchard nets.

Jack remembered Hounsells as a child. He remembered the treacly, creosote smell that came from it; he was told it was a factory for 'fish-traps' and always imagined a fish-trap as something like an underwater mousetrap, baited with tiny sacs of treacle.

Helping to unload the nets, fielding as he did so the half-respectful jibes from Parliament Bench about doing a 'bit 'a shrimpin'', he picked up pieces of Bridport news from the driver. His farm was now in the hands of a 'fat Devon man' who was selling off some of the woods. The driver did not know Jack's great-aunt Bess but he did know Arthur Sweeney – Jack's cousin – who had made himself very unpopular by cutting down two famous oak trees. Jack was more pleased than ever to be free of the land.

The *Maria V* was almost ready. It was time for Newlyn and the pilchards. The summer pilchards, said Croyden, that's what makes or breaks the year. For him it was even more critical; if they failed, he would be forced back to the building sites. From the long-lining he had taken home almost enough to pay off last winter's debts and Maggie grudgingly accepted that he should carry on. With the boat's fifth share Jack had rented a net loft above the East Quay. Already it was filled with gear – some of his pots, a number of dan buoys, a pile of inflatable buffs, countless cork cobles and a couple of miles of warp for the head-rope.

He had also recruited a new crew member. Bran Johns had left to join his brother's boat so they took on Toper Walsh's son, Albert. Albert was a deft, wiry man in his forties. He was a whistler. He didn't whistle on board because it was bad luck but Croyden did allow him to hum. He had an appealing half-smile and an elaborate cipher of nicknames. Because his hair had once stuck straight up like a brush he was called 'Brush' Walsh – but for some 'Brush' became 'Deck-Brush', and in time 'Deck-Brush' became 'Deck' and 'Deck' mutated to 'Dee' and then 'Dee' became 'Double-dee' and simply 'Double'. Most had no idea why he was called Double as he was now completely bald.

In Newlyn, the fishing began well. In the first week they cleared nearly £50. At the end of it, Jack received a letter addressed to *Captain Jack Sweeney, Maria Five, The Harbour, Newlyn* and delivered by a boy from the post office. It was from Mrs Abraham.

Dear Mr Sweeney,
  Thank you for the fish! I drew him quickly – then cooked him. Now I am sitting outside the cottage. It is very early in

*the morning and as quiet as Heaven. Maurice is asleep. He
was up in St Ives and they had a big meeting of painters. They
all get together for a meeting and speak nonsense to each other
and they agree important things and then they go out and
drink and talk more nonsense and disagree about everything.
I stayed here. What is it like catching pilchards, I wonder? I
think of you out on the sea with your nets and here I am
sending some magic messages from Polmayne.*

    Anna Abraham

    *[She had drawn a picture of a line of birds flying over the
horizon towards his boat; as they came closer the birds dived
into the sea and became fish and were gathered up in his nets.]*

Jack lay on his bunk in the mid-afternoon. It was very hot.
He could feel the sun on the deck above. The boat creaked
against its warps. They had landed thirteen thousand pilchards
that morning and now they were tied up in the inner harbour
and everyone was asleep. But Jack could not sleep. He was
lying on his bunk with the letter in his hand and he was
watching a patch of sunlight where it spilled through the
hatch, sliding back and forth against the bulkhead. She's being
friendly, that's all. She is married and she is being friendly.
He tried to tell himself that is just how they are in Iceland
or Russia but he did not try that hard because it was much
more pleasant in the hot afternoon to lie on his bunk and
think of her – and it was pleasant at night when the nets were
out and they were waiting to haul, pleasant in the morning
too when they were motoring in with a hold full of fish.

It was not until the following week that the pilchards
stopped coming. Four nights in a row they drew black nets.
The gains they had made began to slip away. When some of
the St Ives boats announced they were cutting their losses and
returning home, Double suggested doing the same.

'Perhaps you're right,' sighed Jack.

Croyden told him: 'You leave now and you leave without
me.'

Jack knew he could not continue fishing without Croyden. They agreed to give it another week. On the Sunday another half-gale set in from the south and they lost a further two days. The rafted boats in the inner harbour strained and knocked against each other, as did the crews. Croyden and Double came close to blows and Jack told Croyden to go and stay with his wife's family in their tobacco store.

On Tuesday afternoon the wind began to ease. The next evening, in a brilliant blue and orange dusk, the entire fleet put to sea again. The *Maria V* headed west, and with a group of Mevagissey boats reached a place some three miles south of the Wolf Rock. It was a warm night. A light westerly breeze just filled the mizzen. The moon glowed behind a thin layer of cloud. Down to leeward, the other boats took up positions and on the *Maria V* they could hear the murmur of conversation and the single, united voice of a crew singing.

Double rubbed his hands. 'They're about tonight, Jack! I feel it in my bones.'

Croyden glared at him. 'Shut up, Dee.'

They shot the first fifteen nets with ease. The seas had settled and the boat wallowed in the last of the swell. From the bows, the line of cobles stretched out into the darkness. Some way off, receding, was the light of the dan buoy. Double was humming as he paid out the leech. Croyden had his eyes on the head-rope. Every five fathoms he flicked at the line and a coble came swinging up out of the net room, over the gunwale and into the water.

'Come on now, my darlings!' cooed Double at the sea.

Jack leaned out of the wheelhouse. 'All twenty?' Croyden's beret nodded as he worked and he fed out the line and the buoys. Below the surface the mile-long curtain of nets grew.

Croyden had reached the seventeenth buff when he suddenly paused and looked up. Double stopped his humming.

'What is it?' called Jack.

Croyden held up his hand. He was looking up to windward. 'Quick – knock her in!'

Jack pushed the boat forward. Then he noticed it too, a faint oily smell on the breeze. As he eased the throttle, he became aware of a brook-like sound off the starboard bow. The nets spun out of Croyden's hand, the cobles shot overboard. Jack turned on the fishing lights and watched. He could hear the shoal coming nearer. The fish were now very close, speeding towards them like a flash-flood. Then he saw them – the furring of the water, the swarming of fish at the surface. It was a vast shoal!

'Best haul now,' shouted Croyden. 'We'll leave the others.'

The first net came in thick with fish. They fell out and slid over the deck.

'I told you they was here, Croy!' shouted Double.

Even Croyden seemed excited. He was pulling in the head-rope two feet at a time. The first couple of nets were heavy. Fish spilled out of them and Croyden and Double shoved what they could down into the hold.

'Yee–ee!' yelled Double.

'In now,' muttered Croyden with each haul. 'In 'ee come now . . .'

With the third net Croyden began to falter. Jack watched the head-rope tighten on the roller. He brought the bows over it – but it hardly slackened. Croyden braced himself and with Double beside him the net came aboard again. In places the fish were so thick it was hard to see the net at all.

The fourth net had turned over the head-rope as the fish drove into it and it was lighter. Another great mound of pilchards fell on the deck. Then the head-rope tightened again. Jack eased the boat forward. But it did not slacken on the roller. It did not budge at all.

'Hold her!' said Croyden. 'Hold her now!'

Jack steadied the boat on the throttle. He watched Croyden and Double gripping the head-rope, frozen against its weight. The fish were all around the boat. Gannets were diving into the shoal. He looked out beyond the loom of lights and saw the flash of fish-backs far into the darkness. There was no end to the shoal. For the first time he thought: how were they to land such a catch?

He left the wheelhouse and hurried forward. Together the three of them managed to haul a little more. But the weight came again and with each haul they managed less. Still the fish were coming. Another ten inches of net. But now again the head-rope was jammed on the roller.

'Hold her now! Hold her!' cried Croyden.

Then Double lost his footing. They dropped another several feet before he recovered. The scuppers were dipping below the surface with the weight of the nets.

In with the shoal now were dogfish. Hundreds had been drawn to the shoal, driven mad by the plenty. Their brown bodies squirmed amidst the silver. They snapped at the fish. Their eyes flashed in the lights. Some of them came up with the nets and Double knocked them off when he could. Those on deck continued to thrash about among the pilchards, even as they died.

'Out of there, you bastard! Get on now, get on!' Croyden kicked one away and turned back to the nets. 'Come in, my beauties! Come in now!'

The boat was low in the water and heeling hard to the nets. It was difficult to tell which was water now and which was boat. Double shouted, 'Leave it, Croy! Leave the nets!'

There were still twelve nets out. Croyden's face shone in the lights. He was grinning.

'For Christ's sake, Croy!' shouted Jack. 'They'll drag us down!'

'Pull!'

Together they managed a little. 'Again!' shouted Croyden.

Five inches. 'Again!'

Seven inches. 'We're winning!'

Nearly a mile of nets remained in the water, pulling down on the cobles with their weight. And still the fish were coming, shoaling so thickly that they were drowning each other. The surface was full of their bodies. Gannets were diving all around the boat, striking the churned-up water in bomb-bursts and the gannets too were coming up in the nets, and they too were drowned, their necks caught in the mesh as they fed.

'Now! Again!' The sweat was running down Croyden's face.

Fish covered the deck. The head-rope on the roller was slipping back again. The boat was being pulled over. 'Let it go, Croy!' Jack lunged for the rope. Croyden pushed him off. He grabbed the head-rope and alone managed to pull a couple of inches. Jack reached down and slipped a gutting knife from inside the bulwarks. He slashed at the rope. He sawed at it – but Croyden shoved him aside and he fell. The knife spun overboard.

Croyden continued to heave. The net was stuck fast. He tried to reach ahead but the strands of the head-rope were popping apart on the roller. The last one went and the *Maria V* sprang back onto an even keel. The remaining nets stretched out into the shoal. Still the fish were driving into them, but one by one the cobles disappeared from the surface, dragged down by the weight. Croyden watched them go. He remained at the gunwale, even as the boat turned and they made their way back through the fleet to Newlyn.

The next morning, three million pilchards were landed at Newlyn, a post-war record, but for the *Maria V* the season was over. They left Newlyn and headed out towards the Lizard. In Polmayne Bay the Petrels were racing. Jack and Croyden and Double rowed in unnoticed through the Gaps, while a crowd of people stood at the quay wall cheering the yachts as they pushed towards the finishing line.

CHAPTER 8

C royden leaned on the fence and looked at his pigs. Five
was under the stern section of the old dinghy, Three
under the bows. Croyden leaned there for some time and the
August sun was hot on his back. In the end, it was Three
who stirred, Three who rose to her feet and lumbered towards
him. Scabs of dried mud were peeling from her flank. He
rubbed her forehead with his knuckles. 'We lost 'em, old girl.
Nothing we could do.'

With her snout, Three butted fondly at his hand.

He did not tell Maggie. There was no need for her to know
about the nets. He had a little to show for the fishing and he
would give her that and he would be able to carry on at sea.

Double, though, was leaving. When they reached Polmayne
he took Jack to one side: 'I'll not go to sea again with that
madman.'

'But you're in the lifeboat with him.'

'That's different. It's the fish – they do something to him.
You saw it yourself.'

The next day, Jack rowed up the river to Ferryman's Cottage. Rounding the corner he saw the familiar whitewashed walls and the heavy brow of the thatch and the little windows. They were shuttered. A flood board was across the door. The Abrahams had returned to London.

Back at Bethesda, he sat down and wrote a letter, replying to Mrs Abraham's questions about his fishing.

'... It's a see-saw business, Mrs Abraham, sometimes no fish, and sometimes too many ...' Then, although he had intended to make light of his losses to her, he found the whole episode at the Wolf Rock came flooding out.

Three days later came her reply.

... What a calamity! I have been thinking about it and whenever I read your letter it makes me shivering. I will tell you a story and you will understand. My father had a house in a small village in the seaside of the Baltic. He wanted to help the village people. He wanted to give them a grand piano. He took it along the coast in a sailing boat but the piano was too big and the boat turned over and sank and that is how I lost my father, Mr Sweeney. He drowned. So I have always been very afraid of the sea. Be careful, please ...

Maggie Treneer found out what had happened at Newlyn and confronted Croyden: 'So now where's his luck, your Sweeney?' She told him if he went back to sea she'd throw him out of the house. Croyden weighed it up carefully, then took to sleeping in the net loft.

Autumn came early that year. It crouched in the corner of August's darkening evenings; it was there in the cold that lingered after dawn. In the second week of September, the wind freshened from the west and within a few hours had become a full gale. It tore the leaves from the trees and spun them in angry circles around the yards. Apples fell by the dozen and rolled down the leats. It lasted for the best part of two days.

On Parliament Bench, they watched the storm whip up the seas beneath Pendhu Point and Toper Walsh folded his arms and said, 'Well, there's another gone.'

'Gone!'

'Another what, Tope?'

'Another summer.'

'Eeee,' agreed Boy Johns.

With the coming of autumn, the faces on the Bench became fewer. Toper Walsh still put in his daily appearance, arriving before everyone else to sweep the Town Quay and clear up any litter. No one was sure whether this was an official post for Toper, or whether he did it because it gave him some degree of authority. Boy continued to come, saying nothing more than his customary 'Eeee'. But others like Brian Tyler liked to watch the visitors and when the visitors became scarcer so did they. Archie Stephens had grown so wheezy that he seldom left his home now. Dick Treneer went to see his cousin in Mevagissey. (Dick was commonly known as Red Treneer because of his political views and to distinguish him from old Dick Treneer, though it meant he was sometimes confused with Red Stephens who had no political views but had once owned a pair of very red trousers.) Brian Williams had fallen out with Toper. The Crates had taken their toll. It was said that Joseph Cloke and Moor Martin had a bench of their own up there. Tommy Treneer had not been seen since he left Cooper's Yard.

So in September, as the days became shorter and the hotels and guest houses emptied and the Petrels were towed in to Penpraze's yard to have their masts taken out, labelled and stowed in the rafters, and as the Garretts laid up the *Polmayne Queen* and returned to stealing shellfish from other people's pots, and Whaler Cuffe and the others left their summer sheds to take up residence again in their own houses, the Bench began to run out of things to talk about. Not only were there few strangers to criticise but nothing in the town was being knocked down, the autumn storms had been and gone with little destruction, and no one had died since March.

Towards the end of the month things livened up. The lifeboat was called out twice – a false alarm and a schooner put under tow (no casualties) – and then on the afternoon of the twenty-third the Reverend Arthur Winchester was found dead on the floor of his study. On the desk was the conclusion of the latest chapter of his monograph 'The March of Science':

> ... *we are like a man standing on the edge of a great sea. He has been given a boat with which to cross it but he does not appreciate the dangers. This man gives up the land at his peril* ...

The Bench had never acknowledged Winchester in life but now they competed to show their appreciation.

'An inspiration,' concluded Toper.

'A true man of God.'

'From up east, wan't him?'

'London.'

'Ninety-one years old!'

'Some age.'

'They won't come like him no more.'

'Never.'

'Eeee.'

Within three weeks of Winchester's death, a replacement had arrived at Polmayne's rectory. The Reverend Andrew Hooper had spent fifteen happy years as an army chaplain in Aldershot, fifteen happy years in India and now he was going to spend fifteen happy years in Cornwall.

He climbed down from the rectory cart, stretched his long limbs and breathed in deeply. 'Sea air!' he called to Mrs Hooper.

Peering through the lych-gate, he saw the church tower below and the Glaze River beyond it and the graveyard half-hidden by vegetation.

'What did I tell you, my dear! A jungle!'

Hooper had already read the passage in *The Cornish Coast, South* (1910):

The grounds of Polmayne's 14th-century church of St Cuby tumble into a quiet creek to the east of the town. In the 1860s the Reverend Pratt, antiquarian and horticulturalist, assembled the plants for this unspeakably lovely churchyard which, once seen, remains for ever in the mind as the England of one's dreams ...

Pratt's planting, it later turned out, was largely the result of his 'Lent Prayer Tours' during which he would visit the duchy's great houses, conducting informal theological discussions while his driver took cuttings from the gardens' rare plants.

But in his twenty years with the living of Polmayne, Winchester had allowed Pratt's sub-tropical gardens to lapse into a state of tropical disorder. Hooper wasted no time in restoring them. He recruited a team of part-time gardeners. 'Hackers' he called them, and he spent that first winter alongside them, clearing and slashing at the brambles and creeper. 'Assaulting the pagan thorn!' he trilled, and in doing so discovered for himself the half-hidden history of the town.

The granite cross commemorating the victims of the *Adelaide* had almost toppled over; he re-bedded it. Down towards the creek, beside a swampy patch of gunnera, the Hackers came across a group of unmarked graves under an overgrown mound of ship's tackle – rotting blocks, mossy warps, an anchor and shreds of cloth which may once have been sails or may have been clothes. The discipline of the tropics heeded Parson Hooper to burn the cloth for fear of cholera.

Parson Hooper transformed the grounds of Polmayne's

church, and nowhere did he leave his mark more visibly than with his 'Tablets'. Each month, after his diocesan meeting, he would visit the yard of Truro's Pascoe & Sons (Monumental Masons), with a quotation of some sort. The following month he would put the Tablet in the back of his trap, return to Polmayne and install it alongside the main paths of the churchyard. The first month he put in a series of three. The first was by the lych-gate:

> *And I will make thy windows of agate*
> *And thy gates of carbuncles*
> *And all thy borders of precious stones.*

At the beginning of the path's descent:

> *The Path of the Just is as the Shining Light*
> *That Shineth more and more unto the Perfect Day.*

Halfway down, the path took a steep right-hand bend and plunged into a bower of holm oak:

> *They heard the voice of the Lord God*
> *Walking in the garden in the cool of the day.*

Each time he put in a Tablet, Parson Hooper gave a short ceremony. In time, the ceremonies came to be attended by the same group of dedicated Anglican women.

Late in October Mrs Franks returned from several months in India. She was sorry to hear of Winchester's death but pleased to see that Hooper was making such progress in the churchyard. Bending to inspect one of his new Tablets, she read: 'They heard the voice of the Lord God/Walking in the garden in the cool of the day.' When she found Hooper himself in his overalls, she beamed at him. 'So you're the new vicar?'

He smiled humbly. 'Madam, I am the gardener.'

After Winchester's creaking ministry, here was a man of energy and life. As Hooper stood half-singing his prayers of dedication the women looked up at his Asia-weathered face, and vowed to give more of their time to beautifying the church.

CHAPTER 9

On 11 November the *Maria V* left Polmayne for Plymouth. Losing the nets in Newlyn had made Jack even more determined to continue fishing. He had borrowed money and bought a set of used nets from a man in Porth. In Plymouth they began to recoup some of their losses.

By mid-December the winter pilchards came to an end and Jack asked the crew if they wanted to go back to Polmayne. None of them had anything to go for, so they agreed to stay on for the herring.

There were three of them now – Jack and Croyden and a man named Harry Hammels. Crew was hard to come by in Polmayne that autumn; six new houses were being built and the sea-wall was being extended, but Croyden told Jack: 'There's always Hammels.'

Indeed there was. 'Yes, please, Misser Swee, I come Plymouth!' Harry Hammels was something of a mystery in Polmayne. In December 1931 people first started noticing his quick, light-stepped walk along the front, his grinning presence in the coalyard where he found a job. No one knew where he came from. His accent some thought was Spanish, some more Greek-sounding. He himself gave no clues to his past except to say that he had no nationality because all his life had been spent at sea.

Off Plymouth that December the herring were scarce. It was only a year since a group of boats had trawled Bigbury Bay and fished out the spawning stock. Day after day went past without a fish being caught. Croyden moped around the bars of Plymouth. Hammels carved from pieces of driftwood his wooden 'warriors' – which he then sold at the entrance to Hoe Park.

Jack had started a 'Fishing Diary'. In an oilcloth notebook he recorded the weather, details of catches (time, place of shooting and hauling, quantities) and various anecdotes. He had also, since September, been having a lively exchange of letters with Anna Abraham. She had told him that she 'needed news of Polmayne'; he in turn enjoyed explaining to an outsider the ups and downs of his fishing, the goings-on in the town. To begin with, he had held back on details, but she told him: 'I want to know Every Thing, Mr Sweeney, you don't imagine how I miss Polmayne.' And he found himself anticipating with ever greater impatience the delivery of her replies, the particular lilt of her faulty English and her wry descriptions of the artistic milieu of Hampstead.

On 15 December, the *Maria V* struck lucky. In a single night off Start Point they caught fifty-eight cran of fish and earned a total of £160. For almost a week they successfully fished the same spot. They returned to Polmayne in funds. Hammels bought a new French penknife. Maggie Treneer allowed Croyden back into his cottage, but only on condition that he kill one of his pigs. He agreed, but each day found a different excuse to delay the slaughter.

'We are rich,' wrote Jack to Anna Abraham. 'Well, richer than we were – at last we have had some good fishing. This is my second winter here in Polmayne and this morning it is sunny and the harbour is quiet and I cannot think of anywhere in the world I would rather be . . .'

It was the week before Christmas. The town had settled into its midwinter hollow. On frosty mornings the sun rose above the mists of the Glaze River, made a quick dash across the sky and sank back into the sea. They were still days, windless days, and at sundown the water was covered in a rusty light and the gulls came in and settled on it and briefly the whole bay shone orange-red and twitched in the breeze. It looked like the flank of some great hibernating beast, waiting for the spring.

That Christmas, his first Christmas, Parson Hooper proposed holding an ecumenical carol service on Polmayne's Town Quay. He wrote to his fellow ministers: 'When better to unite the congregations of our parish than in this Christmas season?' The United Methodist minister thought it a 'splendid idea', but the Bible Christians insisted that if they were to take part it should be billed 'A Festival of Carols', and the proposed sermons be in the form of a New Year Address.

23 December dawned grey. Soggy clouds hung over a herring-coloured sea. Parson Hooper lowered the sash of his bedroom window, looked downriver and prayed for them to clear. By midday it had worked – a westerly breeze had driven away the clouds.

On the Town Quay the three ministers stood with their backs to the sea. They each clutched a prayerbook to their chest and their robes rippled in the wind. The Town Band assembled beside them. In front, on the broad apron of the harbour, gathered a sizeable crowd. A group had come by boat from Porth and they stood apart from the others.

Whaler Cuffe gripped Jack's arm as he followed his stick along the cobbles. 'Here, Jack . . . or there – what's up there?' They tried several places before finding the right one, where the sound of the band and the singing would be exactly in balance.

At 2.30, Parson Hooper stood on Parliament Bench and spread his arms. The low winter sun shone on his face and gave it a look of glowing innocence. The crowd fell silent beneath him.

'We are gathered together in the sight of the Lord to celebrate the coming of His Son. Lord, you bestowed on us the great gift of Your Only Son and sent him into the world for our sins. We will begin by singing "Once in Royal David's City".'

After that was Thomas Merrit's 'Lo He Comes, the Infant Stranger' and then Major Franks read from St John's gospel. They sang 'Hark the Glad Sound' and with each carol the singing grew stronger.

Parson Hooper climbed up again on Parliament Bench to make the first address. As he began to speak a few clouds drifted in over his head.

'Last week,' he announced, 'I discovered in my study the unpublished tract of my late predecessor, the Reverend Winchester. It is a most interesting document and contains a passage on the coming of the New Year. He likens us at the beginning of each year to the captain of a ship sailing under sealed orders. Those orders tell him the course to steer, but he is commanded not to open them until he reaches a certain latitude. In 1936 we have every reason to suppose that even if we are sailing blind, our orders will be favourable. The world has pulled itself out of its recent mire and we are all stronger for it! So enjoy what you have. I have been in Polmayne only a short time but already I look around me and see an enchanted place and think of it – and we who live here – as somehow blessed . . .'

The United Methodist minister, the Reverend Brendan Jones, followed. 'When we wish each other "Happy New Year", what do we mean? It is not so much a wish as a right of each and every one of you. We have no sympathy with those who frown upon pleasure. We do not hold that the world is worse because it laughs . . .'

Mr Pawle stepped forward for the Bible Christians and said: '. . . I am not expected to be the peddler of intellectual confectionery or the retailer of sweet nothings. It is no use harping about the New Year when nothing in its opening seems worth the wishes spent on it . . .'

Everyone but the ministers could see the coming squall. It dashed in across the bay in a skidding acre of dark water. When it reached the quay, they had just begun 'While Shepherds Watch'. It toppled the music stands of the euphonium and cornet players. The cap of the band leader spun from his head and went wheeling across the quay. Major Franks made a lunge for it, dropping to his knees to try and reach it – but it fell over the edge of the harbour and into the water. He stood and brushed the dirt from his suit trousers. 'Never was much of a slip fielder!'

Then came the rain. It hit the company with a cheek-stinging fury. The fourth verse collapsed. The band was reduced to a series of tumbling squawks as the members ducked. When the rain turned to hail everyone ran for shelter. Major Franks escorted Mrs Kliskey. Parson Hooper tried to make an announcement but no one could hear him. Whaler Cuffe stood his ground: 'Don't go, please! It's only a shower!'

The squall lasted ten minutes. Behind it was a strip of pale blue which widened until suddenly the sunlight burst out of it, shining on the wet roofs and on the road and on drifts of hailstones. But it was too late. The stands were in disarray; sheet music was pasted to the ground or scattered among the boats of the inner harbour. Those sheltering in doorways started to find their way home.

But not all. Some twenty or thirty remained around the quays. The wind dropped, and as dusk spread across the bay the sound of carols rose again. The band had left but the Garretts were still there; the group from Porth was still there, and when they all started to sing, many of the people came outside again to listen. This was what Hooper had intended – the parishes and congregations united in song! All around the harbour, they stood in doorways or leaned from their windows, and with the voices rising from the quay, the sun slid behind the land and the waters of the bay turned from orange to gold.

In the third verse of 'Awake, Awake' the harmony broke down. The Polmayne singers sang their version and the Porth singers sang theirs. At the end Jimmy Garrett glared at the Porth men. 'You sing it the right way when you're with we!'

'We sang it the bloody right way.'

Then one of those Porth men stepped forward and hit Jimmy Garrett on the side of the head. Tacker tried to hold his brother back but Jimmy shook him off. He managed to place himself right in the centre of the Porth men and swing his arms in a most effective way.

In the morning a light frost covered the town and on the cobbles of the Town Quay were scattered tiny beads of frozen blood.

On Christmas Eve, a trading ship sailed into the bay. The *Constantine* was a much-admired schooner in Polmayne, an occasional visitor on her trips up and down the Channel. In the evening the crew rowed ashore. As they entered the Gaps, the vast frame of the ship's master could be seen standing, in a high-collared reefer, in the stern. Captain Henriksen was a bushy-browed Finn, and at the bar of the Fountain Inn he announced that he and his crew would be spending the 'festival' at anchor in the bay.

That day Jack had received a card from the Abrahams. The drawing was by Maurice Abraham and showed an anxious-looking turkey with a speech bubble rising from its mouth: *'Why not have a lark this Christmas?'*

Jack did. On Boxing Day Whaler Cuffe banged his stick on the floor and announced he had been cooped for too long inside. 'I would like to go carousing.' Jack took him to see Benny Stone and they drank brandy and then some others came and they went to the Fountain Inn and Whaler told some improbable stories and the crew of the *Constantine* applauded even though they knew they were supposed to be sceptical about 'Whaler's fabling'.

Polmayne shook itself down that Christmas. The children sooted their faces and went Darkey Partyin'. Jack and Whaler set off to the dance in the Freeman Reading Rooms. They carried on somewhere else and it was almost dawn when they staggered home along the front. Eliza Tucker was sweeping the steps of her store, and stopped to watch them: 'The blind drunk leading the blind!' They were still tipsy at lunchtime and Mrs Cuffe refused to feed them. So they went out again. That afternoon the Town Band left the Fountain Inn for Porth but they took a short cut and the flautist dropped his flute in a stream; the percussionists were found by Ivor Dawkins next morning, sleeping in one of Crowdy's barns.

In the New Year, Jack wrote to Anna Abraham. 'Polmayne was very colourful at Christmas. I would never have believed it possible. When are you coming down here? The town misses you.' He read the letter back and then added: 'And I miss you too!'

The weeks of January dragged by. There was no fishing. No letter came from Anna Abraham. The *Constantine* left on the tenth. In the third week of the month, Croyden went to collect Three for slaughter. Halfway up to Crowdy Farm he turned back and took Five instead. The next day all the flags in Polmayne flew at half-mast. From the bells of St Cuby's church rang a mourning peal and those given to wearing ties picked a dark one that day. At Sandringham the King had died, and Mrs Franks cancelled the Conservative Association's annual dance. But to many in Polmayne the King's death meant little until months later when it became known that *Britannia*, his beloved J-class yacht, was towed out to sea and scuppered.

At the end of January, Jack at last received a reply from Anna Abraham:

Dear Mr Sweeney,
    I would be grateful if you write me no more letters. I hope you understand.
    Yours, Anna Abraham

CHAPTER 10

In early February came a week of relentless rain. The Glaze
River flowed muddy brown into the bay and up at Pennance the ground below the holy well became a shallow lake.
Jack Sweeney was more impatient than ever. It was still early
in the season but when the weather cleared he told the others
that the *Maria V* would start fishing. All they had to do was
load the gear and service the Kelvin. Croyden was happy to
begin; Hammels did not mind either way.

They fished every possible hour. They went out on nights
when others stayed in and returned long after dawn. They
shot sometimes three, four times a night. Once or twice, in
mounting seas, they had to haul in a hurry and race back to
harbour; on other occasions with the fish tumbling onto the
deck, Jack saw the crazed look come over Croyden. But it
no longer worried him. In fact, he saw it as something of an
asset – and he was beginning to understand it.

Then the pilchard market collapsed. Mussolini's Abyssinian

adventure had meant an embargo on Italian goods; the Italians responded in kind and ships filled with Cornish pilchards – food for the Lenten fast – were being turned back.

The *Maria V* was forced to tie up, and Jack kicked his heels around Polmayne. It was still too early for the long-line. On several mornings he rowed out to the *Maria V*. He replaced a series of worn cleats, some old blocks. He sanded down and painted the countless bumps and scrapes on the gunwale. He cleaned and oiled everything that moved and many things that did not. He took to eating on board, then to sleeping. He learned that each and every state of weather and tide tapped out a different rhythm on the boat's creaking timbers. He knew when he woke what sort of day it would be simply from the boat's motion.

One day he was awake at dawn and there was no noise from the timbers and no motion but only the faintest trickle of water past the hull. The tide was flooding and the sun was coming through the forehatch and he rose and rowed up the river, past Penpraze's to Ferryman's Cottage. He drifted for a moment off the shingle bar before rowing on. He followed the river up through its unpeopled narrows to a place where it opened out into a large wood-fringed pool. He had never been here before. It was now nearly the top of the tide and the water was absolutely still. He rowed on into it, breaking its glassy surface. The river divided and he chose the southern branch, the smaller one. Several herons took flight as he entered the creek. The bare branches of scrub oak touched the water and as he rowed further he saw them – the first of the boats. Their rotting hulls lay half-submerged, their bows pointing up the banks and in beneath the trees. Weed and moss hung from their sodden sides. Last year's leaves lay matted on those which still had decks. Many were little more than frames, their shapes discernible only from the bare ribs that pushed up out of the water. The older the boats were the more they took on the colours and consistency of the creek. Jack started to count them. At forty-five he stopped.

He drifted on, his paddles raised, and there were more boats – seiners, schooners, luggers, barges and punts – until the tide turned and began to pull him back.

'Gooth,' Croyden told him later. 'Gooth Creek – where they all end sooner or later. *Good Heart*'s there, they all are, all the seiners and every other bloody boat that's ever worked these waters.'

In early March, the *Maria V* began to fish the ground some fifty miles into the English Channel. One night, Jack was unhooking a large ray and was stabbed in the hand by a spine so suddenly that he slipped and fell on the deck. He was astonished at the pain. Back in Polmayne Dr White told him there was nothing to do but wait for the venom to work itself out and the swelling to go down. It might be weeks.

Jack languished at home. Mrs Cuffe said he had it coming to him. 'Going out in all weathers. It's a blessing, you know. Might 'a been something bad.'

Whaler told him about being bitten by a 'snake-fish' in the Bay of Bengal and hallucinating for four days.

Unable to row, unable even to do his knots, Jack took to walking. He crossed the river and wandered down to the sands of Hemlock Cove. He followed the path out beyond Penpraze's and watched the cropping of the withies. He went inland, up the valley to Pennance where beneath the still leafless beech trees he drank from St Pinnock's holy well and thought of Alice. One afternoon he was ambling down Rectory Lane when Parson Hooper came up behind him in a pony and trap. Jack stepped back to let him pass but instead Hooper pulled to a halt and greeted him: 'Good afternoon, sir!'

The sun was behind Hooper's head and Jack raised one arm to shield his eyes. 'Good afternoon.'

'Mr Swinton, isn't it?'

'Sweeney. Jack Sweeney.'

'Of course, of course! Mr Sweeney.' Hooper lingered there, looking down the lane and smiling.

'And you're a fisherman, isn't that right?'

Jack nodded, and showed him his bandaged hand. 'Not at the moment.'

'Oh.' In his own elation the vicar was unable to find the correct register for misfortune. 'Oh dear ... Er, tell me, Mr Sweeney, can you keep a secret?'

Jack followed him to the lych-gate and Hooper climbed out of the trap and the two of them carried on down the Tablet-lined path to the church. Inside, the air was cool and chalky. At the end of the north aisle, the pews had been pulled back. They were covered in dust sheets. Another dust sheet hung over the wall and Parson Hooper drew it back.

'There!'

A large patch of plaster had fallen away, revealing a section of older, darker plaster behind it. But when Jack stepped closer he saw that it wasn't just plaster. It was a painting. It showed an open boat on a stormy sea. In the boat were a number of crouching figures. Standing on the water beside the boat was a benevolent-looking Christ, and between him and the boat, in the distance, Jack recognised the two jagged summits of Maenmor.

'Came in yesterday morning and half the wall had fallen off. Apparently it's very rare indeed.' Parson Hooper beamed. 'The Bishop is writing to a man in Oxford about it!'

Hooper had just been in Truro and the Bishop had also asked him if he would like to be considered for the post of Dean of the cathedral. He had gone at once to Pascoe & Sons and given them a stanza for an exuberant new Tablet:

> How beautiful it is to be alive,
> To live – to love – to work for God! –
> Till He sends His messanger
> Kind death – to call us home!

That month, word reached Polmayne that the station's first motor lifeboat had undergone sea trials and was ready for delivery. The old one, the pulling-and-sailing *Emily Grace*, had been in service since 1912. She was bought by a man from Skegness for use as a pleasure craft.

The new boat was a Liverpool type with 129 airtight cases made of white deal. She had a six-cylinder engine capable of delivering thirty-five horsepower, with a self-contained reduction and reverse gear and a propeller speed of nine hundred revolutions per minute. She weighed about seven tons, was built at Cowes and cost £3424 – a sum that was met by the bequest of a long-term visitor to Polmayne, Kenneth Lee. It was his name that was painted in gold lettering on the lifeboat's bows.

Coxswain Tyler asked Croyden to help him bring her down from Cowes. With the *Maria V* unable to go out, Croyden had been busying himself up at his piece, avoiding Maggie, planting shallots and sprouts in the saturated soil, wheeling up barrows of seaweed. He had also bought a new pig. But the chance of several days at sea, on five shillings a day, was too good to miss. He went to Bethesda and asked Jack to join them.

It took four days to hop back down the coast – Weymouth, Salcombe, Fowey – and in the spare hours of those passages they examined every inch of the new boat. By the time they reached Polmayne Jack knew her as well as his own *Maria V*. When his hand was better and it came to the sea trials and exercises it was only natural that Jack should help. In early April, Tyler officially invited him to be an auxiliary member of the *Kenneth Lee*'s crew and for the first time in weeks he forgot about leaving the town.

Just after Easter, the new lifeboat was brought into the quays for her dedication. The senior crew stood on board in oilskins, lifejackets and red dress-hats, sweating beneath the hot April sun. Swells of bunting ran above the heads of the crowd. The Coverack and Falmouth lifeboats – the *Three Brothers* and the *BASP* – had come in too and their crews stood on the Town Quay, along with Porth's Volunteer LSA

Company and Captain Williams, Pendhu's Auxiliary Coastguard.

At 3 p.m., two maroons were fired from the station and Major Franks, as Chairman of the Polmayne Branch Committee of the RNLI, formally took delivery of the *Kenneth Lee*. While the spectators sang 'Eternal Father, Strong to Save' Major Franks, the Bishop of Truro, Parson Hooper and his Curate were rowed aboard for the dedication.

Parson Hooper was having a good day. How fortunate that while the post of Dean was open, the Bishop should have had the chance to come to his parish! He had given him lunch at the rectory, shown him the wall painting and for a good two hours managed to avoid mentioning the question of his candidacy.

On board the lifeboat, Coxswain Tyler gave them a brief tour. He showed them the engines, and the end-box, and the watertight containers, and the shelter. It was all very cramped and somehow Hooper's Curate got in front of him so that when Tyler and the Bishop and the Curate crouched down to see the engines, Parson Hooper was left standing above them, craning his neck to try to glimpse it all.

After inspecting the boat, the Bishop stood at the helm and read out the dedication. Those on the quay could hear his voice but not his words.

'Eternal father, Thou walkest upon the wings of the wind. Thou makest the clouds thy chariot. Thou rulest the raging of the sea. Thou speakest and it is still. Vouchsafe thy blessing, we beseech Thee, to this lifeboat *Kenneth Lee* which we now present to Thee. Grant that it may come to the succour of those in distress upon the sea. We commend to Thee also the men of her crew. We thank Thee for the lives they have saved and we pray that they may go forth to the rescue not trusting only in their own strength, but in Thy spirit . . .'

Parson Hooper was standing by the shelter. Behind him he could hear someone muttering. It was Croyden Treneer.

'Whose clever idea was it to bring they damned priests aboard?'

The *Maria V* resumed fishing. They were long-lining down at the Ray Pits and it was going well. Consistently they landed five or six hundred stone. One Saturday they dashed back through a sudden northerly gale with a hold full of fish and the seas breaking over the bows. They took turns at the pump; for a time it was touch and go. They were exhausted even before the gale; that week they had notched up more than ninety hours at sea and when they came ashore Jack hobbled back along the front to Bethesda and fell asleep fully clothed. He woke at midnight, pulled off his boots, then slept another ten hours.

The following week the fishing was just as good. 'No stopping now, Jack!' grinned Hammels. Even Croyden was satisfied, but they were all tired, pursued by a relentless fatigue that Jack suddenly felt unable to resist.

'What about a couple of days off?' he suggested to Croyden. 'Do us all good.'

Croyden was horrified. 'Rest when they's scarce and rest when it blows – but stay in harbour when you can fish and they'll never come back.'

Then an odd thing happened. One morning they came in after a long night on the water and put away the boat and rowed into the Gaps and Jack walked back to Bethesda and he did not feel tired. He did not feel tired the next evening when they left the harbour, nor the next. During the coming weeks he found himself filled with a physical ease he had never known before. Either, he thought, I am so used to this fatigue that I no longer notice it – or I have overcome it.

When in late April an easterly kept them in harbour for a couple of days, he did not mind. On a fine, breezy afternoon he walked up to Pennance. He leaned against the wall of

St Pinnock's well and tore off a leaf of fresh alexander and pressed it to his nose. He saw the first green glow of growth on the beech branches and watched the drift of the clouds on their westward course. It had been a tough winter but now summer was coming and the world looked bright again.

He took the river route back. At Penpraze's yard the shed doors were open and he called 'Hello!' to Peter Penpraze who was sanding down one of the Petrels. The *Polmayne Queen* was propped against the yard's quay wall and the Garretts were painting the transom. Jack cut through the graveyard. Parson Hooper was outside the church, sitting on a bench; he was leaning on his elbows and looking at the ground.

'Good afternoon, vicar!'

Hooper glanced up. His face was drawn, and he shook his head.

There had been a break-in, he explained. He took Jack into the church. In the north aisle the dust sheet still covered the painting and Hooper pulled it back. The face of Christ had gone, chiselled away. A large 'X' had been scratched over the boat and the figures in it; the word 'Alive' was scrawled across the sea.

Parson Hooper suddenly put his face in his hands and groaned. 'Why? Why, why, why!' He pulled his fingers down his cheek, and looked up at the painting. There were tears in his eyes. 'We live in an evil place, Mr Sweeney. Evil, evil! Who on earth could do such a thing?'

Jack left Parson Hooper and, out in the sunlight again, wandered back among the slate headstones. Bright red azaleas bloomed between them. At the top, by the lych-gate, he found Parson Hooper's latest Tablet propped against the bank:

> *How beautiful it is to be alive,*
> *To live – to love – to work for God! –*
> *Till He sends His messenger*
> *Kind death – to call us home!*

2

May 1936

CHAPTER II

⎯⎯⎯◦𝓋𝓋◦⎯⎯⎯

O n a damp May afternoon, the first of the summer visitors arrived in Polmayne. They spilled out of Harris's
Station Bus with their leather valises and their country coats,
and the porters from the Antalya busied themselves in the
square, checking the tags on the cases and leading the guests
up to their rooms.

Mrs Cuffe and the other landladies escorted their visitors
through the town, the luggage wheeled in wheelbarrows by
the same husbands who now had to vacate their rooms for
the summer (Mrs Cuffe had asked her nephew Charlie Treneer
to do the wheeling). Idly they listened to the visitors' animated
chatter about this shop and that house, to their exclamations
of 'I say, that's new!' and 'What is *that*?', and paused with
them as they stopped to read the newly-painted board that
had just been tied to the railings of Town Quay:

PLEASANT DAY EXCURSIONS!
PER
FAST AND COMMODIOUS MOTOR LAUNCH
POLMAYNE QUEEN
(Weather and Circumstances Permitting)

The next morning a group of visitors stood on the quay. They were waiting for the *Polmayne Queen*. Women clung to their hats in the breeze. A swan landed feet-forward in the Gaps, settled down into the water and, with a shake of its tail, swam into the inner harbour. A young girl knelt down and stretched out a hand towards its beak.

Toper Walsh, behind her, was in good humour. 'Mind there, girl! 'ee'll have an arm off you!'

Parliament Bench was filling up again. The coming of the visitors had brought back Red Treneer and Jimmy Stephens and Brian Tyler and a number of others. Edward Harris also began to put in a daily appearance. Harris was a proud and diligent man who saw himself as a cut above the rest of the Bench. He had a watch for a start, which he kept on a lanyard in his waistcoat pocket and for this he was known as Tick-Tock. He was also a lovely speller. Those on the Bench could throw any word at him, even some foreign ones, and he would just send it back, letter by letter. In the summer months, he liked to come to the Bench with a cutting from a newspaper or a photograph from the illustrated press.

Events beyond Polmayne were depressing that May – the war in Abyssinia, growing unrest in Spain. Much more exciting was the forthcoming inaugural voyage of the *Queen Mary*. Each morning when Tick-Tock Harris arrived, they would ask. 'Anything on that ship, Ticker?'

He learned to pace his information. He would take a pair of glasses from his top pocket. ' ... *launched on the Clyde last September ... the largest British liner ever to be built. First transatlantic crossing scheduled for June 1 ... it is hoped she'll take the Blue Riband before the end of her first season ...'*

'But how big's she, Tick? How big?'

'Patience! ... Here – *nearly twice the displacement of the ill-fated* Titanic, *the* Queen Mary's *displacement is 81,237 tons ... Her length overall is nine hundred and seventy-five feet ...'*

'Lord!' said Toper.

'Eeee.' said Boy Johns.

Two new establishments appeared along Polmayne's water-front that May. Mr Tanner opened his grocery store a couple of doors down from Eliza Tucker's general store. As she no longer liked trading in 'hard goods', she was happy to let Mr Tanner sell paraffin and soda and cattle feed and fowl feed. She herself concentrated on sweets and tobacco and barm and home-made bread and an assortment of whatever miscellaneous merchandise caught her eye. In 1935 it had been china dogs and straw hats; this year it was gramophone records.

Near the East Quay, a Mr and Mrs Monk from Exeter converted an old pilchard palace into Monk's Tea Rooms. Mr Monk was of a nervous disposition and had a squint in his right eye. When the tea rooms were empty he would stand in the doorway and look up and down the road, rubbing his hands together. Mrs Monk said that's the way to drive off trade. He told her he couldn't help himself, not at the beginning anyway.

Parson Hooper put the investigation of the church break-in in the hands of the police. He himself became withdrawn. Services were all taken by his Curate. Everyone condemned the vandalism. Even Red Treneer, who had little time for the 'English Church', admitted that it 'weren't right'.

'If I find the bastard that done it,' promised Toper, 'I'll wring his bloody neck!'

It was very wet. In the middle of the month a gale clogged the leats with green leaves and pasted them like paper to the cobbles of Bethesda. Two yachts broke their moorings and at the Antalya an old lean-to collapsed, killing Mr Hicks's spaniel. Time dragged its heels through those blustery days and in the cottages and villas the clocks slowed, their mechanisms burdened by damp.

Then there were the snails. They appeared in mushroom clusters on wet stone walls, on window-panes, their silvery smears criss-crossing the paving stones. They crept and slithered over the redundant fishing gear below the recreation ground, the mountain ranges of old net, the squashy globes of buffs, the causeway withies of broken crab-pots. They made quick work of the potato plants in the town's pieces and crawled in through the lips of the postboxes to chew at the stamps on newly-posted letters.

On the fifteenth, Parson Hooper drove into Truro for the diocesan meeting. The Bishop took him to one side and told him that he had carefully considered his application to become Dean but that on reflection they wanted someone a little younger. The post was to be taken by Hooper's own Curate. Parson Hooper went to Pascoe's and commissioned a new Tablet:

> When the Light of the World stood before them
> They cried: Not this man but Barabbas.

Arthur Treneer died. Agnes Thomas died. Betty Johns did not die as everyone thought she would but rose from her bed to sing 'The Lark in the Morn' at her grandson's wedding.

There were two weddings that May. The Jenkins wedding took place in the Anglican church of St Cuby and the Johns wedding was in the Methodist chapel. Both were followed by receptions at the Antalya Hotel.

On 20 May, Tick-Tock Harris brought a copy of the *Illustrated London News* to the Bench. '. . . *the forward funnel,*' he read, '*is seventy feet in height from the boat deck. The diameter of each funnel is thirty foot and would permit three modern locomotives to pass through it . . .*'

Toper frowned. 'I don't see it.'

'Don't see what, Tope?'

'Don't see why 'ee'd want bloody trains on a ship.'

Towards the end of the third week of May, the French freighter *Charbonnier* was driven onto Pendhu Point. The *Kenneth Lee* rescued all hands. They managed to salvage the ship but not before much of its cargo of tinned food had been lost. The cupboards of Porth and Polmayne became filled with 'Charbon' tins – but because the labels had been washed off no one ever knew whether when they opened one they'd find tinned salmon or cling peaches.

At the Antalya, visitors reported that the hotel was not the same this year. Mr Hicks, they said, was behaving 'immoderately'.

The Garretts had a good fortnight with the *Polmayne Queen*, but on a trip to Falmouth the water intake blocked and the engine overheated. They returned to port safely but for a week the boat was out of action.

A new member of the Petrel fleet was launched with a small ceremony at Penpraze's yard. She was painted canary yellow, commissioned by an art historian from Berkshire and named *Hope*. Petrel racing began on 23 May.

That afternoon Boy Johns's grandson Joseph leaned on the harbour wall not watching the sleek and heeling Petrels in the bay, but reading his monthly magazine:

LADS! The best life for town and country lads (16 to 21 years old) is upon Australia's big and prosperous farms. Greatly reduced steamship passages, only £3 payable before sailing. Apply for illustrated pamphlet to the Assistant Superintendent of Immigration for New South Wales and Victoria, 3 Melbourne Place, Strand, WC.

At the monthly Parish Council meeting it was reported that Cornwall's Public Health and Housing Committee had approved a grant for the building of a reservoir to ease Polmayne's water shortages. The site chosen was Pennance. Major Franks said that 'it would cause a gross violation of natural beauty'. Parson Hooper pointed out that it would threaten St Pinnock's holy well: 'Have we not seen enough sacrilege of late?' The only alternative site would cost a further £30,000. The dam, Hooper was assured, would be well below the spring. Despite the rain the water engineer reported to the Sanitary Inspector that in the previous three weeks Polmayne's reserves had been reduced by six thousand gallons. Work was due to start at Pennance the following month.

It was rain that prevented the Tea Treat of the Bible Christian boys. As a special concession they were allowed to go on the Wesleyan Tea Treat the following week – although not to process near the Wesleyan banners nor to touch the banners' tassels as they marched. Afterwards the Bible Christians asked to go with the Wesleyans again next year as the buns were bigger and had more currants in them.

At 4.35 on Whit Saturday, Mr and Mrs Monk recorded their first full house. Mr Monk was 'a bit fingers and thumbs' that day but all went well. On board the *Maria V*, Jack and Croyden and Hammels took off the dog line and made up a spilter.

Shortly after dawn on 28 May Joseph Johns met his grandfather on the East Quay. Boy Johns gave him £3.9s.6d.

'Thanks, Granddad,' said Joseph.

'Eeee.' Boy watched him as he walked past the Antalya Hotel, up out of town, on his way to Australia.

The police told Parson Hooper that they had arrested three men in Penzance. They were from up-country and they admitted to breaking into St Cuby's. 'It's that damn road,' said Toper. 'Look at the scum comes in on it.'

By the end of the month it was hot. The first tents appeared in Ivor Dawkins's fields. The water engineer recorded a further drop in reserves of eight thousand gallons.

Tick-Tock Harris read from the *Western Morning News*:

Cunard White Star's Queen Mary *is undergoing final prep-*
arations for her maiden transatlantic voyage. She will leave
Southampton on 27 May...

Burnt flakes of cloud filled the western sky. It was late,
after ten. In Hemlock Cove two punts were pulled up on the
sand. Sitting on the cliff above, beside the coastguard hut,
were Toper, Red, Tick-Tock and the others. They had been
there an hour already.

'Anything, Boy?' asked Toper.

Boy Johns had a telescope propped on his knee and he was
looking through it, out beyond Kidda Head. He had said
nothing for all that time and he said nothing still.

'So, Tick, where's this damned ship o' yours?' growled
Red.

Tick-Tock took out his watch for the fifth time and shook
his head. 'I can't understand it...'

It was well after dark before the two punts returned. In
silence they passed back through the Gaps. The next day on
the Bench there was no sign of Tick-Tock Harris, nor the
next. Shame kept him at home after he read the report on the
Queen Mary's maiden voyage: she had not gone straight to
New York from Southampton – a route that would have taken
her three miles south of Pendhu – but had crossed the Channel
to pick up passengers in Cherbourg.

Early on 10 June, the *Maria V* was working ground some
five miles off the Lizard. It was warm and misty. Dawn was
a grey smudge to the east. They were hauling on the tide and
the only sound was the slop of the nets on the deck as they
came back in. To the south were Cove boats, open boats
from the villages of the Lizard, their lights haloed in the mist.
Hammels was humming.

The *Maria V*'s nets were almost in when they heard it.
Hammels raised his head. A faint *thrup-thrup-thrup*. Croyden
secured the head-rope. It was hard to tell in the mist where
it was coming from. It grew louder. It seemed it was moving

across their bow, out of the south-east. No, across their stern. It appeared to echo off the mist. Each of them stood still. They could feel it throbbing across the water, up into the boat and through their feet. A great shadow appeared off the port bow, some three hundred yards to the south. They watched the stream of lights flow past them in the dawn. When the bow wave hit them, Croyden gripped the gunwale to prevent himself going over. Jack held the wheel to keep his balance and Harry fell, striking his knee on a stanchion. He waved his fist at the ship's shrinking stern. 'Great bloody bastard!'

To the south, three of the Cove boats had their lines cut by the *Queen Mary*. By morning news of it had reached the Bench.

'Build these ships too damned big nowadays,' said Toper Walsh.

'Where'll it all end?' asked Red.

They sat in silence for a moment.

'I'll tell 'ee where it'll end,' said Toper.

'Where?'

'Well, Tope?'

'I'll tell 'ee . . .'

But somehow he could not think of what it was that he wanted to say.

CHAPTER 12

J ack Sweeney stood half-in and half-out of the wheelhouse.
It was midday. The long-line was out. The sea lay still all
around them and a few pale-edged clouds drifted across the
sun. Croyden was asleep. Harry was playing the harmonica in
the bows.

During May the *Maria V* had spent more time at sea than
in harbour. They left the bay on countless rain-washed mornings, on sultry windless mornings, on mornings when the low
cloud was still pierced by moon-shards. They returned at
dusk, in the early morning, at midday. Sometimes they would
be gone for thirty-six hours. The ling and conger were plenti-
ful, the prices good. Around the quays word spread again that
Jack Sweeney was lucky and that the *Maria V* was a lucky
boat.

He himself barely noticed anything that month but the sea.
The rhythms of his days were sea rhythms. He had no land
life; his gaze was filled with the waves and their rise and
fall, with gannets travelling against grey skies; he watched

cloud-ranges swell on the horizon and the rain on the boat's fresh paint form into droplets and vibrate with the engine. He heard the water sliding beneath the boat, the slosh of beam seas against it, the creak of the mizzen and the *chug-chug* of the Kelvin. He knew the slow dozing afternoons and the hot noons and the coming ashore late, after midnight, knowing they would be leaving again early the next day. He knew his own concentrations at hauling and at shooting, the precision when the spring tides ran at their quickest, and he watched the line in Croyden's hand tighten and was ready to throttle back as soon as it snagged.

Two or three times that month the weather came in. The wind went round to the east. It freshened and the white-topped seas ran long and high past Pendhu Point and it was not possible to go out. On these days Jack Sweeney was overwhelmed by a frustration that he could no longer keep at bay with the intricacies of his knotwork, nor with the more pressing tasks of the net loft, nor with the hours sitting with Whaler Cuffe outside his wooden shed but only with long walks that had no direction when they began but invariably led either to St Pinnock's holy well at Pennance, or across the Glaze River to Priory Creek and up over the top to Pendhu Point. There above Williams's coastguard hut he sat in the sheep-cropped grass and watched the motionless shapes of the Main Cages.

When they fished, the land was always to the north. Sometimes it dissolved in the haze and at night it was marked only by the loom of the Lizard light sweeping the sky and sometimes by the light of St Anthony Head. At other times they motored down to the Ray Pits and for half a day or more saw nothing but the wide circle of sea and then it came back into view, that thin, dust-grey coast. Jack preferred the mornings when they were setting out, with the open sea before them, pushing south.

That was May.

In early June, the bait became harder to find. They prepared to go to Plymouth. They brought the *Maria V* in through the Gaps and gathered supplies on the East Quay: four drums of fuel, several maunds of spare line, two new dans, a mass of cobles, four bags of Croyden's new potatoes, three pounds of butter and a box of unlabelled Charbon tins which Hammels said he had learned to identify: 'Put 'em in a bucket of water and if one sink quick, he's salmon, sink slow he's peach. He sink very quick and he's no good.'

On the last evening, Jack closed up the net loft and came out onto the front with a canvas bag of tools over his shoulder. The bay was quiet; patches of wind drifted across its surface. They would have a clear run to Plymouth. As he passed Monk's Tea Rooms, he spotted a familiar-looking couple coming towards him. It was the Abrahams.

'Look – it's Jack Sweeney!' called Maurice, and came over and shook Jack by the hand.

Anna was two steps behind him. 'Hello,' she said with a half smile. She was wearing her sky-blue headscarf.

'Well!' Maurice rubbed his hands. 'How's the fishing?'

'It's going well.'

'Off somewhere?'

'Down to Plymouth tomorrow morning, for a few weeks. It's the turbot season.'

'Well, we should still be here when you get back, shouldn't we, my dear?'

Anna nodded.

'Come and see us!'

Jack told them he would do that. He watched them head along towards the Antalya Hotel. Maurice took off his hat at the door and smoothed down his hair and as she went in Anna looked behind her at Jack. She did not wave.

Jack liked the turbot. He liked its predictability, the way that it fed precisely at dawn. He liked the way that when a female was caught and pulled to the surface, the male would often be with her, swimming alongside. Before they brought her on board, Hammels would lean over and hook the male with the gaff and grin as he hauled him in: 'Two for one with lady turbot!'

For a fortnight at Plymouth the fishing was good. But during the third week the bait started to thin. They tried off the Eddystone, and to the south of Rame Head. Often they were late shooting the line, or could not use its whole length. The catches fell away and Croyden became short-tempered.

One sunny afternoon, Hammels returned from hawking his wooden warriors in town. Croyden was re-caulking the deck.

'Look, Croy! Look what I buy!' Hammels held up a pack of cards.

'Get those damned cards away from me.'

'I show you a trick.'

'Piss off.'

'No, Croy – you like this trick. This one help us.'

He cleared a space on the deck and laid out the four aces in a quadrant. 'North – south – east – west. Where knave of hearts falls, that is where wind blows.'

Croyden carried on pressing in the oakum.

'Ha!' cried Hammels.

Croyden glanced at the cards and saw the knave lying on the southerly ace. The boats at their moorings were pointing out towards the sound – south.

'I do again, Croy!'

This time Croyden paid more attention. The jack of hearts again fell to the south.

'Just luck,' said Croyden – but he followed Hammels's hands as he laid out the cards again.

'What's this?'

'This – Bolt Head. This – Start Point. Here Eddystone and Bigbury. Where knave of spade lands, there is fish for bait!'

Croyden shook his head, but he watched as Hammels dealt out the cards. The jack of spades fell on Bigbury.

'Never be there in these tides,' scoffed Croyden.

That night they fished off the Eddystone. Two boats went out into Bigbury and later they saw them burning their flambeaux; they had bait to spare.

So the following night the *Maria V* joined a large part of the fleet in Bigbury Bay, but it was those at the Eddystone who were lucky. Hammels claimed that was where his cards had indicated.

The next evening, Croyden asked casually, 'What do they cards say?'

Harry shuffled the cards. He grinned at Croyden and carried on shuffling them a long time.

'Get on with it!'

Harry flicked out the cards one by one on the deck. Again the knave fell on Bigbury.

They tried Bigbury Bay. It was a clear night and the moon was a couple of days off full. Shortly before midnight they drew a couple of the nets but there was nothing. Two hours later, the same. They drew them all and shifted up to the Eddystone where they had some luck but by then it was too late. They shot half the line without much conviction and hauled it empty. Dawn was a slit of pale sky astern as they motored back along the coast to Polmayne. They had been just over three weeks at Plymouth. They had each cleared about £10.

CHAPTER 13

It was mid-morning when Jack moored his punt and headed back along the front. On the road outside Bethesda, he found Toper Walsh shovelling sand over the cobbles.

'Why the sand, Tope?'

'Whaler's gone poorly!'

During the three weeks Jack had been in Plymouth, a strange illness had crept into Polmayne. It was characterised by vomiting and a series of long, thin rashes on the arms and legs. Agnes Thomas said that it was called Reed Fever and that men were particularly vulnerable. Because that was clear, and because the rashes really did look like little reeds, everyone began to talk of it as the Reeds. Where it came from no one knew, but on Parliament Bench they were quick to point out that it appeared at the same time as the visitors.

Dr White said there was no such disease as Reed Fever and that the illness was caused by a bacillus. Everyone still called it the Reeds.

Whaler's bout had passed after forty-eight hours but in its

wake it had left a series of complaints that he referred to simply as the 'old trouble'. Mrs Cuffe rearranged her guests and he came in from his summer shed. He lay in bed drinking cups of lukewarm water and refusing all offers of help. Mrs Cuffe had asked Toper to spread sand outside to deaden the sound of traffic.

'Can't do nothin' more for him, Jack,' she said.

'Can I see him?'

'He won't see no one.'

The following day Jack spent on board the *Maria V*. He repaired some damage to the wheelhouse door. He spotted in some chipped paintwork. In the afternoon he rowed up to Penpraze's yard for some new shackles and as he came in towards the yard he saw someone sketching on the wharf. It was Mrs Abraham. Sitting cross-legged, she was looking up and down from her pad to the half-painted hull of an oyster boat. The light was in her hair, and she kept pushing its loose strands back behind her ear. She did not notice him until the bows of the punt bumped into the wharf beneath her.

'Oh! You gave me a start!'

Standing in the boat, Jack propped his elbows on the wharf and looked at the drawing. She held it out at arm's length and cocked her head. 'Tell me, Mr Sweeney, why are boats so difficult?'

'Perhaps you must understand them to paint them.' There was a faint hostility in his voice.

'Plenty have managed it!' she said defiantly. 'It's only practice.'

'Perhaps.'

'How was your fishing?'

'Not good.'

The punt shifted beneath Jack and he looked down and straightened it with his feet. 'Mrs Abraham, will you explain to me why did you not want my letters?'

She put down the pad. 'I don't know –'

'You said "write and tell me everything", and then you said "don't write at all". What am I to believe?'

'I was thinking we could just write letters, but – it became more difficult –'

Just then Maurice appeared at the front of Penpraze's shed, tapping his wrist. 'Come on! We're already late.'

Anna stood and clutched the pad to her chest. 'I'm sorry, Jack. Do you forgive me?'

He looked up at her and smiled. 'Yes.'

But she had already gone.

Each evening when Jack came in he asked Mrs Cuffe about Whaler, and each evening she said: 'He's no worse and no better.'

It was already high season in Polmayne. Groups of visitors flowed back and forth along the front, lingered on the quays and filled the beaches. In Mrs Cuffe's dining room, she had to lay on an extra table. One Sunday morning at breakfast she came up to Jack and told him, 'He says he'll see you.'

Jack climbed the stairs. He followed a narrow corridor to a room papered in a pattern of faded red cockerels. On one wall was a picture of a woman stranded on a sea-ringed rock and clinging to the base of a cross; the picture was captioned 'Rock of Ages'. The blinds were down and Whaler was lying in bed with his eyes closed.

'That you, Jack?'

'Yes.'

'Sit down.' He struggled to pull himself up, but did not open his eyes. After ten minutes Jack stood to leave.

'You off now?'

'Yes.'

'Come again, won't you. I like to talk to someone.'

The next day Jack found him in better spirits. He was sitting upright, gazing at the open window. 'Good, good, you've come!'

Jack sat on a stool and leaned against the wall.

'What is happening out there?'

Jack told him the town was full of visitors, and everyone was grumbling about water and it being so dry.

'I know, I know. She tells me.'

They talked about Jack's fishing and then Whaler said: 'Did I never tell you about Floyd?'

'No.'

'Well' – he shifted himself against the pillow – 'Thing we always liked about Floyd was that he could only count as far as five. He never got the hang of it – 3–4–5 . . . he'd say, then he'd stop and go into kind of a daze.

'Anyway, one time Floyd's standing quayside. Portugal, I think it was – maybe Spain. And there's a thunderstorm and Floyd's struck on the cheek by a slab a' lightning! So we all look down at him on the quay and he's not moving. We carry on looking but he doesn't move a muscle. "He's bloody dead!" shouts someone and we all think – Christ, poor old Floyd. But then he jumps up and looks around and he's right as rain – 'cept for a burn mark, here on his cheek.'

Whaler started to laugh. 'But you know what? That lightning's cured him. He's so quick now none of us can keep up with him. And the sums! He can do any sum he likes!'

Jack went to see Whaler whenever he could. There were good days and bad days. On the bad days he'd lie and listen to Jack and he would ask him about his childhood in Dorset and sometimes when Jack was speaking he would interrupt him and ask: 'Tell me, what's it look like?', or 'What's she wearing?', and would not allow him to continue until he had it all fixed in his mind's eye. On the good days he would sit up and tell Jack about the emeralds he'd seen in Colombia, a crocodile farm in Swaziland, pearl-divers in India, and a man in Panama who sold him the seeds of a 'miracle tree'.

The last time Jack saw Whaler was one Saturday in mid-July. The blinds were down and the light was on. Its glow made him feel warm, he said – although the heat of the day itself hung heavy as a shroud in the room. Whaler was weak and pale. He told Jack about the *Belfast*.

'She was a barque we'd sailed to Australia. Failed to find a return cargo so headed east out into the Pacific. Eighth day out we hit a gale . . . struck by a wave and knocked down –'

Whaler started coughing. Jack poured him a cup of his lukewarm water. He sipped at it, then lay back against the pillow and closed his eyes. He lay like that for a long time, and Jack stood to leave.

'Wait, I haven't finished.' Whaler strained to take a couple of deep breaths. '. . . We was drifting for three days, set up a jury rig and sailed to an island . . .'

He took another sip of water. 'We was two months on that island . . . no one there but trees and a lot of turtles. I don't think I ever been happier than on that island.'

Whaler drank some more water. 'Open the window will you, Jack.'

Jack stood and pulled up the blind. He released the casement and felt the breeze on his face. The Petrels were racing in the bay. On the road below the window, the sand that Toper had spread was cut by wheel tracks.

'They don't believe me, do they?' said Whaler.

'Who?'

'They say I make it all up.'

'That's not true.'

'I know what they say. They say Whaler tells fairy tales. But I saw it all, Jack. I saw every last bit.'

Whaler died three days later. They buried him that Saturday. The weather had closed in and thick fog covered the town. Mrs Cuffe had had her best coat dyed black and sat all morning in the parlour with the coffin beside her. Various women came to be with her.

'Cold as 'ell out there,' said Brenda Walsh.

'Damper 'n a sponge,' said Agnes Thomas.

'More like March than July,' said Eliza Tucker.

Mrs Cuffe ignored them. She sat straight-backed before the

coffin. When Jack and Croyden and the other pall-bearers arrived, she watched in silence as they carried Whaler out and down the steps to Bethesda. She did not follow.

At the graveside the men sang 'Rock of Ages'; it had been Whaler's favourite hymn. They sang it again in the Fountain Inn. Everyone agreed that 'a good man had gone', that Whaler had been as much a part of Polmayne as 'the harbour isself', and although they had all spent years deriding his stories, using his very name as a measure of exaggeration, they now competed to show their respect.

'What places he saw!'

'And the rest of his life blind.'

'No one'll ever see the half of what Whaler seen.'

'And he only saw half of what he bloody said he saw –'

'Who was that?' demanded Toper Walsh.

Silence.

'Come on, who said it?'

But the murmur of conversation had resumed, and soon everyone was recalling their best 'Whaler stories'.

Outside the fog had thickened. The southerly wind was driving it on in damp and smoky billows. It cut off one end of the town from the other. It blew over the bay and the deserted quays, up through the hillside alleys, over the roof of the chapel, into the empty space that had once been Cooper's Yard. It rolled in across the damp brown mound of Whaler's grave and in the pine trees above it the wind made a lonely, distant sound. No one was outside. Every two minutes, from the south-east, came the very faint moan of Kidda Head's foghorn.

CHAPTER 14

On Pendhu Point, Captain Williams was singing. On days like this he liked to sing because here on his own with the fog blowing in over the cliffs and nothing in front but milky-white and nothing above but milky-white and nothing all around him but milky-white, he sometimes found it difficult to remember he was alive.

> *Brown cow in the middle of a field,*
> *Brown cow dreaming of home . . .*

He scratched his beard and stared ahead. The window of the watch hut, which on good days looked south over the Main Cages to a horizon that was as sharp and distant as the stars, was now all that existed in this wide, white world. From Kidda Head lighthouse came the moaning of the foghorn, and he hated that foghorn with its intermittent, bovine groan because it reminded him of all the other foggy days that he had sat there, singing into the whiteness.

Brown cow in the sun,
Brown cow lowing for her love,
Poor little brown cow left alone . . .

In his naval days, Captain Williams did not mind the fog as there were always ratings to talk to. His days on watch here were usually broken by a visitor or two leaning in through the door for a yarn, but not in fog. No one wanted to come out to Pendhu if they could not see.

Poor little – poor little – poor little brown cow
All alone . . .

At 3.30 Williams heard the third ship's horn of the day. It was far-off and muted and he thought nothing more of it until it sounded again, much closer. When it sounded a third time, to the east, he pulled on his coat. He took his klaxon and stepped out into the fog.

For a few minutes he stood on the edge of the cliff. The damp wind left drops of moisture in his beard. He struggled to hear anything but there was only the wind at the flaps of his sou'wester and the waves breaking some eighty feet below. He could see nothing. They had probably heard the bell and readjusted their course. That was the thing about the Cages bell – it might mean you were close to danger but it also told you exactly where you were. Keep in the lower half of the quadrant and all you had to worry about was other ships.

Then it came again. Something was moving closer, heading towards the cliffs, but he could neither see it nor hear it. He sounded his klaxon – *Pah – pah – paa-ah!* The letter U: *You're standing in to danger.* There was no reply.

To the east of Williams's hut, the land dropped away to a stream before rising steeply up the far side. He began the climb down and then he heard the horn again. It boomed off the cliffs around him.

Pah – pah – paa-aah! he replied.

He could now see the valley bottom where the waterfall tumbled over a short cliff and the wind was catching its strands as they fell and blowing them back up.

Pah – pah – paa-aah!

This time a deep double sound rang around the cliffs – still to the south-east. He began to run. He reached the valley bottom. As he was climbing the other side, zig-zagging up the path, leaning on the boulders to catch his breath, he heard voices through the fog.

He knew exactly where they were. They were off the Balk – the reef that at low water ran covered in oar wrack out towards the Cages. But he could still see nothing. He stood, breathing heavily. The mist mirrored his own breaths – exhaling great billows of cloud, then thinning. Water was dripping from his sou'wester. The fog came and went, allowing glimpses of the black cliffs, of the grey shifting sea, then smothering them again in cloud. As it thinned so he saw for the first time a darker shade of grey. The fog came in again and all was white and then when it cleared, she was there, where no ship should be. He knew her at once: three-masted barque, high bowsprit – the *Constantine*.

Captain Henriksen and his English wife had been in their cabin, playing a game of chess. They had left Plymouth soon after dawn and made good progress; they would be in Dublin in a couple of days.

'Sir! Sir!' There was a knock on the door. 'Come quick!'

The Captain pushed his rook into an attacking position, then raised his heavy frame from the chair and pulled on his reefer jacket. 'Check, my dear.'

At the door was his First Mate. 'The compass, sir, it's gone strange!'

On deck, Captain Henriksen pulled the collar up to his ears and made his way aft. Fog surrounded his ship and there was a damp southerly wind. At the wheel he tapped the binnacle and the needle flickered and spun. He called for another compass. When that showed the same random spinning, he looked up at the sails and ordered the sheets to be tightened.

They were, he estimated, some two miles west of Kidda Head. He could hear the foghorn astern, off the starboard quarter. He ordered a man to the bows to sound their own horn at intervals. When the helmsman brought the ship round, the sails started to lift at once.

'Close as she'll go, sir!'

He took her off a few points and for twenty minutes they sailed in silence. Mist half hid the mast-tops. Around the ship they could see no further than a couple of swell lengths before the sea disappeared into the whiteness. When they heard the Cages bell, not to leeward where it should have been but off the port bow, the helmsman panicked. He backed up into the wind and the ship stalled.

'Back to your course,' said the Captain calmly. When they had enough way, he would go about.

Just then, from far below them, came a deep groan and the ship juddered as something passed along the hull. It lasted no more than a few seconds and then they were free and sailing again.

'Phew!' said the First Officer.

But in the helmsman's hands the wheel spun idly. 'Lost the rudder, sir!'

Henriksen ordered all hands on deck, and told his Bosun to make a jury. But already he sensed that his ship was lost. They were only minutes from a lee shore, and the wind was still fresh. He went down to his own quarters. Mrs Henriksen asked, 'What did we hit?'

'The Main Cages.'

He looked at the chessboard; she had placed her king out of danger. 'We may have to finish some other time. You must come up on deck.'

'Listen to me, Peter.' Mrs Henriksen had thought often

about this moment. 'You must understand that I will not leave the ship while you remain on board.'

'Don't worry, my dear.'

On deck, Captain Henriksen made his way aft. There was a great deal of shouting and in it for the first time he detected traces of an echo. The light became suddenly brighter. The fog thinned and they saw where they were. On three sides were cliffs.

As soon as he saw the *Constantine*, Captain Williams tensed, waiting for the impact. When it came it was not a single crash but a sickening sound of timbers, scraping and buckling against the rock. The spars shuddered; several men ran to the side. Then the fog came in again and Williams was on his way, running and wheezing back up the hill to call the lifeboat.

The moment he heard the maroons, Tick-Tock Harris set his watch. The conversation around him in the Fountain Inn had ceased to make much sense. Many were singing. But with the double boom of the maroons, the bar emptied in seconds. By the time the first men had reached the lifeboat station the others were spread out along the road in a line of sprinters, joggers, trotters and walkers. Coxswain Tyler had some difficulty picking a crew.

'Bloody favours!' shouted Joe Stephens as Tyler bypassed him and his brothers and picked his own nephew, Dougie.

'You're drunk.'

Jack had left the Fountain early with Croyden and Charlie to be with Mrs Cuffe. They were given lifejackets, as was Double Walsh who never drank. The others picked had not been in the Fountain. They all took their places in the *Kenneth Lee* and Tyler gave the order and they started down the slip.

'Thirteen minutes' – Tick-Tock was standing with the crowd outside the station and he stopped his watch the moment the boat struck the water – 'and twenty-three seconds.'

They passed Pendhu Point without even seeing it. Coxswain Tyler brought the *Kenneth Lee* round until the seas were meeting them beam-on. Jack stood with Croyden in the bows. They had prepared the anchor and Jack was holding its shank on the foredeck to stop it shifting. Down to leeward he watched the wave-backs as they came out under the boat and rolled towards the shore. Somewhere in there was Hemlock Cove and the cliffs but all he could see with the fog was a darting spot before his eyes.

It lifted suddenly. There were the rocks and the seas sliding white up against them and the spray rising and falling back. And there was the *Constantine* with her sails flapping like the wings of a wounded butterfly. She was now listing some way to port.

Tyler brought the *Kenneth Lee* up into the wind. 'Let go!' he shouted. Jack pitched the anchor over the side.

The warp raced out through the fairlead and the lifeboat dropped back. Jack waited for the anchor to strike bottom and the warp to slacken – but it kept on running out. There was a great depth of water between the Balk and the Main Cages.

'Bring her in!' shouted Tyler. 'We'll go in on the engines.'

He edged the lifeboat in towards the *Constantine*. The seas were steepening, breaking high against her stern. She was now not rising with the tide but rocking from side to side as each wave washed through. Her forward holds were filling.

Jack and Croyden prepared to jump aboard. The *Kenneth Lee* caught the top of a wave and Jack looked across the deck. Then they dropped into a trough and he could see only the line of faces at the gunwale and above them the spars and the useless sails. Croyden stood on the gunwale. As they rose he grabbed the *Constantine*'s shrouds and leapt onto the ship.

Tyler pulled the lifeboat back and they came in again. Jack waited for the boat to stop rising and in the second before it dropped and Tyler thrust backwards, he stepped across.

Captain Henriksen faced them. On one side was his First Officer, on the other his wife. He himself dwarfed them both. He wore a white-topped cap and a reefer jacket and tie.

'We have now nine crew,' he told them, 'two officers, myself also and my wife. My rudder has gone. Holds one and two of my ship are flooded and water is passing into hold three. You have capacity for all hands?'

'Yes,' said Croyden.

'How much tide remains?'

'A few feet, perhaps more with this wind. An hour or two.'

The Captain looked aft. Tongues of water were already sliding up across the deck.

'In that case, gentlemen,' he said, 'we should hurry.'

Time and again the lifeboat came in, picked up a man, then dropped back. As the tide approached its peak, so the motion of the seas became more haphazard. They had risen high up the ship's sides and were coming green over the stern. Jack and Croyden stood at the starboard rail, some way aft, where the freeboard was lowest. They held each crew member as he stood on the rail, gripped the stay and waited for the life-boat to come in. 'Now!' shouted Croyden as he released them.

All the while, as his men queued up at the rail, Captain Henriksen stood to one side. Beside him Mrs Henriksen had her arm looped through his; in her other hand she held a leather case with the initials 'PH' embossed on it. The First Officer jumped aboard the lifeboat and Croyden motioned to Mrs Henriksen to come forward.

Captain Henriksen placed his hand at his wife's back.

'Quick, Missus!' Croyden shouted.

But again she said, 'I will not leave before you.'

Henriksen took his leather case and stepped up to the gunwale and Tyler brought the lifeboat in.

'Now!' shouted Croyden.

The Captain glanced back.

'Go on!' urged his wife.

But the moment had passed and as he leaned forward the lifeboat was already dropping away from the ship. Jack leaned over and grabbed him – but Captain Henriksen was too heavy.

Jack did not remember falling. He remembered suddenly being in the water and thinking how very large the *Constantine* looked and how very steep the seas. When the line fell across his head he caught it and looped it around the Captain's waist and, without looking, tied a Spanish bowline. Six hands reached down from the lifeboat and pulled the Captain aboard. Jack already felt the next wave washing him away from the ship. It was breaking as it reached him and it drove him down and slammed him against the side. The water cleared above him and those were the bows of the lifeboat and the line that looped out from them and he was thinking again how very large the *Constantine* looked from down there and he was rising from the water and on the lifeboat they were pulling up his trouser leg and how strange that he felt nothing because there was his shin with a gash down but it was as if it was someone else's leg and not his at all.

CHAPTER 15

B efore the *Kenneth Lee* had even returned to the lifeboat
station, where Dr White put more than a dozen stitches
into Jack Sweeney's shin, the committee of Polmayne's Shipwrecked Mariners' Association were already busy. Between
them Mr Francis Evans, Parson Hooper and Mrs Hooper and
Clifford Thomas contacted the Finnish Consul by telephone,
collected more than a dozen blankets and commandeered the
United Methodists' tea-urn.

Later, when the Freeman Reading Rooms was a mass of
milling bodies, steaming cups and assorted languages, Parson
Hooper arrived and asked for silence. The *Constantine*'s crew
bowed their heads. Captain Henriksen tucked his cap under
his arm.

'Eternal Father, who divided the Red Sea with His power
and brought his people to dry land, we thank Thee for bringing these Thy servants from the perils of the deep. Protect
them this night and always, so that Thou might lead them

peacefully into that final place which is called Fair Havens, nigh whereunto is the city of the Lord . . .'

Parson Hooper then offered to accommodate Captain and Mrs Henriksen at the rectory.

Even though Polmayne's summer visitors already occupied every spare room, and many that were not spare, more than half the ship's company had found billets by the end of that evening. Joan Kliskey put up three at Dormullion. Eliza Tucker erected a camp bed in her store room. Major Franks and Mrs Franks had their guest room occupied by a friend from Bombay but they laid out bedding for one in their dining room. Mrs Cuffe offered Whaler's shed and Mrs Hooper wondered whether it was seemly with him only just buried.

'Take it or leave it,' shrugged Mrs Cuffe.

At the rectory the next morning, Captain Henriksen woke early. He dressed in the same shirt as the day before, the same black tie. He then placed himself in a chair in the corner of the room. He was still sitting there when his wife woke.

'No moping!' she said and after breakfast took him for a walk. The fog had cleared and it was a beautiful morning. In the churchyard they stopped to admire an azalea and some gentians and to read Parson Hooper's Tablets.

How beautiful it is to be alive,
to live – to love – to work for God! . . .

'You see, dear – we should be grateful we survived.'

Captain Henriksen said nothing. He was looking at the latest Tablet. '. . . *Not this man but Barabbas.*'

That day the first reporters began to arrive in Polmayne. The Garrett brothers charged them extra to go to the wreck in the *Polmayne Queen*. 'Dangerous waters,' explained Jimmy.

By the weekend a total of fifteen thousand people had made their way out to Pendhu to see for themselves the FAMOUS BARQUE MAROONED ON CORNWALL'S TREACH-EROUS COAST. The lanes from Porth became clogged with buses and cars. Ivor Dawkins had his labourers place hand-painted signs in the gateways of his mown fields – 'TO THE WRECK!' – then charged sixpence a car for access.

Many of the visitors beat a path to the watch hut where Captain Williams recounted his own part in the events of that afternoon: 'Blind as a mole I was, fog 's thick as paint.'

The *Constantine*'s crew remained in the town. Four were sleeping in the Reading Rooms. In Dalvin's field the number of visitors' tents was still growing and the committee of the SMA wrote an open letter to the Parish Council saying it was 'an iniquity' that the town should fall over itself to charge for tents and put up paying visitors while no space could be found for a few poor shipwrecked sailors. Moreover, the brand new villas along Church Road lay empty. Why should the men not be permitted to stay there?

Parliament Bench responded to the ship's loss as they responded to all loss.

'They won't ever get her off now.'

'Never!'

'We'll not see another barque like her.'

'Not if we live a thousand years.'

But Toper had been thinking. 'They might get her off yet.'

And although the *Constantine* remained fast on the Balk, exposed to the swell, the weather settled and the tides eased and for the time being she was safe. Salvors came in a launch and made their calculations and went away again. They came back and patched up her bows and told Captain Henriksen that if the weather held, they could have a go at refloating at the next spring tides.

For Parson Hooper, the *Constantine* proved a blessing. He busied himself with the crew's welfare, found them all billets, liaised with the Finnish Honorary Consul. The crew's presence in church more than doubled his congregation. He even put a few to work in the churchyard.

And each evening after supper he retired to his study with Captain Henriksen. They played chess and discovered a common interest in the Old Testament. Captain Henriksen said he had found a certain reassuring truth in his misfortune. *'Sorrow is better than laughter,'* he quoted from Ecclesiastes, *'for by the sadness of the countenance the heart is made better...'*

Hooper reached for his Bible. 'Beware, Captain! Beware the worm of self-pity! It can sap your spirit without you even knowing. Here – I thought so. Only two chapters later we have, *"Go thy way, eat thy bread with joy and drink thy wine with a merry heart."'*

Parson Hooper had found purpose again. His faith in Polmayne began to be restored. He resumed his work in the churchyard and one evening read to Captain Henriksen a stanza that the fate of the *Constantine* had moved him to write:

> *Ye who seek out landfall on this earth of ours,*
> *shall surely strike the shoals*
> *and tear the belly of your ship asunder!*
> *For there is no safe haven save in Your kingdom*
> *Where we shall unburden the cargo of our hopes!*

Henriksen went rather quiet. But later that week Parson Hooper proudly took the stanza to Pascoe & Sons and commissioned a new Tablet.

Jack Sweeney sat in his room. With the stitches in his leg and his ankle badly bruised he was unable to walk.

On that first day after the wreck, a number of people made their way up the bare-boarded stairs to his room. Major Franks came and squeezed his shoulder: 'Well done, old man. A splendid rescue.' He handed Jack an envelope in which was his ten-shilling call-out fee.

The Henriksens came. Captain Henriksen stood before him and said: 'I thank you! Thank you...' He then turned and climbed back down the stairs. Mrs Henriksen apologised. 'I'm so sorry, dear. He's finding it all rather trying.'

Mrs Cuffe, whose daily rota had altered little since her husband's death, came up with Jack's food. On the second evening she appeared with a fruit cake.

'Not me that made it,' she explained. 'It was that foreign woman. She left it on the step, with a note.'

I have heard about your adventure and your famous under-water knot and what could I do? I made this cake. It is a very clever cake and will make you better very quick.
   Anna Abraham

Croyden appeared and he alone did not express his concern. When he asked about the leg, Jack knew he was really asking how long before they could leave for Newlyn. The pilchard shoals had already arrived. But one day Croyden came and sat down and lit a cigarette. He had smoked half of it before he said, 'I won't be coming to Newlyn.'

'Why not?'

'It's Hammels. He's a bloody Jonah. We have no luck while he's on board.'

A few weeks earlier, Jack would have given in – but now he called Croyden's bluff. 'We'll miss you.'

The next morning, using a stick, Jack managed to walk out to the front for the first time. Several people he didn't know asked him how he was.

It was a week of very hot weather. As the days passed and he recovered and made his way further around the harbour, so he found himself filled with a restless enthusiasm. He leaned on the harbour wall and thought: I will leave this town, find a trading ship, work passage to America, or Africa or the Indies. Then he hatched a plan to buy a bigger boat, fish the Western Approaches, put into Irish ports. He would go to

London. He even considered going back to Dorset and farming. Each of his whims lasted a few hours.

When the stitches came out, he went to the East Quay and took out his punt. He found if he lodged his bad leg against a stern-frame he could row. He headed out of the bay. What wind there was came from the north and there was no swell. Beyond Hemlock Cove he saw the *Constantine* and its stranded bulk. The sun had not yet risen above the hill and the ship was in shadow. Short little seas rolled along her sides; a line of shags stood drying their wings on her rail.

He rowed on, out into the sun. He heard the first clangs of the Cages bell and at Maenmor came round and looked at the gap between its two peaks. The tide was higher than when he had first done it, two years earlier, and the gap was even narrower. He swung the bows round, brought in the paddles and the rock closed in over him. He ducked, and his ankle twisted against the bottom boards and he cried out. The boat began to spin. He grabbed one of the paddles and jabbed it against the rock. Then he was out again in the sunlight and he caught his breath and looked back at the gap and wondered what on earth had made him so reckless.

Back in the inner harbour, Jack sculled in and anchored his punt. The quays were crowded and he hopped up the steps and there at the top was Anna Abraham. On the cobbles beside her were two baskets. 'So – you can row, but still you can't walk!'

She was on her way back to Ferryman's and he offered to take her there.

Up the river, the heat bounced off the water. The wind had dropped away to almost nothing. The oak trees were thick-leafed, at their greenest, in that brief half-season between fullness and the long drying slide towards autumn. Sitting in the stern, Anna said: 'You know, Mr Sweeney, you look different.'

'Oh?'

'You fit your clothes.'

'Same old clothes!'

'It's an expression. When someone's spirit grew, we used to say it. Maybe they are in love. Are you in love, Mr Sweeney?'

He chuckled, and shook his head.

'Well, something then.'

As they rounded the corner the cottage came into view. 'Is Mr Abraham here?'

'No. He went to Germany. He finished his big painting and he went to Germany.'

Anna prepared a meal of cold ham and salad. They drank cider and sat at the slate-topped table outside the cottage, and the tide turned in the river and the tide-lines that had striped the ebb now tangled in the flood.

Jack bit into an apple and leaned back against the wall. 'I know only three things about you, Mrs Abraham. You are married to Maurice Abraham, you paint, and your father died in the Baltic Sea. Is there anything else?'

CHAPTER 16

～✺～

Anna Abraham had been born Anna Petrovna Shishkin, in 1902, on a small estate to the south of St Petersburg. After her father drowned, her mother was forced to sell the house. She took Anna and her two sisters to live in the city, in a lightless tenement behind the Gostinny Dvor. Following the revolution they wound up in Berlin, then in Paris. In the summer of 1923, the first of several, Anna went south to stay with a painter cousin in Biarritz.

She had spent a lifetime in overcrowded flats. Her companions had been women in threadbare furs, embittered by loss. In Biarritz she threw open a window on the world and saw it clearly for the first time. She stayed in a white house with a white balcony and at the bottom of the street she could see the sea. That first summer her cousin taught her to draw. He said she had 'an instinctive sense of line'. He introduced her to a whole host of writers and painters – Americans, Spaniards, English and Italians. She had always thought it somehow shameful to be an émigré; but here each of them wore their exile like a badge, like an order of merit, and Russian was the highest order of all.

Each May she returned to Biarritz. In 1926 she met the English painter Maurice Abraham and thought that God could not have made a more beautiful man. They were married that September. Anna often asked herself: What have I done to deserve such luck? She was living in a large house in Hampstead which looked over yellowing treetops to the towers and steeples of London. She had an attic room in which she painted – working through a succession of styles until she had something that was hers. At the same time Maurice's own work began to attract more attention. He became, in a minor way, a fashionable painter. He was elected to the Royal Academy and began to travel more widely, and the more widely he travelled the better his work sold. He went to the Near East, North Africa, South America.

Then Anna lost a baby. She had only known she was pregnant for two weeks and already the baby was gone. When it happened the next time, the doctor told her there would not be another. She felt a grief so deep that she could not find the words to express it. She had the sensation she was falling down a well. Maurice went to Germany to stay with his friend, the poet Max Stein.

Over the next two years they drifted apart. Maurice spent weeks at a time in Germany, and each time he came back they found themselves more and more remote. Only in Polmayne, and in Ferryman's Cottage, did they find an enthusiasm they could share.

In the summer of 1935, Max Stein arrived in Polmayne and it became clear to Anna what she had long refused to consider. Max and Maurice were having an affair. Anna Abraham was not an angry woman but she told Max to leave her house at once. She herself left for London and suggested to Maurice that he find somewhere else to live. As much as the betrayal and the hurt, she was haunted by the thought that the only square of earth sacred to her had been sullied.

That autumn, Maurice's mother died and after the funeral he came to Hampstead and asked Anna for forgiveness. He embarked on a three-day monologue, reproaching himself for the years of travelling, his long absences in Germany and South America, for Max. He told Anna he could no longer abide Max's hypocrisy, that Germany under Hitler was a terrible place and he was not going back. He told her he had never for a moment stopped loving her and she believed him. She believed him because she wanted to believe him. It was Christmas 1935, and in the New Year, when she received another letter from Jack Sweeney she wrote back ending their correspondence.

In May 1936, Maurice received a commission from a new hotel in Polmayne and they went down together and all was well. The town was at its bustling best and Maurice rented a net loft big enough for his canvas and divided his working time between there and the cliffs around Pendhu Point. Then a letter arrived from Berlin and he became distracted. When he announced that after his painting was finished he would have to go to Germany, Anna told him calmly to leave at once. 'And there's no coming back.'

For the first time in her life she found herself completely alone. She spent another week in the cottage. She waited for the sky to fall on her head but it did not. She swam and drew and walked and by the end of that week she realised that she had already endured the suffering and that nothing could ever hurt her so much again. She stayed on at Ferryman's.

However hard she tried in coming years, Anna Abraham was never able to remember the first time she saw Jack Sweeney. When he picked them up off the rocks during the storm in June 1935 he was already familiar, one of those sun-browned figures she had watched busying themselves around the quays. It took her some time to see that he too was an outsider. But that first summer she took little notice of him. She was amused by his letters and the details of his fishing, but nothing more. By the time she saw him again in the summer of 1936 she sensed that something had changed in him. He was assured and animated. He fitted his clothes.

'You're well enough to row up Ferryman's, you're well enough for Newlyn.' Croyden had found Jack sitting in the courtyard at Bethesda, working at his knots.

'I thought you weren't coming.'

'I changed my mind.' Reports from Newlyn were good. 'But if we have no luck,' he warned Jack, 'you'll know why.'

Jack told him to take the nets to the barking house. At low water he and Hammels spread them out on the rocks below the Antalya. Jack rowed aboard the *Maria V* and cleaned out the Kelvin. His leg was now almost fully recovered. The following day he brought the boat into the quays and they all scrubbed her down, scraped off the weed and re-tarred her keel. They took on another hand, Croyden's brother Charlie. Two days later they were ready. They would leave at dawn, catch the tide round the Lizard and be in Newlyn by evening.

Jack had seen Anna Abraham on most days. She dropped into the yard and when the *Maria V* was lying against the East Quay she paused to watch them on her way back to the cottage. On his last day in Polmayne she told Jack she would come to the harbour in the afternoon and say goodbye. At five there was still no sign of her. He took the *Maria V* back to the moorings. She had let him down again.

'Stood up, is 'ee?' Toper called from the Bench.

How did he know? How did everyone know everything in this damned town? Jack glared at Toper and returned to Bethesda.

She came at dusk. There was a quiet double-knock and he knew it was her. She had been sketching out at the lifeboat station and the time had gone and, well, she had no idea it was so late. She placed her pad on the table and looked around. She had never seen his room. It was entirely without softness – there were no curtains and no rugs; even the bed looked hard. There were piles of rope everywhere – off-cuts on the chair, hempen coils on the floor, piles of lanyard on the window sills. On the mantelpiece was a collection of shells and driftwood, a piece of old propeller and behind it a picture of a tropical bird.

Anna took off her headscarf. On the table was the mat he had been working on and she ran her fingers over it. 'What is it?'

'A sinnet.'

'Like a poem?'

'That's a sonnet. It's for the mizzen boom – stop it chafing on the stays.'

She shook her head, smiling. 'You know this language is Icelandic to me!'

Crossing to the window she half-bent to look out. The late sun shone on Pendhu Point. The waters of the bay were ruffled by a freshening southerly. Gulls dipped and glided above it.

'Can you see the rocks?'

'Not from here.'

They stood in silence. He was leaning against the table, watching her.

'Let me show you something!' he said. He took a piece of line from the table and stepped up to her. 'Now!'

He tied one end to each of her wrists.

'What are you doing?'

'Wait, wait.' He was grinning. He put his own hands together, as if praying. 'Now, wrap that loop around my wrists – tight, so I can't get them out. See?'

She did so. They stood before each other. He was trapped.

'Now what?' she asked.

'Watch.' He worked his hands through the bight, twisted them and he was free.

'Oh!'

'You know what it's called?'

'Should I?'

'It's the Russian escape knot.'

'I've never heard of it.'

'Another?'

She nodded.

'Give me your ring.'

She slipped her wedding ring from her finger and handed it to him. He threaded a loop of string through it, put each end over his thumbs and said: 'Now – how do I free the ring without lifting the string from my thumb?'

Anna looked at it. She leaned back, examined each end. 'It's impossible.'

'Perhaps.'

Without taking his eyes from hers, he tucked his little fingers inside the loop, pulled tight again and the ring fell away. He caught it.

She shook her head: 'It can't . . .'

He repeated the trick, more slowly. Again he caught the ring as it fell. 'Look, you try.'

He placed the string over her thumbs, then guided her fingers through it. Having pulled the string tight, she shouted: 'Bravo!' Then he leaned forward and kissed her. Neither of them heard the ring fall and roll across the boards.

The day paled in the windows. Even close to midnight, it was still hardly dark. A bluish light fell across the bed and Jack looked down and saw her face against the pillow and it seemed he was seeing her for the first time. Later when he slept again she lay awake listening to his breathing. Down on the beach she could hear the hiss of the waves as they slid up the shingle and then the clink of pebbles as they drew back, and she thought: it sounds like something falling.

They rose at four. She made him sit on the bed for a minute's silence. She said: 'Before a journey. It is a Russian custom, to make sure you come back safely.'

It was still dark when she left him at the quay. Above Pritchard's Beach she watched the *Maria V* head out towards Pendhu Point. She stood there until the boat's lights merged into one. Below her the seas were breaking on the shingle, pulling back and breaking again and she thought again: it sounds like something falling.

CHAPTER 17

T he day the *Maria V* left for Newlyn, a brand-new hotel
opened in Polmayne. For ten months a team of builders
had been working to convert a private house, but because
they were not locals and because they lived on site, a certain
mystery had grown up around the project. Now its doors
were open. It was named the Golden Sands Hotel and its
proprietors were a Mr and Mrs Edwin Bryant.

Mr Bryant was a round-faced, balding man with a penchant
for bowler hats. He also owned a good deal of property in
Birmingham and Wolverhampton. During the dark years of
the Depression he had acquired a number of very cheap ware-
houses, tenement blocks and old ironworks. By the end of
1931 he had added two bankrupt hotels to his portfolio. He
was fond of saying things like: 'When I hear talk of pulling
in horns ... tightening purse strings ... battening hatches, I
know it's time to push the boat out!' His own success was
proof of all his adages.

In July 1932, after thirty months of unrelenting work, Mrs

Bryant had persuaded him to book in for a fortnight at Pol-mayne's Antalya Hotel. They motored down. They were given a room with windows that framed the twin quays like a painting. They were both very happy those weeks. Mrs Bryant liked to sit on her balcony with her eyes closed, while the exploring fingers of the sun ran across her bare shoulders. Mr Bryant liked to walk through the town in his bowler hat. He liked to watch the comings and goings at the quays, trying to work out how the cogs of commerce spun in this sun-splashed seaside town. He liked to watch the young women sunning themselves on the quay wall, their dresses hitched up to the thigh. As the days passed, his passions rose and in the end he succumbed to them: he began to look at property.

Wandering out of the village, he inspected the new villas and the Crates. So much new building! Beyond them was a block of pasture which looked down over the withy beds to the Glaze River. He paced around it, considered the view and dismissed it. He knew what people wanted. In the city they might like something modern, but on holiday they preferred the traditional style. 'In business, look forward,' he mused. 'In leisure, look back!'

On a wet afternoon, he strolled up the laurel-flanked drive of Dormullion House. He counted the upstairs windows. The columns of the terrace, he noted with some satisfaction, gave the façade a faintly Regency air. They were also badly in need of paint. That evening he wrote to Mrs Kliskey. He had the letter delivered by hand. The reply came back to the Antalya at noon the next day:

> Dear Mr Bryant,
> I don't know who you are but the answer is no.
> No, no, no!
>   Joan Kliskey

Up towards the lifeboat station was a half-hidden Victorian house named Pendhu Lodge. The house had been built by an Azariah Dupont, amateur yachtsman, entomologist and founder and Chairman of Dupont Steam Irons in Sheffield. It was now owned by the current Chairman, his grandson Joshua Dupont.

Mr Bryant peered through its gates and saw a group of people sitting on wicker chairs and rugs on the lawn. A young girl in a floppy straw hat was running around among them, chasing a terrier.

Bryant received a courteous answer from Joshua Dupont:

Although it is true that Pendhu is only fully occupied for a brief period of the year it is nevertheless a much-loved family house and greatly appreciated by all members of it – particularly the younger ones. I sincerely hope that Pendhu Lodge will be enjoyed by Duponts for generations to come...

A year later, Mr Bryant read in the paper of the insolvency of Dupont Steam Irons. He wrote again, naming his price. A letter of acceptance came back from a firm of Sheffield solicitors.

Against all the predictions of his architect, the hotel was completed on time. 'You want a job doing well,' Bryant told him, 'you get your own men to do it.'

5 August 1936 was a breezy, sunny day. Mr Bryant congratulated himself on choosing it for the hotel's Grand Opening and Buffet Lunch. At 12.30 the first guests stepped into a hall laid with checkerboard parquet. Several aspidistras umbrellaed out over a stained-oak counter marked 'Reception'. Above the fireplace hung a large, gilt-framed painting. It showed a great lick of a green wave breaking on the sands of Hemlock Cove; the Main Cages were dark shapes in the background. There was a patch of sky on one side where the bare canvas showed through; in the bottom right-hand corner the painting was signed 'M.J. Abraham, 1936'.

Upstairs, one of the bedrooms was on show. Mrs Bryant's imaginative colour scheme was admired by all who saw it –

except Mrs Franks, who called it 'irredeemably vulgar'. The walls were painted sand-yellow, the counterpanes and lampshades were a woody yellow and beside the window was a custard-yellow, plumbed-in washbasin. The butter-coloured towels were embroidered with 'GOLDEN SANDS' in ochre thread. The window looked down over the lawns, between stands of fur-trunked Fortune palms to the hotel's beach – which was neither golden nor sandy but covered in grey pebbles.

One hundred and twenty guests attended the lunch. The Petrel owners came. They stood in a group at the bar and Ralph Cameron with his George V beard sipped at a pink gin. 'Might be time to change watering-holes.'

'The Antalya's become very gloomy,' said the Dane Soren.

'Rather!' agreed Lawrence Rose.

The Hoopers brought Captain and Mrs Henriksen. Mr and Mrs Connors arrived with Anna Abraham. Major Franks and Mrs Franks appeared on the terrace with their house guest of three weeks, a very distinguished-looking Indian man in a white suit and white panama hat. Mrs Franks introduced him to Parson Hooper as 'the Master'.

After lunch, the guests gathered on the lawn below. At half past two, Mr Bryant climbed up on a bench on the terrace and clapped his hands for silence. On one side of the bench was Mrs Bryant, on the other, three feet taller than her, was Lady Banville. The brigantine *Lady Banville*, bound for Liverpool with a cargo of copra and teak, had been wrecked on the Cages in 1862. Her figurehead was spotted rotting in a garden by Mr Bryant. He bought her for ten bob, had her restored, repainted and erected on the hotel terrace. Her eyes were now glossy blackcurrants, her lips re-rouged, and she displayed a spectacular décolletage – in which was stuck a blood-red rose.

'Ladies and gentlemen!' Bryant was without his hat. The wind flicked at the lapels of his dark suit. 'I would like you to imagine, if you will, a town such as Polmayne one hundred years ago – before the railways. In those days it would take the best part of a week to get from here to London. The people here lived in ignorant isolation, depending for their livelihood on the meagre fruits of the sea. All that has changed. Like a beautiful debutante Polmayne stands on the threshold of a – er, "golden" age. Today she is coming out!

'Business, I always believe, is a little like marriage' – for effect, he glanced down at Mrs Bryant. 'Both depend on the principle of mutual benefit. Likewise, here at the Golden Sands we are providing not only repose for our guests but employment and prosperity to a town which is sorely in need of it.'

In the hot sun, Mr Bryant's hairless head was shining with sweat. He paused for a moment and surveyed his audience.

'Several years ago Mrs Bryant and I came here for the first time. I speak for her too when I say I could not have conceived of a more splendid place. Our hope now is that our pleasure will be shared by all our guests. A pleasure shared is a pleasure doubled!'

He turned to his wife. 'My dear –'

Mrs Bryant took a pair of scissors and cut the cord that was wrapped around Lady Banville's waist. Above the ground-floor windows a stretch of sailcloth fell away from the façade. Behind it was a board painted gold and white and broadcasting its little lie to all who entered Polmayne Bay by sea: 'GOLDEN SANDS HOTEL'.

Jimmy Garrett was lying on his bed. He was thinking. His forearm lay across his face. The *Polmayne Queen* was out of action. Her pump had perished the previous week. The propeller shaft needed repacking. She was taking in water at the stem and along the deck and there was no money left for repairs. The wreck of the *Constantine* had helped; if not for that, she would have been out barely a dozen times since May. Even so he had failed to plug his debts. Jimmy was wondering if it was time to sell her. He hadn't bought or sold a boat in a long time and he was ready to trade the *Queen*. But for what?

Tacker sat across the room from his brother on a stool. He was whittling a piece of washed-up timber, and curls of wood lay all around his feet.

'Could talk to Bryant,' he said.

'Who's Bryant?'

'The new hotel.'

Jimmy grunted.

'Give him a share, Jim. We could give him a share in the boat.'

Jimmy lay unmoving, still thinking. After a few minutes he hauled himself up, swung his bad leg round and scratched the great orb of his bald head. 'So where's he to, this Bryant?'

The hotel's oak-panelled office was practically empty. There was only a desk and some packing cases. Mr Bryant leaned back against the desk and folded his arms. 'Well, gentlemen?'

'We got a proposal, Mr Bryant.' Jimmy spoke softly but without directing his gaze away from Bryant. 'You'd know our steamer the *Polmayne Queen*.'

'Yes, I do.'

'Well, we was thinking maybe the hotel could take her on for some of her trips.'

Mr Bryant remained silent.

'She's a lovely boat for excursions, sir!' said Tacker.

'Excursions?'

'Yes, sir! Tin't the same in a bus, taking visitors everywhere in a bus now'days sir, tin't the same, not like being on the water –'

'What are you saying, gentlemen?'

'We're offering you a share in the boat,' said Jimmy. 'We would run it and we could still have our passengers from the quay, but any time you want the boat, you have her.'

'You could have her, sir!' added Tacker. 'We'd take her to

a nice spot for your visitors, let 'em have a nice picnic and we'd run her for you, keep her serviced and trim . . .'

Bryant looked at Jimmy and Tacker in turn. He smiled. 'So, when can you show me this boat of yours?'

CHAPTER 18

Polmayne had never been busier than that August. Fifty-six white tents were now ranked in Dawkins's fields – more than three times as many as in 1935 – and within a week of opening the Golden Sands Hotel had filled every one of its sand-coloured rooms.

The *Constantine* had much to do with it. Every time the newspapers ran a story about the ship's precarious position and the progress of her salvage, another wave of visitors swept into town asking where to find the 'famous stranded barque' before she broke up.

But it was also the weather. June had been fine – high clouds and long warm days. For a while in July, fog muzzled the headlands and on St Swithun's day – the day before the *Constantine* struck – it thickened into heavy rain. Parson Hooper was very pleased. The freshly-cleared gardens were already looking parched. 'St Swithun's Day if thou dost rain/ for forty days it will remain,' he recited at Evensong.

The next two days were damp and foggy and the gardeners

among Parson Hooper's congregation, who made up the largest part, gladdened to his words. But then the skies cleared, steam rose from the newly-tarmaced roads and the crowds returned to the beaches in even greater numbers.

Parliament Bench did not like it. 'Goes on like this and the whole bloody world'll be here.'

'Tin't right, so many people all in one place.'

Tick-Tock Harris produced *Picture Post* photographs of the summer hordes in Nice and Blackpool. He said it was like that everywhere. No one was convinced.

'They pictures are just made up,' explained Toper.

'Eeee,' agreed Boy Johns.

'It won't last,' warned Red Treneer. 'You mark my words.'

'Weather's bound to break.'

But Red was not talking about the weather. For him there were darker clouds just over the horizon. Since the Spanish coup on 20 July he had been collecting for the Republicans and had raised a good deal of money. He was careful not to say it was for the Republicans, but simply for the 'Spanish Cause'. In that way he managed to raise funds from Franco's sympathisers too – and they tended to give much more money.

Then the water started to run out. At seven o'clock on the morning of 27 July, Mrs Cuffe carried her two buckets into Bethesda's yard, cranked the cow's-tail handle and watched the spout produce a trickle of green-brown sludge. Then nothing.

Work had started on the new reservoir at Pennance but it would need the winter's rain to fill it. The extra visitors were helping to drain the existing supplies. Mrs Cuffe took to joining the queue at the pump below the Fountain Inn.

At the Parish Council meeting at the end of July, water was the main topic. Two camps emerged – those who thought that visitors should be told to stay away until there was water, and those who claimed the town now depended as much on the visitors as on water. Chairman of the Council, Major Franks, produced the Sanitary Inspector's report.

'He proposes, gentlemen, that we boil drinking water. According to this report, it seems that our friend the Reed Fever may have popped out just as the water table dropped.'

So that confirmed it. The visitors *were* to blame for the Reeds.

Captain Henriksen sat across from Parson Hooper. His frame filled the leather chair that he had occupied, every evening, since the day the *Constantine* had foundered. As the weeks passed so his bulk sunk deeper into that leather chair. He became more and more silent, more and more convinced that his ship would never float again. Visits from insurers, salvors' reports, letters and valuations filled his days; he could no longer read weather reports in case they told of the shift of wind to west or south that would destroy his ship. He had arranged for a barge to empty her holds. They offloaded twelve hundred tons of grain – less than a quarter of the cargo. The rest was sodden.

Captain Henriksen told Parson Hooper it was a terrible thing to witness the slow death of a ship. 'It is like my own flesh falling off me.'

'Nonsense, Captain! *Du courage!*'

Parson Hooper remained busy. The captain's sinking spirits required his daily counsel. Each morning he went down to the far corner of the churchyard and joined six of the *Constantine*'s crew who were clearing the last jungly recess of the churchyard. Two or three afternoons a week, at Mr Bryant's request, he took tea on the terrace of the Golden Sands Hotel and led discussions with the hotel guests. Then a sailor from the *Constantine* fell for one of the Johns girls. He said he wanted to marry her. The Johns family were against it as she was already engaged to Joe Stephens. Captain Henriksen did what he could but it was Hooper who persuaded them not to run away as they threatened to do, but to wait.

On 10 August he drove into Truro and collected the Tablet

which he had written when the *Constantine* had struck (*Ye who seek out landfall on this earth of ours,/Or shelter from the tempest ...*) and commissioned a new one with T.E. Brown's piece of gardeners' doggerel:

> *A garden is a lovesome thing, God wot!*
> *Rose plot,*
> *Fringed pool,*
> *Fern'd grot –*
> *The veriest school*
> *Of peace ...*

Later that week, over a game of chess, Captain Henriksen announced to him that the salvors had managed to make a full repair of the *Constantine*'s bows. In the next couple of days, they would put more pumps aboard.

'One week, Rector, two maybe – then to sea again!'

Parson Hooper felt a sudden breath of cold air.

In Newlyn, Jack Sweeney had grown a beard. In months gone by Croyden used to tease him for turning up at dawn with his cheeks smooth, because shaving was something that happened only on Saturday evening. But for Jack now everything had changed and the beard was a way to mark it.

Croyden still teased him: 'Makes 'ee look like a bloody Spaniard.' Hammels, who was completely hairless on his chin, was curious about it, and liked to inspect it when Jack was sleeping.

The fishing was very poor. By the time the *Maria V* arrived in Newlyn the early shoals had begun to thin. Jack wrote to Anna:

> *Everyone blames everyone else in Newlyn. The fishermen blame the buyers for the prices, the buyers blame Mussolini and Abyssinia and the shopkeepers blame everyone because the*

boats from St Ives and the East coast have gone back. Now the fish have stopped coming and Croyden and Charlie Treneer blame poor old Hammels for it. If that's not enough there's Penzance council to blame for condemning the houses of Fore St and St Peter's Hill. They want to knock them down and put everyone in new houses. Why can't these people just be left alone?

The next day, he wrote again – this time a hurried note.

We're coming back! Just for a day or two. We'll take the early train on Saturday. It's Polmayne's Regatta & Carnival and Charlie Treneer says he wants his half crown for crewing Petrels – plus winnings and he usually wins. Croyden says he must find water for his piece and I said I'd help him. He has guessed of course my real reason for wanting to be in Polmayne.

*   *   *

That Friday afternoon, at the Golden Sands Hotel, a shiny new Lincoln Zephyr crunched down the gravel drive and came to a halt at the porch. Mr Bryant hurried out of the hotel to open the car door.

'Lady Rafferty . . . Sir Basil.'

Sir Basil Rafferty was a large man with the slightly startled look of a tortoise. He was also the hotel's principal backer. Like Bryant, he had done well in Birmingham out of the Depression and like Bryant he had no experience of the sea – the turf was his passion. When he was invited to invest in the hotel, he agreed not because he believed in seaside hotels but because he believed in Bryant.

'Sounds worth a punt!'

After tea, Mr Bryant took Sir Basil up to Penpraze's yard where the *Polmayne Queen* was leaning against a quay.

'For the guests' entertainment,' he explained. 'Picked it up cheap.'

'Splendid!' said Sir Basil.

'We relaunch tomorrow for the regatta.'

Mr Bryant had told the Garretts that he would take on their boat under a number of conditions. The sides must be repainted golden-yellow, with the bulwarks white. The porthole casements should be picked out in red, the funnels be sky blue with two four-inch yellow hoops towards their top, the woodwork on board be glossed white with some features, such as the wheelhouse, picked out in yellow. The canvas awning would be replaced by a wooden canopy (painted yellow) just aft of the wheelhouse, making a 'saloon' with a simple bar for refreshments. The engine – a four-stroke from Bergius of Glasgow – must be fully serviced and a lifeboat be installed.

'Hospitality and safety,' explained Mr Bryant to the Garretts, 'the twin principles of the hotelier!'

He had also told them he wanted it all ready for Polmayne regatta on the fifteenth.

'Can't do that, sir!' said Tacker.

'If you need extra men, I will pay for them. But I want it ready.'

Tacker looked to Jimmy and Jimmy shrugged, then nodded.

Last, Mr Bryant had insisted on them painting over the places where the name *Polmayne Queen* appeared.

'Good, good!' said Bryant when he saw the boat gleaming bright yellow in the evening sun. 'Look!' he exclaimed, showing Sir Basil where the new name had been applied in gold leaf on the bows – *Golden Sands* – with a gold cove-line running back down the length of the hull.

'Ah!' Sir Basil nodded approvingly.

Tacker Garrett popped his head up over the side. 'Hello, sir!'

'All ready for tomorrow, Tacker?'

'Well, sir!'

Jimmy stood up beside his brother, wiping his hand on a rag. 'Had a little setback.'

'What do you mean?'

'This lifeboat you wanted needs new davits and we had to re-route the fuel pipe round them and we couldn't get –'

'But it will be ready for tomorrow?'

Jimmy shook his head.

Mr Bryant's success as a developer was based on knowing enough about construction to argue with his builders – 'If you want them to jump, learn to say "jump" in their language' – but with boats he was lost.

'Don't worry,' said Jimmy. 'Be finished in time for Porth regatta.'

'Porth regatta's a lovely day out!' echoed Tacker.

'When is that?'

'Two weeks.'

'Two weeks!' Bryant shook his head. He looked across the river, clenching and unclenching his fists. Turning his gaze back to Jimmy, he said, 'You let me down again, Mr Garrett, and I'll have you. You'll be begging for a crust. Good day.'

Jimmy watched the two men go, tiptoeing back through the mud in their polished leather shoes.

CHAPTER 19

The sun rose behind a bank of grey-brown cloud. Beneath it the sea lay sludgy and still. Along the front, Mrs Cuffe took her buckets to the pump, looking at the cloud and hoping it would thicken into rain.

In Dawkins's fields, families woke in their tents to see that the light diffusing through the canvas was not bright and buttery but dull. When they crawled outside they looked to the sky for signs that the cloud might thin.

At six-thirty, Lawrence Rose rowed out to his banana-yellow Petrel *Grace*. The splash of his paddles was the only sound in the stillness of the bay. He climbed on board and hoisted the twenty-six signal flags to dress her overall. As he rowed back towards the Gaps he concentrated less on the bank of grey-brown cloud than on the looking-glass surface of the water and the limp flags reflected in it.

'Not a breath!' he called to Toper Walsh.

Toper was sweeping the quay. 'What's 'ee expect? It's regatta day!'

At seven o'clock a breeze began to tug at the bunting which ran in multi-coloured swells around the harbour. It made a faint clicking in the fronds of the roadside cordylines and rippled the curtains of open windows. Over the next few hours it freshened. The clouds disappeared and by eleven o'clock, when the Falmouth working boats and the cruisers and the Petrels from Porth began to assemble in the bay, it had become a steady southerly. The signal flags fluttered from *Grace*'s mast. The blue bay sparkled in the mid-morning sun, and by common consent it turned out to be Polmayne's best regatta since before the war.

At eleven Croyden and Jack and Charlie arrived back in Polmayne on Harris's station bus. They left the bus in front of the Antalya and climbed the hill to Rope Walk. Croyden's daughters were outside with their mother, preparing for the carnival. The two older ones were staining pieces of sailcloth with coal-dust.

'Look, Father!' they held up the shrouds and made whooshing noises. 'We're the West Wind!'

Croyden smiled. 'Very good. And what's 'ee?' He nodded to Betty, his four-year-old. She was standing in a yellow dress while her mother knelt down to pin up the hem. 'I'm the sun.' She raised her arms and waved them around. 'That's the sun's rays.'

'Keep still!' Maggie took a pin from her mouth and half-turned to Croyden. 'Any luck?'

He toed the dust and shook his head. 'No rain here?'

'Nothing.'

Charlie went to find Ralph Cameron and enlist as crew. Croyden and Jack each took two earthenware bussas and made their way on up the hill to Croyden's piece. The nearest spring to the allotments had long since dried up. A cattle-trodden patch of crusty mud stood in its place. They carried the bussas on into the next field. The spring there was the same. Above the Glaze River the sun was rising to its midday height and away from the wind it was hot. They followed a dusty track down past the tents and reached a granite trough which was full of greenish water; a little bulb of water was rising from the spring above it.

'That's better!' said Croyden. They filled the bussas. As they re-crossed the fields a figure came running down the grass towards them. It was Bran Johns.

'Mr Dawkins' – he was out of breath – 'Mr Dawkins says . . . he'll set his dogs on anyone takes as much as a drop . . .'

Croyden looked at him. He raised the bussa to his lips and drank. He wiped his lips, then drank again. 'You tell your Mr Dawkins he can bugger off.'

At ten minutes to two, Major Franks fired the first gun. The bay was already full of a mass of white and tan sails. There was the flapping of jibs and shouting, and the thud of running back-stays being thrown. Jousting bowsprits sped towards each other. Gybing booms swung across the decks. Spectators along the front and on the terrace of the Golden Sands were amazed (and a little disappointed) that there were no collisions. Sir Basil Rafferty watched it all through his field glasses, trying to work out who on earth was racing with whom.

The various cruiser classes were first off. They were followed by the crabbers and the working boats, and all through the afternoon the crowds thickened on shore in anticipation of the main race – the Petrels.

Three times a week that season the Petrels' cream sails had lined up off the quays for the start. Their dart-thin hulls appeared to fly above the water. Two new additions to the fleet had taken their number to eight. For the regatta they had been joined by four more from Porth. But the two to watch, as always, were *Harmony* and *Grace*. Ralph Cameron usually won in *Harmony*, at least when he could persuade Charlie Treneer to crew for him. For *Grace*, Lawrence Rose had a regular crew in Red Stephens.

That summer, for the first time, the Stephens brothers found they earned more from sailing than fishing. Their lugger remained unused while they pulled on the guernsey sweaters they had been given for racing – Red Stephens's was embroidered with *Grace*. Joe's had the name of the Dane Soren's *Charity*. Parliament Bench nicknamed them 'the angels'.

The twelve boats sailed back and forth along the starting line. Short little white-caps spotted the bay. At three forty-five exactly, a puff of grey smoke rose from the quays and the Petrels fell in beside each other to cross the line. The spectators cheered. They watched the boats beat out to the mark off Pendhu, then bunch up for the run up to the lifeboat station.

On the first round, *Harmony* had a minute over *Grace*; by the time she took the final gun she was five minutes ahead. Ralph Cameron rowed into the inner harbour and was greeted with applause.

'*Harmo-ny*!'

He sauntered up the steps, flashed his airman's smile and clapped a hand on Charlie's shoulder. 'All down to my crew!'

Charlie grinned shyly. He took his winnings straight to the Fountain Inn. Visitors and locals alike congratulated him. 'Thank you,' he said. 'Thank you very much.' Half an hour later, he was bellowing out that he would never sail again. 'Rather drink my own piss than go yachtin'! Bloody pansies' game!'

To raise funds, Coxswain Tyler assembled those of his crew who had been on the *Constantine* rescue and brought the *Kenneth Lee* in through the Gaps. Croyden had fished his brother Charlie out of the Fountain. On board, he and Jack stood on each side of Charlie to stop him falling over.

A steady flow of people passed the gauntlet of rattling

collection tins to see the boat. They were curious, hushed, admiring. They stood on the quay and looked down at the blue-and-orange hull and said to each other how small she looked. The lifeboatmen stood on board like fattened geese, roasting inside their lifejackets and sou'westers.

A group of boys came aboard. Tyler showed them into the shelter. They looked at the engine, the flares, the axe. They went forward, whispering to each other. When one asked a question about the *Constantine*, they all did.

'Sir – did the ship have a hundred sails?'

'Was it a bad storm?'

'Were the waves this tall?'

'Sir, sir – did you have to swim?'

'Only him!' Charlie Treneer pointed at Jack. His face was glaring and shiny with sweat. 'Only 'ee took a swim! Him and the bloody Captain!'

'Did you fall off?'

'Was the Captain in the water?'

'How did you get him back in?'

Jack took a warp and said: 'Look.' He wrapped the rope around one of the boys' waists and with his eyes closed did a Spanish bowline. 'Like that!'

'And me! And me!' shouted the others.

The carnival was next. Croyden and Jack and Charlie hurried back from the lifeboat station to join the parade at the Antalya. In the field behind the hotel, between the frames of two half-built villas, the Walking Class had just begun to file out into the square. Leading it was the Emperor of China (Brian Walsh – First Prize). He was followed by OK But not Saucy (Sue King – Second Prize). There was a spindly, tea-stained Gandhi behind her, and a Bottle of Pop, Miner and Bad Girl, Drink More Milk, Cinema Litter, Russian Peasant, and Scarecrow.

The square was filling. The floats were lining up in reverse order in the field. From the upper windows of the Antalya, guests leaned out to watch. Jack and Croyden stood by the harbour wall. Charlie was slumped between them, murmuring drunkenly: 'Get 'em away . . . they got breeches 'n tags 'n all . . .'

At that moment Jack spotted Anna on the far side of the parade. When she saw him, she put a hand to her mouth in mock horror. 'What is this?' she mouthed, pointing at her chin. As the Walking Class ended, he crossed the road towards her.

'Do you like it?'

'A few weeks on the sea and you come back looking like a mad pirate!'

'As bad as that?'

'Maybe not mad –'

'I can't see!' shouted a woman and Jack stood aside.

The floats were passing in front of them. Speed featured a number of Stephenses as a train, a motor car, and a boy whom Jack thought was a downhill skier but Anna said was definitely a 'parachuter'. Cornish Desert took third prize with its cart-mounted desert (sand from the beach, palm fronds from the churchyard and four miniature wooden camels plundered from the Christmas crib). Several people in rags stumbled beside it, raising empty water bottles to their lips, hissing: 'Water . . . water . . .'

'There's the Treneers!' said Jack.

They had won second prize. On the side of the float was written 'DEPRESSION FROM ICELAND'. Croyden's three eldest girls, with two of Charlie's children and a number of other Treneers, were all whooshing as the West Wind in their grey-stained shrouds. In their midst was Betty. As well as her yellow dress she wore a yellow cardboard ruff, and she was waving her arms in a very convincing way. She enjoyed being the sun and waving her yellow arms as the cart rolled forward and everyone looked up at her and clapped. But she didn't like all the bigger children standing around her making whooshing noises. They too enjoyed the crowd and whooshed with more and more vigour until at last the sun sank and its rays dropped, and it was just visible between the legs of the wind and beneath their shrouds, lying on the bottom of the cart and wailing.

First prize in that year's carnival was taken by outsiders. From the field beside the hotel, pulled by the rectory donkey Job, came King Constantine and his Women. Around the cart were members of the *Constantine*'s crew. They were wearing sack-cloth skirts, high heels, wigs and strings of limpet shells around their necks. They sang Finnish drinking songs. They winked, they flirted, they blew kisses at the crowd. On the cart above them, sitting on a makeshift throne and wearing a cardboard crown, with an orange for an orb and a belaying pin for a sceptre, was Captain Henriksen.

The crowd fell in behind to follow the float and Jack and Anna joined them. Captain Henriksen waved sadly at the people. He clutched his orange, his belaying pin rested on his chest, and the sadder he looked and the more his women hammed it up, the more everyone cheered. By the end the burden of state had lifted from the Captain and even he was smiling.

At the quays the floats assembled and lingered for some minutes. As they dispersed so the St Blazey Silver Prize Band took over with the Floral Dance. The shuffling mass of people began to quicken and spin. Up towards the Golden Sands Hotel, the band turned back and Jack and Anna slipped away and made their own way up towards the lifeboat station.

The last of the sun glowed on the back of Pendhu Point. They sat on the cliff while the sound of the band faded into the distance. The water below them was dark and evening-calm. Anna leaned back against Jack and said, 'How long are you here this time?'

'We go back tomorrow.'

'It's a tramp life, your fishing!'

He leaned forward and kissed her neck. 'We'll have lots of time soon,' he mumbled.

'Ow!' She sat up and pinched his beard. 'This – he must go!'

'He will go.' Jack pulled her to him again. He undid the top buttons of her cotton dress, assuring her with each one, 'He will go, he will go . . .'

His hand slid up her thigh and she settled back onto the grass. Afterwards they lay close together on their backs and slept and it was the cold that woke them and Jack put his coat around her shoulder. She pressed her head against his chest and looked up. The sky was clear.

'Look at the stars. Like sand.'

They lay in silence for a long time and she said quietly, 'What will happen, Jack, what is going to happen to us?'

'We will go to sea and live a tramp life and never go to the same place twice.'

She did not reply and as he held her he felt her shoulders start to shake. 'What is going to happen?' she said through her tears. 'I don't know, I just can't see.'

He could think of nothing to say. He held her more tightly. 'It'll be all right,' he told her. 'It'll be all right.'

When he woke again it was dawn. His coat lay across his chest. Pendhu Point was a pale smudge in the distance and he turned over and Anna had gone.

He rowed up to Ferryman's in the mid-morning. She was sitting outside, half asleep in a wide-brimmed hat, and she opened one eye when she saw him. 'Hello, you.'

'Bad news,' said Jack.

'What?' she sat up quickly. 'What is it, Jack?'

He smiled. 'Poor old Croyden's gone down with the Reeds. We're going to have to stay in Polmayne until he gets better.'

CHAPTER 20

In years to come Anna would think of those borrowed mid-August days as the happiest of her life. She forgot the strange shadow that hovered over them, the stabbing anxieties and doubts, the future that she seemed unable to project, the pain of her wasted marriage, the horror she now felt for her life in Hampstead and the uncertainty of a world that was suggesting itself here in Polmayne. Instead she recalled only the sunny half-week that began that Sunday morning on the bar outside Ferryman's Cottage when she sat Jack in a chair, put a towel over his shoulder and started to snip off the ugly black growth that covered his chin. The hair fell in dark curls around the chair. It dropped inside his shirt and he scratched at it while she cut, until he threw off the towel and ran into the water. He dunked his head and then stood there half-submerged and half-shorn. 'Let me finish it – please!'

She remembered the nights in the room beneath the rafters and the moon in the curtainlesss windows and the pale light on his rising-and-falling chest. She remembered him on Ferryman's beach leaning against his dinghy, eating redcurrants from a jug, and standing in the kitchen talking of the beauty of certain nights at sea. She saw him at the table outside, the ground spread with coils of hemp rope, the slate heaped with off-cuts while he spliced a rope hand-rail for the stairs.

It was a week of very big tides. At midday, they were able to wade across the river and picnic in the woods and before the flood Jack collected lug-worms and then fished for gilt-head bream as the tide rose to its height. In the evening the water was at its warmest and they swam and each day the tide was higher and they watched it seep into the grass, towards the home-made slate oven where Jack cooked the fish.

So the time passed. They rowed, they walked, they slept late and each morning found the dew a little thicker on the thwarts of Jack's boat; each evening the dusk came a little earlier. Across the river, Ivor Dawkins started harvesting the top fields.

On Wednesday, Jack rowed into town. He climbed the hill to Rope Walk and found Croyden feeding his pigs. He was better. They would leave for Newlyn in the morning. 'Expect you're keen to get back to sea,' said Croyden – half teasing, half accusing.

When Jack rowed up to Ferryman's again he brought with him Whaler's sea-chest. 'Have it,' Mrs Cuffe had told him. 'Save me burning it.' It was made of age-blackened mahogany. Jack had already replaced its becket handles but the varnish was badly chipped. On its lid was a lozenge of crude paint-work, done by Whaler himself, and showing, as far as Jack could see, a scene on a tropical beach. Palm trees curved out over a group of three dark men selling to some sailors an animal which looked like a giraffe but may have been a horse.

Anna said she would touch it up and paint the sides. She bent close to look at the scene. 'What is it, Jack, this? Is he a tortoise?'

That afternoon they crossed the Glaze River and walked over to Pendhu and down the cliff to Hemlock Cove. The sea was a deep blue, the sand pale and smooth. They swam out beyond the wave-line and then came in and lay on the rocks.

'When will you be back again?' asked Anna.

'Two, three weeks. Depends on the fish. You'll be gone?'

'No.' She made up her mind in that moment. 'I'll be here.'

Beyond the arms of the cove the long seas broke white against the side of Maenmor. They rose high up its sides before dragging back, to leave the oarweed limp and glistening in the sun.

'Close your eyes!' Jack said suddenly.

'Why?'

'I'll show you something.'

He took her hand and led her over the rocks. She had difficulty treading blind and in bare feet.

'Jack!' she laughed. 'Let me see!'

'Wait – right foot there. Now your left foot.' He guided her step by step around the point, then held her by the shoulders. 'Open!'

They were in another cove. Here there was no beach and no sand, just boulders at the foot of the cliffs. The seas hissed in among them. Dominating the cove were the masts and rigging of the *Constantine*.

Anna stared at it for some moments before whispering, 'It's horrid.' She turned her head, then hurried back to Hemlock Cove. Jack caught up with her on the sand.

'Why did you have to show me that? Why?'

It was spring tides that week, and they brought some strange things down the Glaze River. Into Polmayne Bay came the bloated carcase of a fox, a pair of torn red trousers, a hay-rake, two fish casks, a broken paddle, and an entire oak bough which caused the Petrels to delay the start of their Wednesday-evening race.

Parson Hooper stood watching two punts drag the great

log clear of the yachts. He was returning home from the Golden Sands Hotel where he had been involved in a most interesting discussion. The Frankses were there with their friend the Master and he was putting the case for the existence of a universal morality. Hooper had been quite dazzled by the range of his talk – from avatars to mathematics to German philosophers. Such a mind! He had spoken for a full hour. Hooper looked back at the town. Evening glowed on the sides of the houses. The tide had shrunk the quay walls, narrowed the new defences along the front, and suddenly he had the impression that it was not the tide rising but the town sinking. He broke into a sweat and for a moment felt quite dizzy.

Fatigue, he told himself, just fatigue – and carried on towards the rectory.

At seven-thirty Captain Henriksen came into the study and placed himself despondently in his leather chair.

He made an exaggerated wave action with his hand. 'Today, Rector, no launching. Too much waves.'

'Don't worry – there's always tomorrow.'

'Yes, tomorrow and then one day but no more after. Last possible tides.'

For two days the salvors had tried, and for two days the swell had prevented them. The tides had reached their peak and were now growing smaller again; with September coming it was unlikely the ship would survive until the next big tides.

Thursday was the same. Parson Hooper suggested a game of chess but Henriksen said he was too tired for chess.

'If you cannot save your ship, Captain, what will you do?'

Henriksen folded his arms and sighed. 'I don't know. I was thinking today of that passage in the Apocryphal book of Esdras – "*Come let us go and make war against the sea, that it may depart away before us, and that we may make more woods . . .*" I suppose I will find a little house in a wood and never again look at the sea.'

On the third day the wind held off. At three o'clock Captain Henriksen went to the wardrobe as he had every day that week and unhooked his lightweight sailing reefer. He attached his watch and chain, dusted off his braid cap, and took his cane from the umbrella stand. With Mrs Henriksen he walked to the ferry, crossed the Glaze River and walked slowly over the top.

Three steam tugs were manoeuvring just to seaward of the ship. One by one they dropped in and threw a line to their own men on board. With half an hour to go before high water, everything was in place. The tugs waited, the crowd on the clifftop waited. Fulmar cries echoed off the rocks, and the gentlest of seas ran along the ship's rock-lodged hull.

Fifteen minutes later, a smudge of black smoke rose from the tugs' stacks and the lines whipped up out of the water. As the tugs pulled, a deep creaking noise came from the ship's holds – and the crowd cheered. But there was no movement. The Captain sensed in his own bones the immense stubborn weight of his ship. He looked at the tugs and thought: *this is impossible*.

They pulled again. The line tightened. The tugs strained. Everyone watched for the first sign of movement – but instead there was a sudden crack and one of the lines parted. The two frayed ends sprang back and a collective gasp rose from the crowd.

Captain Henriksen checked his watch; high water had already passed. 'These,' he said to Mrs Henriksen, 'are the last moments of our ship.'

'Look – they are still trying.'

It took them a quarter of an hour to secure another line. The tugs hurried back into position. For some time, there was only the sound of their engines. The water was beginning to ebb. Then the *Constantine*'s top-masts shivered once. A low groan came from somewhere deep inside the ship and suddenly she moved. The fulmars were startled. They left the cliffs and circled their nests. The ship moved a yard, before sticking fast. The tugs pulled again, and with a prolonged scraping that made Captain Henriksen wince, the *Constantine* was dragged over the reef and dropped, bobbing into the water.

The crowd clapped and all at once everyone was congratulating Captain Henriksen. He stood with Mrs Henriksen and said, 'Yes, yes. Very satisfactory. Thank you, thank you.'

They brought the ship into the bay. A few days later, Captain Henriksen announced that they were ready to leave for Falmouth and an extensive programme of repairs. That evening there was something of a celebration at the rectory. Sixteen people – officers of the *Constantine*, members of the Mission and the Frankses – gathered in the dining room. Parson Hooper was persuaded to bring up a case of pre-war claret from his cellar. Mrs Henriksen had ordered a goose from Ivor Dawkins at Crowdy Farm.

After dinner, Captain Henriksen pushed back his chair and stood. 'In Finland, they say we are very famous for making toasts for no reason –'

'Not true!' laughed his First Officer.

'But this evening I have to say we have good reason. This town rescued us and all our company from big danger. It has accommodated us and welcomed us as if we were its own. I particularly would like to thank the Rector whose wisdom and kindness has made dark time possible for me and for my wife and for us all. May God give to him His blessing and may God give blessing to everyone also in this little town of Polmayne.'

The next morning, at eleven, the *Constantine* hauled her anchor. She tucked in close to the lifeboat station, where a large crowd had gathered. On the ship, crew and officers lined the weather rail and raised three cheers. Amidst the crowd, Parson Hooper took off his hat and waved.

The *Constantine* hardened sheets and headed away out of the bay. Picking up a good northerly she struck along the coast for Falmouth.

Parson Hooper watched the ship's stern shrink into the

distance. He stood there long after the others had left, spinning the rim of his hat round and round in his fingers.

From Newlyn that week, Jack wrote to Anna. He told her about the fishing ('prices up to nearly 14/- a thousand'), his crew ('Croyden and Charlie have stopped blaming Hammels'), and then he said to her: 'Why not stay in Ferryman's this autumn? You can paint and I will not be away but will be fishing out of Polmayne . . .'

On Monday, she wrote back: '. . . My sister is coming to Cornwall today. She is going to Tintagel – she always loved King Arthur. She wants me to go but I think I will stay here and paint . . .'.

It was a day of porcelain-blue skies. Small white clouds hung over Penwith, but out to sea it was clear. Jack walked south along the cliffs to Mousehole and beyond. On his left the water stretched to a blade-sharp horizon. What did she want? He felt again the mistrust that had haunted him since last winter. But then, what did he want? He wanted this. He wanted the sea and the blue shapes and the blue shades. He wanted it in its changingness and its grey guises, its capacity to give life and to take it away, its darknesses and depths – and he wanted Anna for the same reasons.

On Thursday morning, manoeuvring back into her berth, the *Maria V* hit the harbour wall and sheared a rudder pin. It would take until Monday to repair. The four of them cut their losses and headed for Penzance station.

It was late afternoon when they reached Polmayne. Jack rowed up at once to Ferryman's. The tide was ebbing and it took him some time but then he reached the corner and came round it and there was the whitewashed front and the low thatch and there were the windows shuttered and there was the door with the arch of a padlock securing its latch.

She had gone – of course she had gone.

CHAPTER 21

A nna Abraham at that moment was some forty miles to the north, seeing off a gentleman visitor on the steps of a Tintagel guest house. Silver-haired and silver-tongued, Dr Sanders was talking to her in soft, encouraging tones.

It was less than twenty-four hours since she had received the telegram – COME TINTAGEL SOONEST V ILL MARIA – and now the doctor was telling her that he could find nothing physically wrong with her sister.

'The problem is here,' he said and tapped his temple.

Dr Sanders saw a number of such cases every year. Having spent a lifetime wrapping themselves in Arthurian tales, first-time visitors to Tintagel often lapsed into a state of 'acute depressive torpor'. He had once written a paper on the subject for the medical press: 'Myth and Melancholy at Arthur's Tintagel'. The paper had done him no favours, as his conclusion was entirely unscientific: people like this were unable to cope with the earthly realisation of their dreams.

'It's like seasickness, Mrs Abraham. As soon as they leave Tintagel they feel better.'

So it proved for Maria. By the time they reached Bodmin Road station the next morning, she was chiding Anna.

'It's a man, isn't it?'

'Perhaps.'

'Nice?'

Anna nodded.

Maria looked up into the oak trees and smiled. She had never liked Maurice. And Anna's mysterious involvement, which drew her deeper into Cornwall while she herself returned to London, went some way towards reviving her bruised sense of romance.

'*Schastlivo!*' she called as Anna's train slid westwards out of the station.

Harris's Station Bus was waiting at Truro. It was very hot inside. Anna found a seat on the shaded side. The windows were open but it was still hot. They were waiting for three men from the train, one of whom was having an argument with the station porter. The men wore flannel suits and in the end two of them dragged their argumentative friend away and ran for the bus.

'Almost missed it!'

As the bus pulled off the men came swaying down the aisle. They flopped into the seats beside and behind Anna.

They introduced themselves. They were off-duty Guards officers. The one next to her was called Lee, another Travers, and the other was Birkin. In a week's time, they said, Birkin was getting married, and he and his friends were booked into a hotel for a final spree.

'The Golden Sands – you staying there?' Lee asked Anna.

'No.'

'I say, are you Spanish?'

Anna shook her head and turned to look out of the window.

'Well, you sound Spanish. Does she sound Spanish to you, Birkin?'

'Never been to Spain.'

'Refugee, I suppose. Damned hot in here – can't we open a window?'

'They are open,' said Travers.

'Funny, I thought they were dark in Spain, but you're pale. Very charming though. Isn't she charming, Birks?'

Birkin was asleep.

In Polmayne, the bus pulled to a halt in front of the Antalya Hotel. Several people stepped out of the shade to meet it. Mrs Cuffe greeted a couple and their son. The boy's face was half-hidden by the sail of a model yacht, and he was crying.

Three porters had come with barrows from the Golden Sands, and the Guards officers joined them and another couple from London and they all followed the barrows along the front.

Anna set off for the shops. She was surprised to bump into Croyden Treneer. He looked at her raffia hat and her small leather valise and said, 'He's over there.' He flicked his chin in the direction of Bethesda.

He was back! She cut through the alley just as the boy with the model yacht came rushing out past her. She knocked on Jack's door.

Nothing. She knocked again. Had she misunderstood Croyden? Had he meant that Jack was still in Newlyn? He wasn't due back for another two weeks at least. Maybe Croyden had come back earlier, the Reeds . . .

The door opened. Jack stepped out of the shadows.

'I thought you were in Newlyn!' She stepped up and wrapped her arms around his neck and kissed him.

'And I thought you'd left for good.'

Parson Hooper was driving the dog-cart back from Truro. On the hill below Pennance, Harris's Station Bus rattled past him and Job jumped forward and Hooper had to grip the reins to stop him bolting. But then the bus was gone and Job resumed his walk. In the close and thundery heat the sound of his hooves made the parson drowsy and his hat nodded down towards his chest. The reins fell into his lap. In the back of the dog-cart was last month's Tablet: *A Garden is a lovesome thing, God wot!/Rose plot,/Fringed pool,/Fern'd grot . . .*

Without the crew of the *Constantine*, without Captain Henriksen, Parson Hooper had slipped back into his early-summer mood. Polmayne had become an alien and friendless place. He had not even taken any lines for a new Tablet. Never in all the years of his ministry had he felt so isolated.

'We're not wanted here,' he had told Mrs Hooper. 'Do you know what the fishermen do if they see me on the way to their boats? Do you know?'

'No, dear.'

'They turn round and go home. I am bad luck. *Bad luck!* Imagine what that feels like.'

Anna and Jack rowed up to Ferryman's. It was hot and close and Anna pulled up her sleeve and trailed an arm in the water. The clouds were heavy overhead. Anna started to sing. She sang in Russian and then stumbled over the words. 'I forgot this song until now. It was one my grandmother sang us.'

'What's it about?'

'If I remember – it is the story of a Cossack and he steals a noble lady from her husband and her big house and he takes her away in his boat. Then later she becomes a bandit also and one day in a war or something she comes to raid the estate of her husband. I don't remember exactly what happens then – I think he shoots her and then he shoots the Cossack, or maybe the Cossack shoots him or maybe she shoots the husband and herself – anyway they all end up dead! It's quite a sad song.'

They came round the bend in the river and the boat eased up the shingle and Anna threw her shoes ashore and went on ahead to unlock the cottage. She stood for a moment on the slate floor. She closed her eyes and let the coolness seep up her calves. When Jack came in, he took her hand and without a word led her across the room and up the stairs. On the narrow iron bed, he sat her down and knelt before her. The shutters were still closed and in the shadows her face glowed in the heat. He wondered why, when he had tried so often, he had failed to remember her features, failed to remember the exact curve of her lips and her long nose and her smiling eyes.

'Don't go.' He gripped her hand. 'Don't leave here.'

'Ladies and gentlemen!'

On the terrace of the Golden Sands Hotel, Mr Bryant called for silence. Beside him stood Mrs Bryant and the Raffertys and Lady Banville with her pout and her painted *décolletage*.

The afternoon had dragged into evening. Thick grey cloud hung over the town; already it felt like dusk. Veils of midges followed the guests as they milled around the hotel lawn. Everyone was short-tempered.

Mr Bryant had arranged another reception, this time for the commissioning of the newly-refurbished *Golden Sands*. Dozens of visitors were added to the fifty-odd guests staying in the hotel. Parson and Mrs Hooper were there. The Guards officers were there; they had been asleep and their flannel suits were creased. The knot of Petrel skippers were discussing next day's Porth regatta when Mr Bryant clapped his hands.

'Dear God!' hissed Ralph Cameron. 'Not another of his damned speeches!'

'Ladies and gentlemen! Thank you all for coming this evening.' He paused. 'When Mrs Bryant and I first came to Polmayne, we were drawn here for one reason and one reason only. Indeed it is the same reason you are here – all of you.

Those who are visitors or guests or have chosen to live here, or to bring your children here or sail your yachts. Indeed, it is the same reason this very town exists and has existed since dim antiquity.'

Mr Bryant pointed over the heads of the guests, over the lawn and the shingle beach to the water. It stretched grey and soupy into the gloom.

'The sea! It is the sea that pulls us here as powerfully as a nail to a magnet. One has only to think of the many ways in which it provides for us – feeding us with its fish, cooling us when we bathe, exercising our bodies, soothing us when we hear it on the rocks at night. From cradle to grave it provides for us all in a dozen different ways.'

'Hear, hear.' Sir Basil was finding it hard to concentrate in the heat. But it helped to bob his head up and down in agreement.

'Get on with it, for God's sake!' muttered Cameron.

'No doubt Sir Basil here will remember a comedian we had up our way before the war – Tommy Thomas?'

Sir Basil nodded.

'You will remember then his routine of a publican whose refrain was always, "If the guests is happy, then we's is happy" – at which he would grin and jangle the change in his pocket.' Mr Bryant chuckled.

Sir Basil dabbed at his forehead with a handkerchief.

'"If the guests is happy, then we's is happy." Well, that is our motto at the Golden Sands and that is why I have taken on an enterprise which I am sure will yield great dividends not just for visitors to the hotel but for the entire town!'

Mr Bryant and Sir Basil and their party then made their way down the terrace steps, down the hotel's well-watered lawn towards the beach and the newly-built jetty.

They heard it before they saw it – the shrill *poop-poop* of a foghorn in the slate-grey dusk. Around the point came the *Golden Sands*: golden-yellow sides, sky-blue funnel with yellow hoops.

Mr Bryant stood with the Raffertys by the jetty. 'There she is!'

'Splendid!' Sir Basil clapped; a few others clapped too.

Lady Rafferty was fanning herself with a mother-of-pearl fan. 'Is that it?'

On board Jimmy Garrett stood at the still-unfinished bar, silently dispensing drinks. Tacker darted back and forth, pointing out the new features.

The Guards officers stood at the bar and Travers said, 'I like this boat, don't you, Lee?'

'I like it too. What about you, Birks?'

Birkin was waving his empty glass at Jimmy. 'Barman!'

Jimmy ignored him.

In all, more than eighty people made their way along the jetty that evening and on board the *Golden Sands*. Mr Bryant gave the Raffertys a detailed tour of the boat. 'Ladies' convenience here. Covered seating here at the back for thirty people . . .'

'Marvellous!' Sir Basil asked lots of questions. Lady Rafferty asked none. Behind the wheelhouse was the new lifeboat and a rather complicated piece of plumbing. 'And what's this?' asked Sir Basil.

'That is, er . . . Tacker!'

Tacker came out from under the awning and said, 'Fuel intake, sir. Had to reroute him, sir.'

'It's the fuel intake, Sir Basil. It's where they take in the fuel.'

'Oh really! I can't stand another minute of this.' Lady Rafferty told Mrs Bryant to take her back to the hotel.

From far out to sea came the first growl of thunder.

CHAPTER 22

Anna Abraham lay on her back. She kicked at the water and the splashing echoed in the creek. She gazed up at the cave-grey ceiling of cloud above her. The whole sky looked ready to drop on her head. How long could it stay up?

It was she who had woken first. In the heavy heat of early evening she rose and put on her bathing suit and came down to swim. When Jack heard her, he pushed open the upstairs window and leaned on the sill.

'Come into the water!' she called.

'I have a better plan!'

They went rowing. They rowed upstream, around the bend above the cottage where the river opened out into a broad lagoon. It was mid-tide. Oak-woods bordered the river, the trees' boughs hung down over a steep foreshore. The water was as flat as a table. Anna had never been up here. She followed the strokes of the paddles and watched the crease of the bow-wave spread out towards the shore.

At the top of the lagoon, the river divided.

'Which way?' asked Jack. 'Main river, or the side creek?'

'Er . . . Side creek.'

The creek's edges dovetailed into the dusk. Jack made three strong strokes and let the boat glide into it.

'What's it called, Jack?'

'Gooth – Gooth Creek.'

They drifted up between the oak-lined slopes. The tide pushed them on. A curlew screeched, slewed off over the trees. As they rounded the first bluff Anna saw the boats. They had become the same grey as the rocks and mud. There were dozens, scattered along both banks. Among them were several larger ones – their spars had been stripped and only the bare hulls remained, lying side-on and half-submerged.

'What are they?'

'Seine boats, fishing boats.'

For generations, he explained, boats had been laid up here by the people of Porth and Polmayne. In the war, many were brought up here and remained when their owners failed to return.

'In the town, they say that someone's "gone to Gooth" when they're too old or too ill to go out.'

'Ugh!' said Anna.

'You want to go back?'

She nodded. But at the main river she said, 'What happens up the stream. No more boats?'

'No more boats.'

They pressed on, on into the heavy grey evening. One or two slender canes broke the water's surface. The river swung to right and left, narrowed a little, but the woods on each side never thinned. Where streams came into the creek, the woods receded and gave way to beds of blond reeds. They came to a place where the river widened, and Jack shipped the paddles. He stood and the boat rocked from side to side.

'Careful!' said Anna.

He made his way towards her and stretched his legs out

165

along the boat. She twisted round and hung her feet over the side. Her head rested on his stomach.

'Jack,' she said, 'I have made a decision.'

'Yes?'

'You said stay here in the autumn and, well, I think I will stay.'

He kissed the top of her head. 'Good.'

'On one condition.'

'What's that?'

'You do not let any more beard grow on your chin.'

They lay for a long time in the stern and listened to the splash of jumping mullet. Then from over the oak-woods, over the hill, came the sound of thunder.

'We ought to go back,' said Anna.

'No,' said Jack. 'Let's wait here, let's wait for the rain.'

At six o'clock the first large drops fell on Polmayne. They fell on the roofs and in the courtyards and they spotted the tarmac of the front and the cobbles on the quay. They brought with them a sweet, vegetable smell. Those on Parliament Bench upturned their palms and Toper Walsh gave a small cheer and Boy Johns went 'Eeee!' In Basset's Yard, Mrs Stephens tilted her face to the skies and said, 'Thank the Lord!' Even Mrs Cuffe at Bethesda gave half a smile as she cleared the feeds to her water butt.

Then it stopped. The heat of the cobbles shrunk the drops to nothing and only the dust and the smell were left. On the Bench they shook their heads and leaned on their elbows again. They cursed the clouds and scowled at the Porth boat, the *Andrew Eliot*, which was now pushing in through the Gaps.

Every year, on the night before the regatta, the Porth Male Voice Choir performed in Polmayne. It was meant as a conciliatory gesture between the two towns but it rarely was. Fifteen men in green jackets trotted up the steps and nodded at the Bench and made their way up to the Freeman Reading Rooms. There they agreed to shed their jackets and sang in white shirts and ties and the audience of visitors joined in the choruses. Six people had left before they finished, faint with heat. Afterwards the men took their green jackets and made their way to the Fountain Inn.

Since early evening, a large crowd had been gathering outside the Fountain, escaping the heat of the tap room for the open air. Those who wished to talk found they had to raise their voices to make themselves heard, and what with the heat and the talking they returned more often to the tap room, and each time they did they managed to talk even louder.

Only the Porth singers did not talk. They stood in a circle, glasses in hand, and every so often one of them would start singing and then the others would join in.

Up at the Golden Sands Hotel the reception was over. It was almost dark by the time Jimmy and Tacker Garrett saw off the last of the guests and brought the *Golden Sands* back to her moorings. When they reached the Fountain Inn, Tacker added his voice to the Porth singers. Those who didn't want to sing but wanted to talk found that they had to raise their voices even higher. And from the Fountain Inn the talking and singing spilled out of the alley and down to the quays. In the breathless air, it joined the talk of those on the front and spread back into the side-alleys and up over the net lofts and into the lanes to merge with the voices of those who were talking inside. As night drew its curtains across the day it seemed as if the whole town was one vast room and everyone in it was a part of the same inescapable hubbub. No one slept. Those men with the Reeds turned this way and that in bed, rising to open the window because of the heat, then rising again to close it because of the noise.

A host of long-buried resentments came to the surface that Friday evening. For months Mr Hicks had watched the numbers in the Antalya restaurant fall away, losing custom to the new hotel. His dining room was almost empty. His chef was playing cards with the kitchen staff. When a couple of new guests told him that they too would be 'trying out the Golden Sands's cooking', he collected their bags and threw them onto the street. 'You want to dine at the Golden Sands, you can bloody well stay there!'

The Town Quay was full of people walking up and down. Having walked up and down, many of them leaned on the wall. Toper Walsh was watching a very fat boy eating a cold sausage.

'Christ, what they children get fed now'days! They never bloody stop eating.'

'Why shouldn't he eat a sausage?'

'You never had a sausage, Tope?' asked Tick-Tock Harris.

'Course I 'ad a sausage! Course I have. Anyway, Tick, you ain't even from 'ere.'

In Rope Walk Maggie Treneer discovered from Croyden that his piece had become a desert. 'How in the name of God do you expect to feed us this winter?'

Having no answer, Croyden took his brown beret and left the house for the Fountain. There he found his brother Charlie and Double and Edwin Pentreath and the Tylers and they stood in a circle. Double said he was going up to the new reservoir at Pennance in the morning. There was water there, he said, and Ivor Dawkins had lent them his water-cart but they needed hands to help. They all told him they would go and then Charlie said, 'I tell 'ee, all this talk of water's making me thirsty.' And he rejoined the crowd queuing in the tap room.

Up at the Crates, Old Mrs Treneer and the Moyles and a few others were standing outside the new houses when a blood-coloured glow appeared behind Pendhu. They had not even noticed that the thunderclouds had gone and now here was the moon, fat and pitted beside the church tower. 'What a beauty!' cooed Mrs Moyle.

'A peach!' said Mrs Treneer.

Inside, in the middle of his empty room, Tommy Treneer

168

sat rocking on his stool. He was cursing the stiletto of light which had cut through the gap in the curtains. 'Gone to Gooth,' they all said of Tommy in the town, but because he never went out he had no idea. He scratched his bare arm and the flakes of dried skin drifted down in the moonlight and he muttered about 'damn labbetts and larrs'.

By eleven the day's heat had gone. In the fields of Pendhu the corn shocks stretched fingers of moon-shadow across the stubble. When the Fountain Inn closed, the singing continued. Those in the alley followed the green jackets of the Porth choir, still singing, down to the Town Quay where the *Andrew Eliot* was being brought into the steps. The singing turned to jostling as they stood on the quay and the Garretts glared at the choir and for the first time the Porth men stopped singing and hurried down the steps to the *Andrew Eliot*. As she backed out through the Gaps and slid onto the rug of silvery light in the bay, the singing resumed. It rose in pitch until the taunt in it was audible not only to those still on the quays but to all those who lay unsleeping in their beds, trying to shut out the remaining murmur of the streets and the rose-red light of that harvest moon.

'Fare-well Pol-mayne – Fare-well, fa-are-arewell . . .'

3

Saturday, 29 August 1936

CHAPTER 23

‑◦⧫◦‑

Shortly before dawn, the first pale light brushed Polmayne's quays. For some time everything was still. The
boats lay to the tide. The front was empty. Beyond the bay,
beyond Pendhu, the grey of the sea was one with the grey of
the sky.

Even in this deadest of dawn seas, the Main Cages picked
out a swell where there appeared to be none. It came in from
the east, each wave mounting as it approached the first of
the rocks, the Curate. The crest steepened and began to curl,
and just before it broke the water was sucked away from
around the rock and it was exposed, a brief black island hung
with strands of draining white. Then the wave fell, swamping the Curate, and it was rolling on to Maenmor and its
jagged satellites. There too it rose and a shadow grew beneath
its crest and its waters spread high up the rock and it was
sluicing through the gap before dropping again beyond
Maenmor and disappearing into the flat grey waters to the
west of Pendhu.

As the sun rose, it took the stars one by one. It splashed orange on the underside of each cloud and tortoiseshelled the entire eastern sky. Within an hour the last of the clouds had gone and along Polmayne's whitewashed front the first of the day's warmth began to glow from the walls.

Up over Pendhu hill came Captain Williams. He was whistling a nameless tune. He unlocked the door of the watch hut, took off his cap and put it on the table. He scratched his beard. Unlatching the window, he pushed open the louvres and blinked in the sudden glare. The sea below was as bright as glass. He swung the telescope along the horizon but could take it no further east than 120 degrees because of the sun. From his frail he took a cold lamb cutlet and unwrapped it from its greaseproof paper. He felt tired.

At a quarter to eight Captain Maddocks telephoned the hut.

'Morning!' said Williams.

'Morning.'

'Millpond!'

'Harry Flatters. All set for this afternoon?'

'All set.'

For the past two years Captain Maddocks had been a starter at Porth regatta. His deputies assisted him, and the agreement was that if the weather looked fine he handed over responsibility to the auxiliary watch huts.

'Should be quiet,' said Maddocks.

Captain Williams put down the receiver and swung the telescope again. There was less glare now and the early haze had gone. Just south of east he could see a dark line on the horizon. Within half an hour it had spread, criss-crossing the water with paler channels like a flood plain. When it reached the shore, the breeze pushed up the cliff and in through the open window of the hut. Captain Williams closed his eyes and let it blow on his face.

He woke with a start. Far to the south-east, the first white-caps had begun to flicker. His lamb cutlet remained uneaten;

he was not hungry. He wrapped it up, put it away and prepared himself for a long day of duty.

Dawn at Ferryman's and the water stood motionless in the
river. The world was mirrored in its surface – the pines hung
down from the hill and beneath them was the pale-blue sky and
a scattering of early-morning clouds. A heron appeared wide-
winged in the trees and rose to meet itself on the foreshore.

Jack had woken early. He stepped outside and stood bare-
foot on the shingle bar. It was cold. Summer was coming to
an end. The pilchards were almost over and then there was
the dog-fishing. He hated the dogging – the days getting
shorter and that snaggy line and the relentless rhythm of the
tides. But now it looked different. Everything looked different. She was staying. They had talked late last night and she
said, 'What is there for me back in London?' She told him
she wanted to remain here and paint and Jack offered to build
her a work-bench and bring her firewood and prepare the
house for the autumn.

He stepped into the shallows. He turned and looked at
the window under the eaves but could not see her. Upriver,
skidding across the surface of the water, came the first ripples
of an easterly breeze.

'Easterly, Jim, 'ee's gone easterly!'

Jimmy Garrett lay on his bed, one arm across his face.
Sunlight filled the window. Tacker stood in the doorway.
'Do's go?'

There was a slight movement around Jimmy's mouth as he
tried to moisten his lips. He reached out for the empty cup
on the floor and Tacker took it and filled it with water from
the bussa. Jimmy sat up and reached for his block of tobacco.
He nodded.

Tacker carried the newly-repainted board out to the Town

Quay. There he lashed it to the railings with coir twine. At the top of the board was painted:

PLEASANT DAY EXCURSIONS
PER
FAST AND COMMODIOUS MOTOR LAUNCH
GOLDEN SANDS!

Where '**GOLDEN SANDS!**' was written, you could make out beneath it the traces of '**POLMAYNE QUEEN!**'. Below the lettering was a square of blackboard, where Tacker slowly chalked up the day's itinerary:

Saturday – Porth Regatta. All the fun of the fare!
Depart Town Quay 12.30 promt

'Got a "p" in it!' Tick-Tock was sitting with a couple of others on Parliament Bench.

'What has?'

'Prompt.'

'I put a bloody "p" in it.'

'Another one, Tack!'

They were sending him up. He knew they were just sending him up. He pitched the chalk at them but it bounced off the top of the wall and fell into the sea. He then headed round towards the East Quay and his boat.

'Hooligan!'

'Wouldn't catch me going Porth,' said Toper.

'Your mother was born Porth, wan't her, Tope?'

'Don't mean I have to go there.'

Croyden woke to the smell of fish. All around him were maunds and line and everything smelt of fish. When he returned to Rope Walk the night before, he found Maggie had slipped the bolts. He did not remember coming down to the net loft, but here he was, cheek pressed against a tarpaulin. Raising himself, he licked his lips, but his mouth was dry. He made his way home to Rope Walk.

Hannah and Betty were playing outside. Each of them grabbed one of his arms.

'Father, Father! Look!'

On the floor inside sat a young herring gull. It had the muddy-brown feathers of that year's hatch and moved hardly at all. A trail of creamy excrement was spattered across the slate flags.

'It's ill, Father! We found it!'

Croyden sat down at the kitchen table. 'Where's your mother to?'

'Town.'

'Fetch's a can.'

Hannah brought a Charbon tin and Croyden jabbed a marlin-spike into the top and it was salmon. He handed it back. 'Another.'

That one was peaches and he drank down the syrup, then widened the hole to get at the fruit. By his feet Betty was prodding the young gull with a fork. 'What's it got, Father? Will it die?'

'There any milk?'

'No milk,' said Hannah.

'Water, then.'

She put a saucer on the floor and poured a little water into it from the bussa. The bird started to drink. When the saucer was empty, it looked around, then dropped its head and let out a barely audible mew.

'Look, Father! It's getting better.'

She filled the saucer again. The bird carried on drinking.

They watched it hop out through the door, sit for a while in the sun, then spread its wings and fly away.

'Poor bastard's only thirsty,' said Croyden. He called for another can, and they brought two more before he found one with peaches inside.

*　　*　　*

177

Shortly before eight, Coxswain Tyler headed up past the Golden Sands Hotel towards the lifeboat station. He leaned back to slide open the first of the double doors and there was the *Kenneth Lee*, her blue bows shining in the early sun.

The boat's rudder lay beside her on two trestles. Flattening his palm, Tyler ran it over the primed surface and could not feel the join. On Thursday evening they had struck the back wall coming in from exercise, and he had scarfed in a new piece of timber that night. Now from the store he fetched paint pots and brushes and stroked on the first coat of gloss. He then climbed on board, took out each of the plugs and checked the spark. Having fired up the engine, he telephoned the Secretary: 'Be up Pennance till later,' he said. 'Collecting water. Brad's on call.'

Outside on the bank, he squinted up the flagpole and hoisted the RNLI ensign. The breeze picked it up at once and he looked out beyond Pendhu and saw that a swell was already running. It was after nine by the time he left the station and went up to Rope Walk to find Croyden.

At about the same time, Anna and Jack were leaving Ferryman's. Anna had her sky-blue headscarf round her neck and she was wearing a jacket of pale orange linen, sitting in the stern of the dinghy and talking about her planned studio.

'I don't like an easel, Jack. I need something about this angle' – she raised her forearm about thirty degrees. 'On a table . . . and storage, lots of storage for brushes and paints.'

'We'll have a look in my net loft.'

When they reached the quays, Jack dropped her off on the steps and sculled out again and threw the anchor astern. Parliament Bench watched the two of them as they passed.

It was dark in the loft and the air was thick with the smell of rope and cutch and fish. Jack pushed open the front hatch and the sun came flooding in.

'Now!' he clapped his hands and stepped over the warps

and buoys to the back. It surprised even him to see what he had accumulated over the past year or so: crates of rocks, shells, egg-like pebbles, countless old rowlocks and shackles and cleats, wreck-wood, a broken enamel tea-tray, one of a pair of Scotch hands. He held up a canvas drogue and pinched the bottom. 'What about this – for brushes?'

'Perfect!' Anna leaned forward to catch it. She put it in a maund. There it was joined by part of an old medical chest – for painting outside – a frail, a piece of trammel net and, propped against the basket's side, to be used as a painting board, the recently-replaced forehatch from the *Maria V*.

As Jack dug deeper into the shadows, Anna told him what she had done so far with Whaler's sea-chest. 'I have painted the sides – the harbour and white birds here, other things here, also some people. Also your three boats – the *Maria V*, little dinghy and the big lifeboat. And birds too, with fishes and lobster. I have cleaned the top and it is much better, but, you know, this animal, maybe it is a dog of some kind –'

'Jack!' A shout came up from the street below. He leaned out through the hatch and there were Croyden and Tyler.

'There's water up Pennance!' called Croyden. 'We got a horse and tank. If you was free –'

'Everyone else is crewing over Porth or down with the bloody Reeds,' added Tyler.

Jack stepped back into the loft, and Anna said, 'Of course you must go. We can do this later. We have lots of time.'

All morning the sun climbed higher into a cloudless sky. The wind rose with it and by eleven the bay was a stippled silvery blue. Side by side, Red and Joseph Stephens walked out along the Town Quay. They were wearing their racing guernseys; on Red's chest was 'Grace' and on Joe's was 'Charity'.

'Look who it is!' shouted Toper Walsh. 'The bloody angels.'

'Off up Porth then?'

'Yachtin' for the gentry, is 'ee?' taunted Red Treneer.

They ignored them. They carried on to the end of the quay where the Petrel skippers were standing in a group, watching the bay.

'Porth's in the lee of it –'

'We'll have it on the nose going round –'

'We can still get inside the Cages on the flood –'

'It'll be wind against tide –'

'It'll be fine. Don't worry.' Ralph Cameron checked his watch. 'But we must leave now.'

They each gathered their crew. Joe Stephens went with the Dane Soren, Red with Lawrence Rose. Cameron had persuaded Charlie Treneer to join him with an offer of a guinea bonus for a win. Half an hour later, with a roll each in their mainsails and the wind astern, the six Petrels sailed out of Polmayne Bay. They hardened their sheets around Pendhu Point and reached open water already hard-pressed. From the coastguard hut Captain Williams watched them go, watched the progress of the icing-white sails against the blue sea. By the time the Petrels reached Porth, the wind had dropped. They were in the lee of Kidda Head and there was little sea to speak of. A couple of punts put out from the quay and as the skippers were rowed ashore Lawrence Rose said, 'Not a bad breeze out there.'

'Not bad at all,' Cameron nodded.

'But dying now,' complained the Dane Soren.

They joined the skippers of the Porth boats in the dining room of the Kidda Head Hotel. Ralph Cameron looked at his watch. It was exactly twenty to one.

'Perfect,' he said, and went to the bar to order his first glass of Plymouth gin.

Outside the Stephenses and Charlie Treneer opened their frails in the shade of the sea wall, and ate in silence.

*   *   *

Anna too went to Porth regatta that day.

When Jack left for Pennance, she took her sketchbook out to the lifeboat station and for several hours sat in the shade of the slipway, alternately eyeing the curves of Pendhu Point and the distant peaks of Maenmor, and looking down to reproduce them on the page. She worked fast. It had been a long time, she realised, since she had drawn with such freedom.

It was the heat of midday that drove her back into Polmayne. She drank a glass of lemonade in Monk's Tea Rooms and through the window watched the *Golden Sands* come into the quay. She had intended going back to Ferryman's, but stepping out into the sunlight she spotted Tacker's notice on the Town Quay:

Saturday – Porth Regatta. All the fun of the fare!
Depart Town Quay 12.30 promt

It was twenty-five to one. Tacker himself was freeing the bow-line and as she ran round to the steps he reached out and took her arm.

'Almost missed it, my lover!'

They crossed the bay and pulled in to the hotel jetty. A group of twenty or so people stood waiting. The three Guards officers were there in wide-brimmed hats and floppy linen trousers. Mr Bryant was wearing a grey suit and Mrs Bryant's face was shaded by a brand-new hat of Leghorn straw. The Raffertys stood with them. Lady Rafferty, in a brown tweed suit, was adjusting the flame-coloured angora scarf at her neck. A barman, in starched monkey jacket, followed them all on board.

The sun was high overhead and most of the passengers settled themselves in the shade of the new deckhouse. As they pulled out to sea, they caught the cool of the breeze.

'That's better!' said Mrs Bryant.

'We'll see about that.' As a veteran of several Atlantic

crossings, Lady Rafferty knew better than to trust the weather at sea.

Two nannies were sitting together while their charges darted in and out between the rows. 'Come out here, where we can see you!'

The couple staying at Bethesda were there and their son was holding his model yacht and saying, 'Mummy, how long till we get there?'

An elderly couple from Wales sat in the front, side by side, in a benign and smiling silence. The Frankses were beside them with the Master and he was in contemplative mood, wearing his crisp white suit and leaning on his cane. Mr Bryant was introducing Sir Basil to Parson and Mrs Hooper.

Anna had made her way aft to the last line of benches. Away from everyone, she leaned on the rail and watched the town's confetti of houses as they slipped astern.

At the bar were the Guards officers. Two of them were facing it, ordering cocktails. Birkin, bridegroom-to-be, was in the middle. He was looking back over his fellow passengers. 'I say – there's that Spanish girl!'

'Here,' Travers gave him a large gin, but within a minute he had finished and was wiping his moustache. 'Mind if I go and see her now?' he asked. 'She's all on her own.'

'Steady, old man.' Travers placed a second gin on the bar beside him. 'They're good for you.'

'I'll have another and then I'll go and talk to her. She's awfully lonely.'

Just then they came round Pendhu Point, and the first of the easterly swell began to nudge the hull.

CHAPTER 24

⬥

At Crowdy Farm everyone was out harvesting. Jack and Croyden and Coxswain Tyler wandered through the empty stackyards. They found the water-cart promised by Ivor Dawkins and then they found the horse. He was in the paddock. He was standing head-down in the shade of a barn wall. The ribs showed through his flanks and he was asleep.

'Oh God!' groaned Tyler.

'Be hard pushed to pull his own tail, him,' said Croyden. 'Damn 'ee, Dawkins!'

'Don't Parson have a horse, Jack?' asked Croyden. 'Think he'd lend'n?'

'It's worth asking.'

'You ask, Jack. You're one o' his.'

Jack found Parson and Mrs Hooper just leaving for Porth regatta. Hooper agreed – provided they brought some water for him. 'My new plants are just wasting away!'

Job was happy in the loose boxes. He was not at all keen on going outside with Jack into the hot sun. He moved slowly

up towards Crowdy and even slower when hitched, but
Croyden slapped his haunch as they left the farm, and clicked
his tongue and urged him on. 'Come on, boy!'

They followed the marled track to the main road and then
along a steep-sided valley. Away from the breeze, the heat
clogged in the still air. The empty cart bounced and rattled
behind them. A stream ran parallel to the road, dry since June
when the dam was begun. Then they climbed and came out
on top and caught the wind and Job came to a halt. They let
him graze the verge and Croyden and Tyler leaned on a gate
and looked over the fields to the sea. They could make out
the haze-wrapped shape of Kidda Head and the dusting of
sails around Porth harbour.

'Charlie crewing?' asked Tyler.

Croyden nodded.

'He's a devil for the yachtin', in't he?'

'Only for the money.'

After another mile they left the main road and cut down a
ferny slope back to the valley bottom. The track was deeply
rutted, the mud as hard as rock. Several times Job stopped and
they had to lean against the back of the cart to help him heave
it out of a hole. Where the valley narrowed they came out into
open ground and there was the dam – half-built, head-high.

Croyden lobbed a rock over the wall. There was a pause,
then – splash!

'We're in luck!'

A terrier came running up to them, circled Job and yapped.
Edwin Stephens appeared from above the dam with his two
boys and Double Walsh.

'What happened?'

'Dawkins's horse were no good,' explained Tyler.

'You got the buckets?' asked Edwin.

'You was going to bring buckets!'

'We got no buckets!' As Cox, Tyler had a deep fear of
inefficiency. 'Just like a bloody Stephens – hopeless!'

Edwin confessed it was his fault, but said it didn't matter, there was plenty of time. He sent his boys back to town to fetch buckets and they all watched them run off down the track, the terrier after them. By the time they reached the trees, the boys were walking.

Jack unhitched Job. There were white lines of sweat where the traces had rubbed. He led him round the dam wall and down to the pool of water above it. Job dropped his neck towards it, let his whiskers brush the surface, then pursed his lips and drank. Jack hobbled his legs and followed Croyden and Tyler up to the well.

Since Jack had last been here in the spring, Pennance had changed almost beyond recognition. The valley was now open to the skies. The grove of beeches had been cleared. Their great pale trunks now lay in log-piles on the slope. The trees' sawn-off stumps were dotted across the scoured soil. In the middle of this waste ground remained the slate grotto of St Pinnock's well, its open mouth still bearded with ferns.

One by one they ducked into the darkness of the well. It was cool inside and their splashes echoed off the walls.

'Best water in Cornwall,' said Croyden as he emerged.

'I reckon,' concluded Tyler, 'that's the best water in the world.'

Croyden leaned against the side of the slate canopy and looked down towards the dam. 'How high's that wall to be, Cox?'

'About twenty-five, thirty foot.'

Croyden looked at the dam and he looked at the well. 'The last we'll see of this. A year's time and 'ee'll be under.'

Tacker Garrett stepped into the *Golden Sands's* wheelhouse. The door was rattling with the engine. Jimmy was staring straight ahead. They were coming into the open sea and beginning a slight roll.

As the Main Cages appeared, Jimmy could see the disturbed

water between the rocks and the land. In the half hour since the Petrels had pushed through, the flood tide had strengthened and the seas were chaotic.

'What about going outside?' asked Tacker.

'And arrive this evening?'

Tacker went astern and told the barman to clear the bar. Since the swell had begun, the passengers had all found their seats. Only the three officers remained at the bar.

'Bit of a sea ahead,' Tacker told them. 'Best sit down.'

'Right you are!' said Travers.

Birkin said, 'Think I'll go and sit with the Spanish lady.'

He made his way along the rail to the stern. When he reached Anna, he sat down heavily beside her. 'Hello!'

'Hello.'

'I heard that you might be a little bit lonely.'

'I'm not.'

'It's just that you looked aw–' The boat dropped suddenly to starboard, '– awfully lonely here on your own.'

'I'm happy alone.'

The boat lurched again. Birkin looked at his feet. 'Feeling a bit funny. Do you feel a bit funny?'

'No.'

Birkin sat in silence for a while, looking at his shoes. Then, glass still in his hand, he stood and made his way back up the aisle before flopping into a seat two rows forward.

'Tacker!' called Mr Bryant, and when Tacker reached him he asked quietly, 'What is happening?'

'Nothing to worry about, sir. Just a bit of lump.'

'Lump?'

But at that moment the motion stopped. They had entered the smooth water before the tide-race. Mr Bryant looked relieved. 'That's better!'

'Well, sir, not exactly –'

The boat fell sharply to port. An excited cry went up from the children. Lady Rafferty put a handkerchief to her mouth. 'I knew it.'

The *Golden Sands* was now in the tide-race. Her movements became rhythmless. She would rear up, then roll; or a sudden wave would thrust up from nowhere against her sides, spraying the decks.

Tacker stood in front of the passengers. He leaned back against the bar and folded his arms. 'Soon be through it!'

For ten minutes the *Golden Sands* tumbled about, bows bucking and plunging. The engine raced when the stern rose from the water. Jimmy stood at the wheel, impassively playing the helm and throttle to avoid the worst of the seas. They were almost clear of the race when a sheer-sided wave dropped away from them and they fell down it. Screams of surprise echoed around the deckhouse and a pair of bottles smashed together beneath the bar.

'Oops!' Birkin dropped his glass and it started a long roll across the deck before shattering against a stanchion.

There were two bangs amidships. Tacker pulled aside the awning and went forward to look. The new lifeboat had come free and was swinging on its davits. The boat had struck the wheelhouse several times. He secured it and rubbed his fingers over each impact – only paint and some small splinters came away. But the kelson of the lifeboat had also dropped against the new fuel pipe, and the cap was swinging on its chain.

Jimmy shouted from the wheelhouse, 'Any damage?'

'No!' Tacker screwed the cap back on, but the thread was bent. He twisted it hard and it lodged and he went to the rail and lit a cigarette. They were now free of the Main Cages and the boat's motion had eased. He watched the foamy patch around the Curate rock slip astern. Ahead was Porth and the long curve of land which sheltered it from the east wind and the swell.

He finished his cigarette, flicked it overboard and made his way astern. The passengers watched him come back into the deckhouse. 'Don't worry!' he told them. 'Be in Porth in no time!'

And he grinned proudly, as though it was he alone who had stilled the troublesome seas.

Just east of Pendhu Point was a group of three farm labourers' dwellings on their own which, because they were built in a terrace, were known as London. The four-acre field below was also called London and here Ivor Dawkins was driving his binder, harvesting a drought-stunted crop of Cornish oats.

Around the field were several others. Some were scything the crop's edges to make way for the binder; others were following along behind, gathering the sheaves and building them into shocks. Many of them were working bare-chested, shirts knotted around their waists. Several dogs were running in and out of the oats chasing rabbits and fieldmice, and the children were chasing the dogs and shouting and beating the ground with sticks.

With the crop so short, Dawkins was having trouble setting the blades. When they struck a rock for the third time he stopped the machine and climbed down. He took off his cap and wiped the sweat from his forehead. The sheavers brought a flagon of cider and they all took a rest in the shade of the binder. When the yellow shape of the *Golden Sands* appeared beneath the hill, Dawkins said, 'Christ, that's some bloody colour Garrett's painted his boat!'

'Belongs to that hotel now.'

'Hicks's place?'

'No, that new one.'

Bran Johns was looking to the east and the cluster of distant sails around Porth harbour. 'Porth regatta today.'

Dawkins shook his head and squatted down to fix the blades of the binder. 'Bloody useless song and dance.'

CHAPTER 25

~❦~

By lunchtime, Porth was filling with people. In a trail of straw hats and caps and striped blazers and white cotton blouses and blue summer jackets they were making their way down the hill from the field where the buses and cars had parked. They were thicker around Thomas's bakery where Edgar Thomas stood outside, selling pasties and sandwiches from a table. Towards the quay were more standings, offering Corona and Nicey and sticks of brown rock laid out under coloured awnings. Beneath a parasol was a tricycle and a box marked 'T. Wall' where a clutch of children were queuing for ha'penny ices. Yards and yards of bunting fluttered above the heads of the crowd. Signal flags ran in multi-coloured waves from window to window, over the road and back again. Union Jacks, ensigns, naval ensigns and Cornish regimental banners hung from upper storeys. The St Blazey Silver Prize Band were erecting their stands beside the Kidda Head Hotel. Captain Maddocks and the Racing Committee had set up shop above the old lifeboat slip, in a direct line with the start.

They had a table lined with trophies and above it an elaborate canopy made from a brand-new length of white tarpaulin. A starting cannon stood on a small purpose-built plinth. Porth had made great efforts in the name of its perennial cause: to be better than Polmayne in whatever way possible.

Into the throng stepped the passengers from the *Golden Sands*. They climbed the quay steps and spread out into the crowd.

'This way, dear,' Sir Basil Rafferty steered Lady Rafferty towards the Kidda Head Hotel. The Hoopers and the Frankses followed them; the Master was telling Parson Hooper about his recent walking tour of the Auvergne.

Anna had planned to lose herself somewhere along the front. She wanted to take out her sketchpad and sit alone in the shade and wallow in the warmth that had followed her every step that day and that had nothing to do with the sun.

'I say!' Birkin fell into step beside her. 'My friends and I – we would like to invite you to luncheon.'

'That's kind, but –'

'We'd be so pleased, Miss. You wouldn't have to stay for long.' Birkin sounded hurt. 'It's just that it would make us happy. Men on their own often make rather boring company.'

She smiled. 'All right. Just for a while.'

The dining room of the Kidda Head Hotel was dominated by a large and gloomy painting of a ship in a storm. A buffet lunch of ham in aspic and salads and cold beef was arranged beneath it, afloat on its own sea of white damask. In the middle of the table were two large fish mousses moulded in the shape of lobsters.

Lady Rafferty set herself up at one end of the bay window. Relieved to be ashore, she ordered champagne. When it came, she took from her handbag a folded envelope and tapped some powders into the glass. She then scrutinised her fellow guests.

'Who are they?'

Mr Bryant bent to follow her gaze. 'Mr Harris and Mr Williams, Porth Parish Council –'

'And there?'

'Yachtsmen. They have –'

'Will they be racing?'

'Yes, I believe so.'

'Bring them over, will you?'

Conversation rose in the room and merged with the sound of laughter and the chink of knives and forks on plates. In the far corner, Anna pretended to eat but in truth she had no appetite. Birkin had rediscovered his high spirits. He was telling a story about a boating trip with some soldiers in his regiment, or maybe it was his brothers, Anna wasn't sure. He and the others had lapsed into a private dialect that she did not understand.

Lee tried to include her. 'So, what do you eat in Spain?'

'I'm not Spanish. I'm Russian, but –'

'Ah! Good food in Russia?'

'I don't live in Russia.'

'Told you,' said Birkin. 'She's Spanish!'

Anna suddenly wanted to leave. 'Actually, where I am from everyone eats nuts and berries. We roast wolves. Sometimes –' she dropped her voice to a whisper and the men leaned closer to her '– people eat their own babies.'

'Lord!' Birkin blinked. Travers looked down. Lee blushed.

'I think I will go outside.' She thanked them and left the dining room.

Bryant returned to Lady Rafferty, bringing with him Ralph Cameron and Lawrence Rose and the Dane Soren.

'So, gentlemen,' she looked up at them in turn. 'What's the form?'

'It's been pretty tight all season,' volunteered Cameron.

'What he means, Lady Rafferty, is that he's been winning –'

'Everything,' said the Dane Soren.

'He wins here and he'll have won the season series.'

'Again.'

Cameron flashed a smile. 'In these light airs, really it's anyone's race.'

'So, Mr Cameron, what are your colours?' Lady Rafferty was beginning to look forward to her afternoon.

'Pea-green,' said Lawrence Rose. 'And mine is –'

'Splendid! Does anyone have a book on it?'

They each looked at each other, embarrassed at the mention of boats and betting. 'Well, not exactly.'

Outside, Anna paused on the hotel step. She blinked in the sun. The front had emptied somewhat and she made her way down to the beach. There she took out her sketchpad and gazed at the sparkling bay and the boats lying motionless in its shelter. It was very bright. She closed her eyes and listened to the gulls and the gentle kiss of seas on the sand and the distant barking of a dog and soon she was asleep.

At the dam, all was quiet. The Stephens boys had not returned. Croyden was leaning against the wall, his beret pulled down to his eyes. Stretched out beside the well, Tyler was scratching at a piece of slate with a stone; he blew away the dust and there, in full sail, was a mackerel driver.

Jack had wandered up from the spring. He stood on one of the stumps and surveyed the damage. Sawdust ringed each of the stumps and the entire top of the valley was scarred from the weight of the trees falling and being cut up and dragged over the ground. He carried on up the slope and sat in the grass. Far to the south, in the V of the valley was a triangle of blue sea below Kidda Head. He lay back and squinted at the sky and all that broke his vision was a tiny feather of high cloud drifting in from the east. He gazed at it for some time and soon forgot the destruction all around him. He felt the warmth of the sun on his face, then he too fell asleep.

Some three miles to the south-west, through the gateway to London, came lunch. Around the open sides of a wain sat women and children from Crowdy Farm. In their laps were baskets of sandwiches and saffron cake. The dogs ran up to bark at the wheels and the legs that dangled from it. Ivor

Dawkins brought the binder to a halt and everyone laid down their forks and scythes and converged on the wain. They all sat in a row, in its shade. Having eaten, they rested for a while and the dogs lay beneath the axles and some of the children lay with them, half-listening to the low hum of adult talk.

Polmayne too paused. On Pritchard's Beach the visitors had sought out the shade. The shops were closed; few people were out along the front. Parliament Bench was empty.

In Porth Bay, not even the gulls were moving. The wind had died and the Petrels lay rafted together, their sails loosely stowed. The anchor chain of the *Golden Sands* dropped vertically into the silky waters. Tacker was stretched out, face down on a bench. Jimmy sat in the wheelhouse, looking out to sea and idly passing a pebble from hand to hand. On Pendhu Point, Captain Williams had pulled closed the louvres of his hut and his head rested on the table. It was just for a little while, he told himself; he'd been feeling strange that morning but if he rested for a few minutes he'd be better. It was very hot in the watch hut and stripes of sunlight came through the shutters and lay across his bare forearms where his skin was covered in the first tell-tale rashes of the Reeds.

At two-twenty exactly the first puff of smoke rose from Porth's breakwater. A moment later, its loud report bounced off the façade of the Kidda Head Hotel and echoed around the harbour.

All over the village, people stirred. They packed away their picnics, pulled shut the doors of their cottages, and made their way down to the harbour. On board the Petrels they were raising their sails, dropping their moorings and drifting across the bay. There was still very little wind.

In the hotel many of those having lunch had made their way to the first-floor lounge. With its large balcony, it offered the best view of the racing.

The three officers, awash with gin, stumbled out of the

hotel and into the afternoon sun. Birkin spotted the T. Wall tricycle. 'Anyone care for an ice?'

From beside the hotel, the St Blazey Prize Silver Band started up with the hymn 'Grace'.

Five minutes after the first gun came another. The Petrels were already close to the start-line, crossing and recrossing before each other in a slow parade. The air was so light that the cries of 'Ready about!' and 'Lee-o!' and 'Gybe-o!' could be clearly heard ashore. The haze had thickened; Kidda Head was now no more than a grey shadow in the brightness.

Anna was leaning over her sketchpad, drawing in lightning sweeps of the page. She was looking up and down at the boats as they manoeuvred offshore. She had no idea what they were doing, but she saw in their silhouettes and their movements an arcane ballet whose steps she was trying to submit to paper. By the time the start gun sounded and the boats fell into line beside each other, she had covered a dozen sheets.

On the hotel balcony, Lady Rafferty was equally baffled. But in Major Franks she had found a fellow racing enthusiast and they had discreetly exchanged five-guinea wagers – he on Lawrence Rose and *Grace*; she on Ralph Cameron's *Harmony*.

'Have they started?' asked Lady Rafferty.

Franks had his binoculars on the boats. 'Yes. *Grace* is down to leeward, but she's being luffed already –'

'Speak English, man!'

It was becoming hard to see. The boats were moving away from the harbour, out towards Kidda Head, and the sky and the water and the sails all coalesced in the white haze. Anna watched them become fainter. She looked at her drawings and was pleased.

On the hotel balcony, with the race out of view, silence fell. Parson Hooper, who found silences embarrassing, looked down on the heads of the crowd and exclaimed, 'Well! Everyone seems to be enjoying themselves!'

Lady Rafferty glared at him.

Major Franks was still just able to follow the race through his binoculars. 'They've rounded the mark . . . they're on their way back!'

'Who's winning?' demanded Lady Rafferty.

'*Harmony* – half a length over *Grace!*'

She smiled.

The boats were reappearing from the mist. The two front-runners were together. Fifty yards astern was *Chastity*, the new Porth boat. Five or six others were bunched behind her. There were a couple at the rear. They were all moving so slowly that they seemed almost stationary. Their sails hung in loose folds, the bight of their mainsheets brushed the water – but yard by yard, they were narrowing the gap to the line.

Harmony was keeping her advantage, but *Grace* was closing. As they came closer to the village, everyone could see clearly their two hulls, green and yellow, and then the white of *Chastity*.

Along the front and on the quay, the Porth supporters were urging on their boat. 'Bear away, *Chastity*! Bear away!' Those from Polmayne were crying out '*Grace!*' and '*Harmony!*'

On the balcony, Lady Rafferty was now standing. She had told Bryant to support Ralph Cameron's *Harmony*, and he too was shouting '*Harmony!*'

'Luff her, *Grace!*' hissed Franks. 'For Pete's sake, luff her!'

On the quay was Captain Maddocks. He alone maintained a judicious calm, co-ordinating his spotters and waiting with the gun for the first boat's bow to cross the line.

There were only three in contention now. With a hundred yards to go, *Chastity* was third but beginning to close the gap. Ahead of her, *Grace* drew level with *Harmony* – then pulled ahead. *Harmony* had borne away a little, seeking the tide. She lost ground at once, and Franks nodded with satisfaction.

No one saw it coming. They were all watching the three lead boats. They did not see it as it crept around Kidda Head, peeled back the haze and darkened the sea-surface.

It reached *Hope* first, the back marker. Dr Jones and his crew had long since given up and were lying with their legs up over the combing. When the sails suddenly filled and the boat leapt forward, they were caught unawares. The breeze pressed on towards the bulk of the fleet. As it reached each boat, the helmsman felt it and he watched the sails fill and everyone sat up.

When the wind came to *Chastity*, it drove her through the water and she at once gained twenty yards.

The Porth supporters raised their voices.

Grace was still in front. The wind reached *Harmony*, slamming her boom to port; she began to bear down on *Grace*. Cameron pushed her upwind until *Grace* too caught it and tried to get ahead of *Harmony*'s bows. Cameron had right of way and held his course. The points of the boats' bows sliced through the water towards each other. The heeling shape of their sails converged. The crowd fell silent, waiting for the collision.

A few yards short, Lawrence Rose could see he was not going to make it.

'She's gone ahead!' said Franks. 'Dammit – *Harmony*'s ahead!'

'Yes!' hissed Lady Rafferty.

Grace's bow passed harmlessly astern of the green-hulled boat and *Harmony* surged on to the line.

But as they duelled, *Chastity* had gone through. She came in ahead of *Harmony* by a length and the Porth supporters raised such a shout that the sound of the winning gun was almost drowned out.

On the balcony, Lady Rafferty and Major Franks avoided each other's gaze.

CHAPTER 26

I t wasn't the racing guns that woke Tacker – those he could
sleep through. Nor was it the yachts which before their
start had come so close to the *Golden Sands* that their sail-
shadows slid over his sleeping form. Nor was it the shouts of
the skippers or the clamour from the harbour that had been
rising in tempo throughout the race. It was a much slighter
sound – the very faint creak of timbers.

He opened his eyes. Lying on his side he saw the stern-rail
and beyond it the houses of Porth. They were moving. The boat
was swinging on her anchor. He sat up at once. Two red stripes
ran down his cheek. He hurried forward to the wheelhouse.

'Coming in again, Jim!'

Jimmy nodded. He had been watching it, had seen the first
flurries of wind on the water, had seen it work its way boat
by boat through the Petrel fleet. Now he was watching the
sea out beyond Kidda Head where the flickering white-caps
had just begun to appear.

* * *

Up at Pennance they welcomed the breeze. They had formed a human chain. At one end, Croyden stood on the half-built dam wall, lowering the buckets into the water, hauling them up and passing them down to Jack who, balanced on the rocks, passed them on down to Edwin Stephens. In this way the buckets swung down the line until they were raised up to Tyler who poured each one through a funnel and into the tank.

They made quick work. At one time or other most had worked together on the lifeboat, and although the afternoon was at its hottest, they settled into a practised rhythm and found that it required little effort. Double Walsh started singing in his own tone-deaf way:

> So merry, so merry are we.
> There's no man on earth . . .

'For Christ's sake, Double!'

> – like the sailor at sea . . .

'Dee!'

> Blow high, blow low, as the ship sails along.
> Give the sailor his grog and there's nothing goes wrong.

Then Croyden let one of the buckets slip. It fell on Jack – soaked him.

'Ooops!'

Jack picked up the bucket and threw what was left of the water at Croyden and he stepped aside but it caught him on the shoulder. He dipped the next bucket in and stood on the dam and swung it out towards Dee who was still singing. A silvery arc shot out and for an instant those underneath saw it above them, frozen against the clear blue sky. Then it flopped down and caught all those who failed to jump clear. Croyden threw another.

'Oy!' Tyler was standing on the cart, shouting at Croyden.

'No harm in it, Cox!' called Double, whose shirt was soaked in cooling water. And he slopped a bucket up at him from below. Tyler jumped down from the cart and avoided it, but then Croyden caught him with a bucketful. Soon the whole line had divided into two battling groups, led by the perennial rivals Tyler and Stephens. The encrusted ground softened into mud and soon they were all laughing. Even Tyler was laughing. Something had lifted, some months-long anxiety. They knew now there was enough water here for weeks.

The forty-gallon tank took another half-hour to fill. When they had finished they trooped back up to the well. All of them were glad of the damp on their clothes and the wind that chilled it. They drank and filled bottles and sat down for a rest. Jack went back to the dam and untied the hobble from Job and led him back to the shafts and they began the journey back.

It was hard going. With the tank full, the cart had to be eased over each rut and bump of the track, but once on the main road it was easier. They followed the road up the valley and through the dappled sunlight of Kestle Wood. Job was struggling. A couple of them gave a push against the tank and when they reached the top they sat down and drank from the bottles.

'You fixed that rudder yet, Ty?' asked Stephens.

'Good as. Just one more coat of gloss.'

A couple of cars drove past, full of visitors. They all waved and the visitors waved back.

There was one more slope. The road dropped towards Polmayne and before the Crates it climbed again. Job managed twenty yards before it steepened. He came to a halt. The cart started to roll backwards. His hooves scraped on the tarmac. 'Hold it – quick!' shouted Jack, and Tyler jammed stones under the wheels. The cart stopped. Job found his feet again and they all paused and sat down. They passed the water around and then four of them stood against the back of the tank and took the weight. The others slipped out the stones and they heaved the tank up yard by yard. Jack was up at the front with Job. Tyler came up and they all urged him on: 'Come on now, boy!'

Everyone was pushing. They brought the tank over the top of the hill and left the main road and went through the gate towards the pieces. The strip of parched allotments curved down over the hill.

Before they transferred the water they unhitched Job and fed and watered him and then they all sat down in the grass.

'Well!' said Stephens.

'Well,' agreed Double.

Croyden lay back and looked at the open sea. Out beyond Pendhu they could see the tops of the waves turning. The haze of early afternoon had gone and Croyden knew that even if they were down at Newlyn there would be no fishing in this easterly.

'Be another two days before he goes round again.'

'Are you ever wrong about the weather, Croy?' teased Jack.

'He can smell a gale!' laughed Stephens.

'Better than his own pigs,' said Double.

Croyden smiled, but said nothing.

Beyond Kidda Head the sea was now a sharp and brilliant blue. In the wheelhouse of the *Golden Sands* Jimmy made his decision. He took a blue-and-white signal flag from the locker and limped forward to the mast.

In the upper lounge of the hotel, tea was being served. The afternoon sun flooded in from the balcony where the Polmayne Petrel skippers, back from their race, were looking out over the bay.

'Don't fancy it,' said Lawrence Rose.

'Tide's with it –'

'We should leave the boats here –'

'Nowhere safer than Porth in an easterly.'

Cameron looked from one face to the next. 'Right. We're agreed? We can return to Polmayne on the Garretts' boat.'

'Hey-ho!' It was Lawrence Rose who saw the flag go up the *Golden Sands*'s mast. 'P flag!'

'Someone call Bryant.'

Bryant came out, blinking in the sudden sunlight.

'Your boat's just hoisted the P flag.'

'The P flag?'

Rose explained: '*All persons report on board as the vessel is about to proceed to sea.*'

Bryant took a watch from his waistcoat. 'No, that can't be right. It's barely gone four.'

'I think you'd be advised to heed your skipper.'

'I think he'd be advised to heed me. We said five-thirty. My guests –'

'Listen, old man.' Ralph Cameron put a hand on Bryant's shoulder and led him to one side. 'The wind's getting up. It might all look pleasant in here, but I can assure you if you leave it much later, your guests will not thank you when you get out there.'

When Cameron spoke like this, people usually agreed with him. Mr Bryant said, 'Well, it's damned inconvenient!'

He went inside to where Sir Basil had joined his wife and the others. Major Franks was telling a story and Sir Basil's shoulders were shaking with laughter.

'. . . so the fellow was hopping about with this wretched spear through his boot!'

Everyone laughed.

'Come and join us!' Sir Basil was holding a paste sandwich. 'The Major here's telling us about Tanganyika.'

'Thank you. Er –' Bryant pressed his palms together. 'We've a slight change of plan. We must make our way to the harbour.'

Sir Basil said, 'Just finish my tea!'

'It seems the boat must leave immediately.'

Lady Rafferty said, 'Why is it that boats always make men such tyrants?'

Outside, the wind was gusting harder. It was shooting down off the headland, darting across the sheltered water in dark, feathery patches. The halyards of the Petrels had begun to tap against their masts.

The Garretts hauled their anchor and brought the *Golden Sands* into the harbour. The tide had dropped down the quay wall yet there was still enough water for passengers to board straight from the steps. But the rowing races were now in full swing. As the *Golden Sands* approached the quay six praams were also converging on it.

'Clear off!' they shouted.

'Back away, Garrett!'

Captain Maddocks's voice came crackling over the address system. 'Will the *Golden Sands* please stand off until the heat is finished!'

Jimmy ignored it. He gave several loud blasts on his fog-horn and the praams below him scattered right and left. Two race officers shouldered their way along the quay and stood on the steps as he came in. 'Take your boat away, Garrett!'

Jimmy checked his bows and stern. He then looked to the men on the quay. 'You'll have to move there – my passengers are coming through.'

'Remove your boat at once, Mr Garrett!'

Tacker jumped ashore with a line and Jimmy came out of the wheelhouse to lean on the rail. 'You want fifty more mouths to feed tonight? More stern, Tacker!'

Tacker shoved past them.

'Five minutes, Garrett. We'll give you five minutes. Then, I can assure you, we will come and untie your lines ourselves.'

At the hotel, Mr Bryant went into the kitchens and had a word with his barman, Pearce. 'Go and ask the cook – hurry, boy!'

Cameron and Rose took it upon themselves to gather in the rest of the passengers. They went to the Racing Committee and asked to make an announcement.

'Will all passengers for Polmayne please make their way to the quay! The *Golden Sands* will be boarding at once! Repeat – the *Golden Sands* will be leaving for Polmayne immediately!'

On the beach Anna packed away her sketchpad and made her way round to the front. Birkin was slumped like a starfish on the sand, and Travers and Lee pulled him to his feet and led him to the quay. The elderly couples, the nannies with their children, the boy with the model yacht, the guests of the hotel, the non-residents – all hurried along the quay and down onto the *Golden Sands*. There they took up their former places on the benches. Some carried on through the deckhouse to the open stern where for the first time they were aware of the hostility of the crowd staring down at them.

Tacker came and counted heads. They were all there, plus the Petrel skippers and crew. Cameron and Charlie Treneer stood ready to cast off.

'Wait!' called Charlie. A white coat was pushing its way through the crowd. It was Pearce. In one hand he had a wicker hamper and in the other a bag of ice. He jumped aboard.

Jimmy put the engines into reverse – Cameron and Charlie Treneer brought the lines in and the *Golden Sands* backed her way out of the harbour, followed by a series of jeers.

In the stern the passengers caught their breath.

'What a palaver!' sighed Mrs Hooper.

Lady Rafferty found her place. 'Hopeless, hopeless . . .'

Sir Basil was muttering; he was still a little baffled.

Parson Hooper looked astern at the cloudless sky. 'It's going to be a lovely evening! What nicer way to spend it than on a boat?'

By the bar Tacker was talking to Bryant and Bryant was nodding. He stepped forward and opened his arms: 'Ladies and gentlemen – please . . . please . . . I must apologise first of all for our rather hasty departure. Please ask at the bar for anything you'd like to drink. Thanks to the Kidda Head Hotel, we also have a little nourishment.' Pearce was unwrapping two large fruit cakes from the hamper.

'Good man!' said Sir Basil.

As the boat gathered speed westwards, away from Porth harbour, so the easterly wind appeared to drop and in the warmth everyone's spirits rose. That morning they had come over as strangers, but now from the deckhouse rose the sound of a dozen conversations.

CHAPTER 27

At the allotments they were all slowly following the trenches, watering. The leaves behind them were dotted with tiny orbs of moisture. Double began singing again:

So merry, so merry – so merry are we –

'Dee-ee!' shouted everyone.

When they had finished they drained the rest of the tank into a big granite trough and pulled an old door over it. Jack harnessed Job but Tyler said, 'I'll take him back. I got to go that way.'

Five minutes later Jack shouted, 'Oh God!' and ran off after Tyler and brought him back. 'We forgot the Parson's share.'

So they pulled the door off again and transferred a few gallons back into the tank and Tyler and Job set off once more for the rectory.

Croyden lit a cigarette and lay back on the bank. Smoke

spilled out of his mouth, blew up over his face and away downwind. Jack retied his boot and stood to leave.

'You're in a hurry.' Croyden squinted up at him.

'Things to do.'

'Down Ferryman's?'

Jack smiled. 'Nine tomorrow morning. We'll take the Station Bus.'

'And if it's still easterly?'

'We'll see.'

Jack set off down the path. As he reached the fence he heard Croyden call after him, 'If 'ee's late, I'll know where to come!'

Jack turned and saw them all in a line on the bank. Croyden was sitting up with the others and Double was below him, wrestling with the Stephenses' terrier. Stephens and his sons were to one side, waving goodbye.

Jack pushed his hands deep into his pockets and carried on down the hill. It was late afternoon. The haze had cleared. The roofs of the town dropped towards the bay and one or two gulls glided out over them. At Bethesda he would pick up cord and timber and some nails for Anna's paintbox, then up to Ferryman's and Anna would be there painting on the foreshore or maybe inside in the kitchen or maybe lying in the sun. He quickened his step.

Anna was on a bench across from the Hoopers. The sunlight came through the eyeholes in the awning and dots of it shifted across the folds of her jacket. The engine rumbled away below, shaking the deck and leaving a faint smell of fuel in the air.

Parson Hooper stood to go to the bar. 'Can I bring you anything?' he asked Anna.

'Some lemonade? Thank you.'

Mrs Hooper moved her knees as her husband passed and said to Anna, 'You're down at Ferryman's, isn't that right?'

'Yes.'

'And – don't tell me –' She put a finger to her lips. 'You're from Finland?'

'Russia.'

'Russia! Of course!' She sounded excited to discover Anna was Russian, but could think of nothing to say. 'And you're married to the painter, Maurice Abraham.'

Parson Hooper returned with a tray of lemonade and some cake and handed them round.

'She's from Russia, dear. Mrs Abraham's from Russia!'

Parson Hooper sat down, tugging up the knees of his trousers. 'Goodness!'

'We lived in India once,' said Mrs Hooper.

The *Golden Sands* had left the shelter of Porth Bay and was just beginning to sway on her keel. Astern, through the open back of the deckhouse, the village had shrunk to a nugget of white buildings. Kidda Head glowed green in the late sun, its flanks spotted with sheep.

The passengers had fallen quiet. Parson Hooper looked at those around him. 'I trust everyone enjoyed themselves today?'

He leaned forward to a girl with pigtails. 'What about you, young lady? Did you like the boat races?'

The girl turned and buried her face in her mother's coat.

On the other side of the boat, Lady Rafferty was holding court. She was seated on the front bench and in the open area before her stood Bryant and Sir Basil and some of the Petrel skippers.

'What I can't understand,' she said to Lawrence Rose, 'is why you let Major Cameron through.'

'Mr Rose is a gentleman,' explained Cameron.

'He was on starboard,' explained Rose. 'It was his water. Rule of the road.'

'Well,' said Lady Rafferty, 'it didn't do either of you any good. And it didn't do me any good. Now, Mr Bryant,' she continued, 'I was thinking. What do you think about a boat for the hotel?'

'We have this –'

'No, this is a workhorse. I'm talking about one of those yachts, a thoroughbred.'

'But you hate boats, my dear!' pointed out Sir Basil.

'I wouldn't have to get in it. We could let guests race it or watch. It would be an elegant advertisement for the hotel.'

'Well –'

'Penpraze can build one in three months.' Lawrence Rose was always keen to swell the class.

'What could we call her?' asked Sir Basil.

'*Golden Sands II*?' suggested Lady Rafferty.

'No good.' Rose shook his head. 'It must be a virtue.'

'What about *Thrift*,' quipped Cameron.

'Yes, Mr Bryant,' smiled Lady Rafferty. 'How about building a boat and calling it *Thrift*?'

Mr Bryant frowned. 'I'm not sure. We'd have to look at the cost.'

Lady Rafferty threw back her head and laughed.

The wind had freshened. The seas were now pushing up under the *Golden Sands*, raising her stern and then dropping it as each one went through, rolling on to the west. As the boat began to pitch, so those people standing made their way back to their seats. Bryant was embarrassed and he left Lady Rafferty and the Petrel skippers and went and sat with Mrs Bryant. Cameron and Rose sauntered over and leaned against the bar.

A woman in a yellow hat turned to look for her child; he had found the boy with the model yacht. 'Come back, Edgar!'

The awning lifted and the Master made his way aft. He had been up alone in the bows. He returned to the benches and, sitting down, propped both hands on his cane. Beside him was the elderly couple from Wales. They had taken the same seat as in the morning and were still smiling their benign smiles, still hand in hand.

On the bench in front of them were the three Guards officers. Travers and Lee sat impassively; Birkin was asleep between them. His head was lolling against his chest. As the boat's pitch increased, he opened his eyes and tried to focus. 'Urf!' he said, then fell asleep. When he woke again, he said, 'Bit squiffy.'

'Come on, old chap!' Travers and Lee took him forward, out under the flaps of the awning to the starboard companionway. Birkin sat down heavily on the box beneath the lifeboat.

'Well done, Birks!'

'Good show, Birks!'

Birkin's head lolled forward. 'Be's right as rain,' he slurred. 'Don' mine me, jussa bit –'

The boat lurched hard to starboard and Birkin lurched with it. He stumbled against the rail opposite, where he checked his fall and retched over the side. After a few minutes he turned and stood a little straighter. 'All gone.'

'Good man!' said Lee.

As they went back the *Golden Sands* dropped into a deep trough. They all grabbed at the rail and Birkin tripped, banging his toe against the fuel cap.

'Ow! Ow-ow!' He hopped around, gave the cap a kick and shouted, 'You bastard!'

'Come on, Birks!' Travers took his arm and led him back into the shelter of the deckhouse.

Loosened, the cap began to work its way off. It was soon swinging free on its short brass chain.

The *Golden Sands* was pitching heavily now. In the blue light of late afternoon, the seas were breaking all around her. Anna tightened her headscarf and left the Hoopers and the benches and went astern, out into the open.

A gull skimmed over the ridge of a coming wave, dived

into the trough, then arced up high to hover above the ensign.

She gazed out beyond it, at the endless plain of water. The waves were running behind and beside the boat, and as far as she could see they were rising into white crests that flashed above the blue and grew thicker towards the horizon. She thrilled at the sight of such seas and the vagrant motion of the boat beneath her. When the first wave slammed against the transom, she stepped back and watched a lazy column of spray rise above her, break into a thousand shards and splash into the boat.

'Careful, Miss!' In the corner of the stern were Red and Joseph Stephens in their 'Grace' and 'Charity' sweaters. They were smoking.

She continued to watch the shifting seascape before her. Two, three, four waves back she could see the approach of the larger ones. She followed them as they came in, as the stern dropped into the valley before them and the dark scarp of water rose to block out the land behind and she felt the surge as it picked up the stern and drove them forward. Sometimes the waves were steeper and broke with a slow swish of white water on either side, and she learned to predict them, to move to right or left as the spray rose. Then came one that thumped hard against the stern and she could do nothing. A great curtain of water flopped down and soaked her. She took off her headscarf and shook out her hair – but her jacket and dress were wet through.

'Best be in out of there!' Red Stephens threw his cigarette over the side. He came over, peeling off his sweater and handing it to her.

'No, no.'

'Go on, take it – I have this.' Beneath his 'Grace' jersey he wore another, a much older one, embroidered with the name 'Ratona'.

* * *

When the first sea fell into the boat, it sent a slosh of water forward which buffed against the bench uprights. It washed over the shoes of those too slow to raise their feet. Several people cried out as they felt it cool against their legs.

Ralph Cameron predicted it. He stepped forward and picked Lady Rafferty's handbag from the deck, calmly suggesting to those around her that they might like to raise their feet a few inches.

Only Birkin did not flinch. His head was now lodged against Lee's shoulder. The water submerged his shoes and ran on against the bar and out beneath the awning. There it flicked at the fuel cap and slopped in through its mouth.

In the wheelhouse the Garretts saw the water. They saw it run forward into the bow, before falling back as the stern dropped again. It drained out through the scuppers. Tacker went astern and Bryant called him over.

'Well?'

'Twenty minutes, sir! Another twenty minutes and we'll be in under the point – be calm as a duckpond in there!'

Tacker looked up at the rows of heads around him. Then he bent down again. 'Tell you what, sir.'

'What, Tacker?'

'I'll sing 'em a song.'

Bryant frowned.

'Always like a song, sir. Keeps their minds off it.'

'All right.'

Tacker went and stood before the bar. He cleared his throat and looked out at them all. Over their heads he could the sea beyond. He began:

> *Now what do you think I made of a red herring's head?*
> *I made so fine an oven as ever baked bread.*

He was right. One by one the passengers turned to watch him and when Charlie Treneer joined him and their combined voices filled the space and rose above the sound of the engine, they were completely absorbed. The Stephenses came forward and joined in, and although Cameron and Rose had moved off to one side, they knew the chorus:

> Hark! Hark! How dost thou lie?
> And so do you as well as I.
> Why hast thou not told me so?
> So I did long ago.
> Well, well and well, well.
> And thinks I to myself:
> It's a jolly herring!

Lady Rafferty did not mind the singing but she did mind the motion. With each drop of the boat her gorge rose, and with the fumes from the engine she said to herself: 'Dear God, don't let me be sick, not here, not in public.' She closed her eyes and tried to focus on the lines of the song.

> Now what do you think I made of a red herring's ribs?
> I made forty cow-stalls and forty ox-cribs . . .

Anna had returned to her seat beside the Hoopers. She held her orange jacket over her arm. Across her chest were the white sewn-on letters 'Grace'. She had rolled up the sleeves but the jersey hung heavy on her shoulders and reached down to her thighs. It smelt of pipe-smoke and work. She sat watching the singing for a while, then turned to look back out to sea.

> Now what do you think I made of a red herring's tail?
> I made as fine a ship as ever did sail . . .

Another wave rose above the stern-rail and fell on board. The water flooded forward. Tacker, still singing, raised his hands, and the passengers lifted their feet. He saw it gush around his own boots and over those of Charlie Treneer and the Stephenses beside him. He left them to carry on singing and ducked out beneath the awning.

As he climbed down through the hatch the engine's *thut-thut* cut out the sound of singing. His feet landed in water. He flicked on the light and saw a pool of it swilling about in the bilges. He turned on the pump. It was still ten, fifteen minutes to Pendhu and they were shipping water at quite a rate. But the pump was a new one, and with each roll of the boat the pool shrank. When he heard the pump sucking on air, he turned it off.

He was halfway up the ladder when he heard a knock in the engine. He paused on the rung, listening. Nothing – it was smooth again. It continued at its steady throb. He came back into the deckhouse and rejoined the singing. By now all those unaffected by the ship's rolling had picked up on the final chorus, and Tacker stood at the front and waved his hands like a conductor.

> *Why hast thou not told me so?*
> *So I did long ago.*
> *Well, well and well, well.*
> *And thinks I to my-self:*
> *It's . . . a . . . jol-ly . . . HE-RRR-ING!*

'Bravo!' said Parson Hooper, clapping.
'Bravo!' The Master tapped his cane on the deck.
'Bravo!' said the Dane Soren.
The Welsh couple smiled.
Charlie Treneer took off his cap and bowed to the audience and Tacker bowed too and the clapping grew louder before subsiding.

The wind plucked at the deckhouse's scalloped awning. A loose block banged against the rail. Apart from the sound of the sea, there was silence.
Silence.

CHAPTER 28

—⟅∽⟆—

In London, they were cutting the last half-acre. Ivor Dawkins, forearms red and sunburnt, shirt half-open to the wind, had been bouncing in the seat of the binder for hours, for days, for weeks. But here was the last half-acre of the last field, and the summer's work was done.

For some time he had been watching the *Golden Sands*. He had seen her pull away from Porth quay, cross the harbour and enter the open sea. On the up-rows he saw London Terrace and the pipe-smoke clouds above it; on the down-rows the sea and the single yellow shape pitching across it.

Neither occupied him. Nothing occupied him very much except this last harvesting, this last oblong of oats. He watched the flails and the horses' heads and listened to the whirring of the canvas belt as he reached the terrace and turned for the down-row. The yellow shape was a little further to the right. He wondered idly, who would get there first? Would he have cut the last stalk before the boat reached Pendhu? Or would he still be sitting here in the binder's seat as it came inside the rocks and disappeared round the headland?

It was close. He still had, what, twenty yards – and twenty yards was fifteen rows. The boat was well over halfway to the headland. It would be touch and go. He flicked the reins, turned at the bottom and drove the pair hard up the hill. Their hooves drove into the soil. The slope steepened, London came closer. The blades cut quicker; the flails flailed faster; the tines of the sheaver spun more urgently and, foot by foot, the line of stubble behind him advanced. He reached the terrace and turned, and there was the boat just half a mile away. The sun shone on its funnel and its bows. It was dipping and surging in the swell. It was going to beat him to it.

Silence.

Tacker appeared to react before it happened. Most could not understand why he was dashing forward again when they were expecting another song. But the Stephenses knew at once. Charlie Treneer knew. The Petrel skippers knew.

Jimmy leaned out of the wheelhouse. He saw Tacker pulling up the hatch. 'That hose again?'

'Could be!' And Tacker dropped down to his shoulders, found the rungs of the ladder with his feet, and ducked inside.

Jimmy eased himself back to the helm. Without power the *Golden Sands* was beginning to yaw. He tried to keep her straight but his steerage was going. Charlie Treneer had come forward. Mr Bryant was behind him, but before he could speak Jimmy told Charlie, 'Go drop us six fathoms of chain, will 'ee?'

As Charlie left, Bryant stepped into his place and said, 'Why has the engine stopped?'

Jimmy said nothing. He was thinking. If the hose had gone again, Tacker could bind it up in a few minutes. He had only thirty fathoms of chain and there was at least that much water. He wasn't trying to anchor; he just needed the weight at the bows to stop them going broadside. Broadside in that swell would be very uncomfortable.

Mr Bryant leaned through the door. 'Answer me!'

'Be all right, Mister,' boomed Jimmy. 'Don't 'ee worry!'

Charlie was on the foredeck freeing the lashings from the anchor. Red Stephens came up and helped prepare the chain. The wheel was now loose in Jimmy's hands. The boat's motion was changing and they were swinging and it wasn't the bows dipping any more, but the sides; their pitch was turning to roll. The boat dropped onto her topsides and there was a series of slow clatters and shiftings as everything loose on board moved to port. Charlie stumbled. The anchor slid overboard and the chain rattled out over the gunwale. Red took a bight from the loose chain and flicked a couple of hitches over the post. The chain snapped tight on them.

But the boat was still beam-on to the seas. Jimmy watched the angle of the chain as it entered the water. They all watched it. Very slowly it began to stretch out. The *Golden Sands* was sliding downwind, swivelling as she did so on the weight of the anchor. Another shadowy sea rose and the boat tumbled down before it. But now the sea anchor was working. It checked her roll and they rode over the crest. When she dropped down into the next trough she was pointing into the wind.

Tacker was still below.

Half a mile astern was the white water around the Main Cages.

'Tell me, Bran, has she stopped or no?'

Ivor Dawkins had pulled the binder to a halt. He was leaning on his knees and squinting out to sea. Bran Johns followed his gaze. He put the sheaf he was holding to the ground and shielded his eyes.

The *Golden Sands* was swaying back and forth in the swells. Bran lost her for a moment as she dipped into a trough

216

but then her bow rose and she climbed up over it. She had no way; there was no white water at her stern, none at her bow.

'Well,' said Bran, 'if she's in trouble, she's in the right place.'

Dawkins glanced at him and Bran nodded towards the headland. 'Williams'll have her in his telescope.'

The passengers were silent. As the boat began to wallow so they wallowed too, half aware that the engine had stopped, that the ceaseless bucking of the boat had altered, that there were plenty of people in the know to deal with it.

Lady Rafferty was feeling less ill. Without the sickly fumes from the engine, she could breathe easily again. Sir Basil was sitting with her, patting her hand. 'Back in no time, my dear!'

In the hiatus some of the children had slipped free of their parental clutch and stood in a group before the bar. They were trying to keep their balance as the boat heaved about, holding out their arms and crying 'Whooooo!' and 'Eeesh!' whenever the deck tilted beneath them. They giggled as they felt the weightlessness in their stomachs when the boat dropped.

Then one of them fell and knocked his head on a bench. He stared for a moment before crying out. Parson Hooper half-stood to assist but the woman in the yellow hat was there already. 'I told you, Edgar! Now just stay here.'

Cameron came aft with Joseph Stephens; the passengers all turned to watch them.

'What is happening, Major Cameron?' asked Lady Rafferty.

'Blocked hose – they'll soon clear it.' He threw up his hands and smiled. 'Engines! Why didn't we ever just stick to sail?'

* * *

Tacker was crouched in the bilges. It was very hot. Without the engine there was no electric light. He had taken off his coat and he had lit the emergency lantern and hung it from a hook. The shadows were swaying with the boat and he was trying to follow the hoses with his fingers. He had been there several minutes before Red pulled up the hatch and came down the ladder.

'Bring's that light, Red!'

Red unhooked the lantern and held it out and squatted down himself. Close up, he could feel the glow of heat from the engine. 'What's the trouble?' he asked.

'Pff!' he shrugged and shook his head.

The line that had leaked before was intact. Tacker sat back and frowned at the mass of steel before him. Sweat ran down his temple and he wiped it with his sleeve. He shook his head. Switching off the fuel tap, he worked the pipe free from its nozzle. At that moment the boat rolled and Tacker dropped the pipe and fell, reaching out a hand to the bulkhead. Red twisted so that it was his back that fell against the boat's side. He had managed to keep the lantern steady, even as his head dropped close to the frames. For a moment as he pushed himself up he could hear the rush of water through the timbers.

'The anchor's out,' he said. 'Bringing us head to wind.'

Tacker nodded. He eased open the tap and let the fuel drip out into his palm. Raising it to the light he could see, against his skin, paler bubbles in the black pool. He wiped a finger on his thighs, then dipped it into one of the bubbles and put it to his tongue.

He held it out to Red, and Red tasted it too.

'Salty?'

Red licked his lips. He nodded.

Parson Hooper glanced at his watch. They had been stopped now for five minutes. He looked at those around him. They

218

were like people in a station waiting-room, still and resigned. Most of them were watching Mr Bryant and Major Franks and Rose and Cameron who were leaning against the bar and gripping it with the boat's motion. But they were standing. It was their standing, realised Hooper, that was reassuring the passengers. If only he could get across the aisle, across the open area beyond, he could stand too; he could add his own calming presence to theirs.

Anna saw him try to rise, then sit back. She turned to look out over the stern. The boat was facing in a different direction. Through the back of the deckhouse she could now see Pendhu Point rather than Kidda Head. Evening had painted its cliffs the colour of honey. The seas were driving towards it, rising in white surges at its base. She could see Hemlock Cove and the cove beside it where the ship had gone aground and to the left of that were the shapes of the Main Cages. She could see the rocks, could see what they were doing to the water. But what colours – what a white and what a blue! And what a sky! Anna had been gliding through the day, and now with the approach of evening she was gliding still.

Jimmy said nothing. His face was as blank as ever. As Tacker lurched into the wheelhouse and told him that seawater had got into the engine, that to start it again would mean draining it and flushing it through – hours of work – Jimmy gave no response.

His options were narrowing. The sea anchor was stalling them. He could put out another but it would only slow them a little. They were drifting downwind at nearly a knot. The ebb tide was taking them in the same direction, increasing all the time. He guessed that they had half an hour, forty minutes at most, before they reached the Main Cages. If he kept the helm down hard, he might gain a little steerage from the anchor and avoid the Curate. But as for the other rocks, it was pot luck.

Tacker suggested lighting a flare. Jimmy shook his head. It would panic the passengers and panic Bryant. 'Anyway,' he grunted, 'Williams'll see us. Raise M and V.'

Later, Bran Johns was unable to recall the exact moment when he started running. He could see himself standing at the binder with Ivor Dawkins and both of them watching the *Golden Sands*, and then he was bounding down through London, through the stubble, and the dogs were running with him and he was scrambling over the wall to the cliff path.

He ran swiftly. The dogs followed him for a while, then stopped and trotted back. From time to time, he glanced over the wind-stunted hawthorn – to seek out the boat and the churn of water that would appear at her stern when the engines restarted. But she was still drifting. She was in trouble; that was clear now. The rocks were less than half a mile to leeward, and down-tide.

He reached the slope above Hemlock Cove and saw the path drop down seventy, eighty feet to the stream. Opposite him was Pendhu Point and the watch hut on its end. He descended in a series of leaps, jumped the nearly-dry stream before zig-zagging up the far slope. No more than a third of the way up, he was already struggling. His throat ached. He felt dizzy. He was not even sure he could do anything once he reached the hut. Maybe Williams wasn't there. There was no need for a watch on a fine day like this. But Williams was always there, and he had probably rung through to the lifeboat already – but where were the maroons?

With each step his boots scuffed higher against the dusty earth. But the top still seemed far off. 'Come on!' he told himself. The slope steepened and at the top were lichened boulders and the path ran between them and then out across the grass to the headland.

The hut door stood ajar. Inside, the shutters were closed. Williams lay slumped on the table.

'Captain!'

Williams remained unmoving.

'Captain! Captain Williams!' Bran was so short of breath he found it hard to speak. He put one arm against the door frame and bent at the waist. Williams did not move. Bran stepped forward and pushed open the shutters and the hut filled with sunlight. He saw the lines of rashes on Williams's bare forearm. 'Captain! Captain!'

Williams stirred. Someone was standing a long way away and calling '. . . tin . . . tin . . . tin.' He dragged his head up.

'Captain!'

His hair was sweat-flattened against his head. His mouth was dry.

'Look!'

Williams followed Bran's pointing arm and saw only a huge light that burned and filled his vision. Something was inside his head, trying to beat its way out. He covered one eye with his hand and slowly the cliff appeared and the sea and the dark shape of Maenmor and in the midst of it all the yellow hull. He responded not consciously but with the instincts of something rehearsed a thousand times in his mind; he never thought it would happen twice in one summer.

The mortar tube stood in the corner. A box of maroons was on the shelf above the window and he stood to retrieve them. He handed two to Bran and told him to place the mortar in the hole outside, to point it up and slightly out to sea, to light the touch-paper.

He himself picked up the telephone and rang through to the exchange. Two rings for the Lifeboat Secretary, three for the Cox and five for the boat.

'The *Golden Sands*,' he heard himself say. 'Three-quarters of a mile sou'sou'east of Pendhu. Requires immediate assistance.'

'The LSA?'

Williams looked out to sea again. He could hardly open his eyes with the throbbing in his head and the light before him, but the yellow shape was well offshore. She would be moving parallel to the shore. If she was going to strike at all it would be the rocks.

'No,' he said. 'Send the boat.'

Then he heard the maroons – first one then another – and he sat down again and took up his telescope and raised his brow to try to loosen the mask that seemed to cover his face.

On the *Golden Sands*, Jimmy Garrett saw the grey trail rise from Pendhu, then another. The boat would be on its way. But he was filled with indignation: why should *he* need assistance?

CHAPTER 29

———

Jack was on the Town Quay. He had been to the net loft and he had come out on to the quay and he was now hauling in his punt, gathering up the painter in long, loose coils. The wind was fresher. Short little seas were lapping at the boats in the inner harbour. It was still easterly – easterly and an ebb tide would mean a hard row up the river. Beside him was the maund full of odds and ends for Anna's studio. This time tomorrow he would be on his way down to Newlyn, if not already there, but now he was going to Ferryman's and nothing else mattered.

'She's not at home!' Toper and the others were on the Bench. 'She went up Porth dinner time!'

'Took the Garretts' boat, Mr Swee!'

'For the regatta!'

Jack carried on with his coiling. All right, so he would go to Bethesda and look out for the boat and they'd row up to Ferryman's together later on. He pulled in the punt, loaded the maund and turned to wave to the Bench.

That was when they appeared, high over the capped and hatted line of Parliament Bench. Two green stars in a sky too bright for stars; two late and muffled thuds on the wind. From the direction of the lifeboat station came a couple of much louder reports, echoing off the town's walls, rolling back from the headland.

Toper let out a yelp and Boy stood on the bench to look over the wall.

'Anything?' called Treneer.

Boy peered out towards Pendhu and the open sea beyond but could see nothing more than a speckling of white crests on the swell. He sat and shook his head.

Tick-Tock Harris was looking at his watch. He had set it the moment he heard the maroons.

'A visitor, swimming,' speculated Toper.

'A yacht.'

'False alarm.'

'Eeee.'

Jack was already on his way.

On board the *Golden Sands*, the group of men were still standing at the bar. Parson Hooper had given up trying to join them. It was Lawrence Rose who saw the maroons through the back of the deckhouse – the brief blooms of green above Pendhu Point.

'Help's on its way,' he said quietly.

'What do you mean?' asked Bryant.

'Lifeboat.'

The mention of the lifeboat only alarmed Bryant even more. He could not wait any longer. He stumbled out under the awning to the wheelhouse. 'Mr Garrett,' he barked, 'you will explain to me exactly what is happening!'

A flicker of contempt crossed Jimmy's face. 'Tack!'

Tacker had been examining the fuel intake to port and he came into the wheelhouse from the other side, wiping his hands. 'Damned cap's off, Jim, must have poured in down –'

He stopped when he saw Bryant.

Jimmy said, 'Perhaps you can take Mister here somewhere else.'

Tacker led him out to the forward deck. Mr Bryant gripped the rail to steady himself. The wind had freshened further. The bows were kicking hard against the anchor chain but the seas were still long, with long rounded tops and smaller waves which rolled over them and half-broke over their backs.

'Well, sir,' said Tacker.

'Yes?'

'Looks like the engine's gone.'

'What are you doing about it?'

'Not a lot we can do, sir.'

Bryant looked at him. There must be something else, something he didn't understand. 'But you've put the anchor out. At least we are not moving . . .'

Tacker said nothing. Bryant knew suddenly that it wasn't true, that they *were* still moving. And for the first time, above the mysterious constraints of the sea that he had made no progress in fathoming, he saw the plain logic of their position: they had no power and they could not stop. It was a simple enough equation, and in the heat of the late afternoon it left him with a feeling of cold terror. What could he tell the passengers?

'Lifeboat's on its way, sir. They'll tow us in.'

Bryant clutched at that. 'So it's just a question of waiting?'

'That's it, sir. Be here in no time!'

Bryant went back through the deckhouse awning. A silence had settled on the passengers. Most had felt the first shadows of doubt, sensing with the passing of each minute that their situation was becoming more dangerous. And with the doubt came the need to know. They watched Mr Bryant stand to face them from the bar.

'Ladies and gentlemen, you have probably noticed that we have had a little breakdown –'

'What, exactly?' someone shouted.

'It seems it might be difficult to repair –'

At once a murmur of questions rose from the benches. It grew indignant.

Bryant held out his arms: 'Please! Please –'

'What do you mean, difficult?'

'Who's in charge here?'

The woman in a yellow hat pointed to the boy on her knee: 'He must eat by six, you know!'

'I wish someone would just explain . . .'

'Oh good God,' Lady Rafferty scoffed. 'A little problem and the whole world goes mad!'

'Quite right, my dear,' said Sir Basil, who had become somewhat subdued.

Then from the second row of benches, from beside Mrs Franks, came the unwavering voice of the Master. 'Perhaps you could explain to us, Mr Bryant, what was the flare above the headland?'

Bryant was relieved to be asked. 'A boat is on its way from Polmayne. If we should need assistance they will be on hand. Please bear with us – everything is being done to ensure our swift return. And Madam,' he smiled at the woman in the yellow hat, 'you may rest assured that the young man will get his supper!'

At once the chattering rose again from the benches. Bryant sensed the collective relief that now filled the deckhouse. He had done his job. He went up to the Raffertys. 'I must apologise – these things can't be helped.'

'Of course, of course,' said Sir Basil.

'Piffle,' muttered Lady Rafferty.

Anna too did not believe Bryant. She knew he was telling them only part of the truth. But she still had the strange feeling that she could step away from it at any time.

Opposite her, Parson Hooper clapped his hands. 'Now, children, what about a story? Would you like that, children, a nice story?'

In the front row of benches Birkin stirred. He grunted, licked his lips, and transferred his head from Lee's shoulder to Travers's.

'Mr Bryant,' the Master spoke again. 'By my estimate we'll be on those rocks before they get a boat to us from Polmayne.'

Everyone fell silent.

Bryant straightened up. 'I can assure you, sir, that there will be assistance here very soon.'

'. . . so, when they were in Egypt' – Parson Hooper was faltering – 'the Lord sent many plagues. Do you know what they were, children, what strange plagues there were?'

The children looked at the vicar and saw only his nervousness, and they looked to their parents and saw it there too, and soon it was spreading among the benches like a contagion.

Jimmy was alone in the wheelhouse. He was standing with the weight on his good leg and he was making calculations. Both hands held the wheel and his face was impassive. What was their speed through the water? Next to nothing – but not quite nothing, judging by the helm. The wind was giving them a little westward way. And over the ground? A knot perhaps, no more. How much more ebb would there be, and which way was it taking them? West, of course, but was there any north in it as it approached the rocks, or was it yet working round to the south? South, he thought, and was playing the helm for every inch of south he could get. Less than half a mile separated them from the Curate rock, maybe a third. And what was that in time now – twenty, twenty-five minutes?

Two minutes had passed since the maroons went up. If they had a good launch the lifeboat should be away in another ten. It would take them a quarter of an hour to reach the *Golden Sands*. More, perhaps, with wind and tide against them. So – twenty-five minutes.

For the first time Jimmy considered his own lifeboat. It had broken free on the way over, but it was still all right.

Ten, fifteen people at a time – three or four trips – but who was to say they could land anywhere in this sea? No, they were better off here, on board the *Golden Sands*.

Even so, he leaned out of the wheelhouse and told Tacker to see that the lifeboat was ready. They might need it in a hurry. Glancing aft, he saw the rocks shadowy against the sun, closer than he'd thought. He went back to the wheel and tried again to use what little way they had to head them south. But something had changed. The wind had veered. A tiny shift, but enough. All the effort with the helm had worked against him. The wind was now pushing them back onto the Curate rock, and he realised that if he had left it, if he had not played the helm, they would have gone clear of the Curate, clear too of the other rocks and drifting into open sea.

Then he saw the ship.

It was not a bad launch. Harris stopped his watch when he saw the boat and said, 'Eleven minutes and twenty-five seconds!'

Coxswain Tyler had been with his sister. He had been sitting in the sun outside her house at the Crates, and Job and the cart were on the newly-seeded verge before him.

'They've gone again.' His sister was in the kitchen, and her account of their mother's feet came through the open window. 'Swelled up like turnips. Grandma was the same, her legs was just as bad, remember?'

Tyler felt the day's warmth in the concrete step beneath him, felt the fatigue from his own exertions, and he was only half-listening, kicking at the loose gravel with his boot. 'Mmm –'

Just for a moment when the maroons went up, he paused on the step. Job flinched at the noise and shuffled his hooves. By the time Tyler's sister came to the window, she saw only her brother's back as he ran down the road.

It took him exactly seven and a half minutes to reach the house. The launch crew were well ahead. Second Cox Brad

Harris was already there, and as he spoke to him Tyler was pushing his arm into his lifejacket. He came out of the office doing up the straps just as Croyden and the Stephenses and Double and the others arrived from the allotments. Jack had arrived with them, and several other irregulars and some runners.

'Where's Red to?' Tyler called.

'Up Porth – crewing!'

'Joe?'

'He's there too.'

'Bloody Stephenses!'

'I'm here,' said Edwin Stephens.

Tyler ignored him. 'Brian?'

'Got the Reeds. So's Thomas.'

Tyler shook his head. He crossed the floor and took down the lifejackets. He pushed one at Croyden, one at Jack and one at his own nephew Dougie Tyler. Grudgingly he tossed the last two at Edwin Stephens and his son. Standing beside the ladder he slapped the shoulder of each man as he climbed on board: '. . . five, six, seven . . .'

Tyler was last aboard, and he gave the signal. The *Kenneth Lee* started its slide and hit the easterly swell and they all ducked as the spray rose over them. Tyler knocked her into gear and she was already rising to meet the next sea.

First they saw the curve of distant smoke from her stack, then a flash of her white bridge in the sun. She was rising and falling with the swells. A tramp steamer off Kidda Head, three miles away and on a heading to clear the Lizard, sou'sou'west.

Jimmy retrieved two red flares from the shelf above the wheel. He left the wheelhouse and shouldered his way past Red Stephens and lit them one after the other. They shot up and shone briefly some fifty feet above the water. He returned to the helm and watched the steamer's undulating course. Three miles at ten knots – fifteen, twenty minutes, but with the wind with them and the tide . . . . She was now abeam of them. She disappeared in a trough and her bows emerged and they all waited to see if they were coming round. They were not. She was keeping her course.

'What's the service, Ty?' Croyden was in the bows and he shouted aft, over the noise of the engine. Jack was with him up for'ard, and down the benches each side were the Stephenses and Double and the others. Their faces were red and glowing from the day at Pennance. They stared ahead or at their feet and waited for Tyler to reply.

'*Golden Sands*. Disabled upwind of the Cages.'

Jack did not at once equate the *Golden Sands* with the Garretts' boat, the boat he knew as the *Polmayne Queen*. He thought of the hotel first, then he thought of the boat and the Garretts – and then he thought of Anna.

Upwind of the Cages.

Of Jack's four call-outs, three had been false alarms. There had been the *Constantine*, but with the half-dozen exercises he had taken part in, this place, this squatting beneath the lifeboat's foredeck with the smell of damp and linseed from the lifejackets, was not one he associated with danger.

It'll be a false alarm. If the engine had gone, they'd fix it. How many times had something gone on the *Maria V*'s Kelvin and they'd idled for a while and sorted it out? They would come round Pendhu and there would be that new yellow of the Garretts' boat and she'd be on her way back, the sun shining on her bows as she surged forward with each of the following seas.

CHAPTER 30

On the for'ard deck of the *Golden Sands*, all eyes were on the steamer. Red and Tacker and Joseph Stephens were preparing the lifeboat. They had pulled back the cover and were checking the davits, but had stopped while they watched the steamer. Charlie Treneer and Lawrence Rose and Ralph Cameron watched too. They could see her profile with the bridge amidships and her gantries and the smoke blowing sideways. She was abeam of them and in her far-off rise and fall each of them tried to see the first shift in her course.

'Any more o' they flares, Tack?'

Tacker dashed to the wheelhouse. Jimmy was standing, eyes ahead, hands firm on the wheel. He did not stir as Tacker fumbled in the locker by his legs. 'Christ, Jim – there's some bloody damp in 'ere!'

He fished out a flare and wiped it on his trouser leg. He took it into the open air. Red and Joe and Rose huddled with him inside the coaming. The first match blew out. So did the second. The third flickered against the touch-paper and went

231

out, and the next. Time and again Tacker tried to light it, but the matches flared and went out. Red took the barrel of the flare. 'It's bloody sodden, Tack!'

Rose smacked his hand on the gunwale. 'What sort of tinpot ship is this?'

The seas were butting against the bows. As each one came through they could feel the weight of it trying to drag the boat round, and they all knew that all that kept them from rolling over was the sea anchor.

'She's coming!' Cameron was standing against the foredeck.

Rose looked up. Cameron was pointing to the steamer.

'She's coming round!'

The others came to the rail and they could see that the gap between them and the ship was narrowing as she swung round towards them. On the wind came two blasts from her foghorn.

'Hurrah!' cried Rose.

Cameron went aft to tell Bryant. There was an odd hush among the passengers.

'How long, Major Cameron?'

'Ten, fifteen minutes.'

'Then what?'

'They'll put us under tow.'

The news spread fast through the deckhouse. Travers raised Birkin's sleeping head from his shoulder and went to stand with several others in the doorway.

'You can see her!' he called back. 'Coming straight for us! A mile away!'

'Thank God!' said Mrs Bryant.

Even the Master agreed that there was a good chance she would reach them in time.

The pitch was changing, but so slightly that only Jimmy noticed it. Everyone was concentrating on the steamer, but as he played each of the seas with the helm, Jimmy could feel it. The seas were becoming shorter. They were steepening. Deep beneath the *Golden Sands*, the sea-bed was beginning to rise – towards the first of the rocks, towards the Curate.

The steamer was close now. Those in the bows of the *Golden Sands* could smell her coal-smoke on the wind. Still a few hundred yards off, she swung round and began to drop back, stern-first. Five or six men were standing high up at the ship's stern-rail. Beneath them the black paint was chipped and scabs of rust glowed in the late sun and the name was painted in white: *Hopelyn*, Newcastle.

Jimmy told Tacker and the others to shorten the sea anchor.

Back in the deckhouse the passengers had sat down. The boat's motion was becoming wilder. Only Travers stayed on his feet. He was leaning against the jamb of the companionway door and the still-freshening wind was flicking at his hair. '. . . three hundred yards . . . they're coming in backwards now . . . two hundred . . . one fifty . . .'

'That's it!' said Major Franks. 'Come on!'

'. . . one hundred . . .'

'Come on –'

'Please!' Mrs Franks put a hand to her chest. 'Stop him! He's giving me flutterings.'

'. . . eighty, sixty . . .'

Beside Mrs Franks was the Master. He looked into her eyes and began to whisper.

'. . . fifty . . . They're going to send a line . . .'

'They're sending a line, my dear!' repeated Franks.

But Mrs Franks was not listening. She was looking at the Master. 'That's better. Yes, much better . . .'

The *Hopelyn* was in place. One of the seamen raised his arm. From the bows of the *Golden Sands* they watched an ellipse of heaving-line rise from the stern and uncoil against the sky. It flopped down into the waves – twenty yards off. They saw the scuff of water as it was pulled back aboard the steamer.

The figure of the seaman stepped away from the rail, out of sight. They were dropping back; the stern of the ship was coming in closer.

The man threw the line again and it drifted out above them. The last of the coils spun out and fell, slapping down across the *Golden Sands*'s foredeck. Red and Tacker both grabbed at it. They began to haul. Others joined them. High up on the *Hopelyn*'s stern they saw where the line was attached to a loop of wire hawser which came flopping down into the water, across the seas between them and up onto the *Golden Sands*. Tacker reached for the spliced eye, but already the two ships were moving apart. The slack was slicing up through the water. Tacker leaned forward.

'Quick, man!' shouted Cameron. The line slackened for a moment, then began to tighten again. Tacker took the eye in one hand and jammed it over the mooring cleat. He jumped clear. The line pulled tight and the eye narrowed and creaked. He raised his arm.

In the last half-hour the wind had strengthened. Those in the bows could feel it harder on their faces. They could see the lines of spume streaking the water, and the dark corrugations that moved through the troughs and covered the ridges and slopes of the sea all around them. But for now they were watching the hawser. It made a shifting angle between the boats – now slack, now taut. Then they saw the sudden surge of white water at the *Hopelyn*'s stern and she began to move. The line flicked a curtain of spray upwards, and very slowly the *Golden Sands* made her first forward progress for thirty-two minutes.

Cameron started to clap.

'At last!' hissed Rose.

'Yee-eee!' cried Charlie Treneer.

Tacker looked over his shoulder and raised his thumb to the wheelhouse. Jimmy nodded.

When Cameron went aft, Sir Basil looked up at him and said: 'We're moving!'

234

They could all feel the boat going forward beneath them, and a ripple of applause spread across the deckhouse.

'About time,' said Lady Rafferty, and closed her eyes.

Tacker and Red and the others were on the foredeck. Five of them were hauling in the remaining anchor chain. It was tricky to keep a grip on the deck and haul at the same time, and now with the boat's forward motion the bows were slamming down hard into the swells. Each time they fell, the spray came over the bows and fell on them. But they didn't mind; not now that each second took them another yard from danger.

In the wheelhouse, Jimmy was still struggling with the helm. He was trying to keep the bows steady to lighten the tow. Each time they rose from a trough the warp sliced down into the crest and he lost sight of the steamer. Then they topped the wave and the hawser stretched across the trough to the ship. The glass in front of him was streaming with spray. The bows came up and the wire jerked tight against the cleat. It slackened as they cleared the crest and dropped down into the next. They fell hard to port and the wire jumped clear of the brass fairlead. Jimmy threw the wheel. He watched the warp rasp along the gunwale, then cheese-wire down into the wood. He felt the enormous weight of the two ships moving away from each other. The line strained against the cleat. Those in the bows had pulled the anchor in and Tacker was lifting it down off the bows. He propped it on the deck and held it and he too watched the cleat – watched it rip out from the foredeck, bang against the prow and shoot overboard.

The *Golden Sands* fell back. They were lifted up onto the next wave and for an instant those in the bows saw the whole scene – the steamer off to starboard, the far smudge of Kidda Head, the line of land to the north, the cliffs of Pendhu and the white water around the Main Cages. Then they dropped down a dark slope of water and rolled far over onto their beam. Tacker fell. With a heavy clanking the anchor somersaulted down the deck. It slammed into the bulwarks and toppled, catching Rose on the shin. On the wind his cry carried down through the boat.

Down in the scuppers, Tacker looked up at the weather rail high above him. He was sure they were going over. He saw the anchor tumbling towards him and he rolled to avoid it. Water bubbled up from the scuppers and he thought: 'We're going. We can't go back from this.' But the boat stopped at the very edge of her balance – then dropped back onto her keel.

On board the *Kenneth Lee* they were coming under Pendhu; in the lee of the cliffs it was suddenly calm. The sun-coloured rocks rose above them. Echoing overhead they could hear the cry of gulls and fulmars.

They watched the edge of the cliffs ahead and the sea opening out as they came round. One by one the Main Cages slid into view. They could see the seas high against Maenmor, rising fifteen, twenty feet up the rock before falling back. Each time the swells came in they smothered the smaller rocks beside it.

Jack picked out the disturbed water to the east and the *Golden Sands* beyond it and the steamer to one side. 'They're under tow,' he thought. 'They're not far off the rocks but the steamer has them in tow.' At that moment the lifeboat cleared the lee of Pendhu and the first of the swells picked her up and for a moment everything disappeared in the spray. When they came up again, Jack saw that there was no line between the two boats.

Tacker hauled himself up out of the scuppers. Rose was clutching his leg and together with Cameron they took him aft and sat him on a bench. There was confusion in the deck-house, but when they saw the men come in the passengers fell quiet.

Parson Hooper pursed his lips and looked at Rose. His hair was wet and water dripped from his chin. As he hopped up to the bench Hooper could see the darker stain swelling at his calf. The woman in a yellow hat turned her boy's head away.

'Oh Lord!' Mrs Franks put a hand to her mouth when she saw Rose.

'Now what?' said Lady Rafferty, opening her eyes.

Cameron rolled up Rose's canvas trousers. There was a gash three inches long and they tied a clean rag round it, dipped in seawater.

Rose forced a smile and said, 'Get that anchor over again!'

Bryant leaned forward. 'What is happening, Major Cameron?'

Cameron looked at him. Fear had rid Bryant of his harshness and his face was wide open, almost boyish.

'They'll be bringing the steamer in again.' Then Cameron stood and went forward.

The *Golden Sands*'s movements were chaotic again. She was being raised up to the top of the seas, rolling back as they pushed through. The steamer was dropping in towards her. Tacker and the Stephens brothers and Cameron stood at the foredeck.

'Come on, you bastard!' Charlie Treneer shouted at the steamer. They scrutinised the figures at the stern-rail. One of them would send over the heaving-line again and it would drop on the deck of the *Golden Sands*, they would haul it in and this time make sure the wire was secure on the samson post. A couple of hundred yards to the north would be enough, enough to clear the rocks, just a couple of hundred yards . . .

Then from beneath the *Hopelyn*'s stern came the boiling of the propeller. She began to push forward again – away from the *Golden Sands*.

'No!' cried Tacker. 'You can't leave us!'

One of the seamen at the rail raised his arms and pointed

over the *Golden Sands*. Tacker realised then. They all realised. They had been watching the ship for so long they had not seen how far they had drifted. But the men on the *Hopelyn* could see beyond the *Golden Sands*, over the top of the deck-house to the rocks. They were running out of water.

Tacker and Red reached for the anchor and heaved it over. It was the last thing they were able to do.

The Curate rock was twenty yards astern. Above it the swells were half-breaking and pulling back, but even in the troughs the rock was not visible. It lay eight feet below the surface, and Jimmy was steering straight at it. The sea anchor had worked. It brought their bows head to wind and he had given up trying to avoid the rock and was using all his steerage to aim straight for it.

Tacker was paying out the anchor when he realised what Jimmy was doing. 'Jim!'

Tacker secured the anchor and ran to the wheelhouse. Jimmy was leaning out of it, siting the white water astern and working the helm with his left hand.

'For Christ's sake, Jim – port the helm!'

Jimmy shoved him aside. Tacker fell, and watched his brother go into the wheelhouse and jam the door closed. From the outside they all pushed at the door, but it wouldn't give. Jimmy was leaning against it.

'What the hell are you doing, Garrett?' Red Stephens kicked at the door.

Three of them shouldered it and the hinges gave. The Stephenses held Jimmy while Tacker took the helm. But it was too late. Only two seas now separated them from the surf and the rock beneath it.

Few of the passengers were watching. Each of the countless ups and downs of their progress from Porth harbour had served to numb them a little more. A fatalism had settled among them. One or two of the children were whimpering.

Parson Hooper had his head bowed and was whispering in panic: 'Help, help, oh please God, help me . . .' Mrs Bryant and several of the others assumed he was praying and bent their heads.

The Master had his palm pressed against Mrs Franks's forehead. Her eyes were closed and he was muttering in a strange tongue and all those around him were watching him and listening.

The Dane Soren and Travers and Lee were the only ones looking astern, the only ones able to face the coming rocks. The noise of broken water now filled the deckhouse.

Anna studied the stitching of her borrowed jersey. The end of the sleeve was frayed. She was frightened now. She closed her eyes. She prayed. She hoped that when she opened her eyes she'd be somewhere else entirely, but here was the boat again, here was the noise of the surf, the frayed sleeve and the stitching – and the fear.

The stern of the *Golden Sands* dropped sharply. Anna let out a cry at the suddenness of it. Two children beside her screamed. The boat was right over the Curate. The next sea broke hard against the bows and even with the sea anchor the boat swung round and was rolled onto her side. They saw the water breaking over the stern and felt the boat being driven down and they could see over the rail into the boiling water below. They all waited for the strike.

CHAPTER 31

The low sun shone brightly on the Cages and on the creamy crests of the waves, but into the eastern sky had slid a bank of high cloud.

Tyler was watching it, driving the lifeboat as fast as he could. He was cutting the throttle as they came over the wave-tops and as they plunged down the backs. Then he opened it again and they drove through the troughs and all they could see down there was the slope of the next wave. Croyden and Jack were pulling down the jib and it was beating loudly and flapping as they gathered it in their arms. Each time they topped a wave they could see the *Golden Sands* a little closer to the Curate rock. They watched her rise and fall. They saw the broken water all around her and as she dropped into each trough she all but disappeared and they expected to see her jolt at the rock and come up sluggish and half-swamped.

The last sea before the Curate was high and steep and the *Golden Sands* slid down it, swinging round stern-first and falling. Through the deckhouse those who looked could see the white water coming up towards them, even as it drained from the rock. Travers and Lee and the Dane Soren watched the bubbling mass, watched it rising. They braced themselves. The boat heeled to the gunwales. There came a slow cry, more like a moan than a scream, which joined the roar of the surf until the two sounds merged into one. A number of people fell from the benches. From the bar came a shattering of glass.

The water was draining from around the rock and they waited to see the dark shape beneath it. They waited to see the flap of weed and the stillness of the rock but it never came. The next sea picked up the bows and drove the *Golden Sands* on over the Curate and left her in the quieter water beyond.

The tide was running fast and they were soon clear of the rock. They were now in a kind of lagoon, ringed by a broken reef. Beyond it the swells continued their march. All around them was disturbed water but in the middle the seas were long and smooth and not breaking. Three hundred yards downwind was the high double peak of Maenmor and the evening sun was slicing through the gap. They could see the spray rising high against the rocks. They were still drifting.

Jimmy Garrett knew exactly what he'd been doing. If he managed to get them over the Curate and out into deeper water again, then the trailing anchor might just find a purchase on the rock. There was no choice. The tide was quickening, and if they missed the Curate there would be nothing to stop them driving on and breaking up on Maenmor. The Curate was a single rock. Around Maenmor were smaller rocks and reefs, marked by a mass of broken water.

Jimmy pushed open the door of the wheelhouse. It fell away from the upper hinge. He leaned over the side. Seven or eight fathoms of anchor chain were out. As they cleared the Curate, it stretched away and tightened. He felt it hold for a moment, then loosen. When it stuck again, he took a mark from one of the inner rocks against the land. He watched it; the rock did not move. The wind would be working in their favour now, keeping the chain tight, and in these flatter waters there was less motion to dislodge the anchor. Jimmy looked again at his marks and they had not moved. They were fast! For the first time since they lost the engines he had a degree of control.

'Christ, Jim!' said Tacker, but he was smiling.

Charlie Treneer gave a little leap when he realised what had happened. Joe Stephens lit a cigarette and Red Stephens muttered, 'Bloody Garretts . . .'

Cameron was exhilarated by the risk, and looked at Jimmy and shook his head in admiration. 'Utter madness!'

Jimmy paid no attention to any of them. He checked the angle of chain. 'Another few fathoms, Tack!'

Tacker eased out a further length and the boat settled back away from the rock. Her bucking calmed. He opened the engine hatch and dropped into the darkness below. He stepped off the bottom of the ladder. The water was ankle-deep. He had expected more. But with no power for the pump, there was nothing he could do about it.

Among the passengers it took some time to realise that they were still.

Parson Hooper looked around him. 'Are we moving?'

Lawrence Rose shook his head; he tried to move his leg. It was propped up on the bench, and he winced. 'That's the anchor holding us. Solid ground.'

'Ah!' Hooper put his hands on his knees. 'We've stopped!'

'Really stopped?' Mrs Hooper looked up at him.

'I think so.'

'What now?'

'Well . . .' said Hooper.

Everyone was quiet. The movement and the noise at the Curate had ceased. To be free of it now, in still waters, felt like victory. They loosened the grip they had held on the benches, on each other, and many were struck by a profound tiredness.

But the horizon was still a ring of surf. It reached the boat with its river-roar. Travers stood and went astern and watched it.

'The lifeboat!' he called out. 'I can see the lifeboat!'

One or two turned to watch. Others heard him but could not bring themselves to look out over the water. The woman in a yellow hat pulled her son to her: 'The lifeboat's coming, Edgar. The lifeboat.' Rocking him in her arms, she started quietly to hum.

The *Kenneth Lee* was battling with the seas, trying to find the best route through the rocks. Tyler knew every inch of the waters around the Main Cages from potting, but he had never been among them in such a swell nor at mid-tide – even on exercise. He cut in about thirty yards up-wind of Maenmor. The waters were confused and for some time he steered a hesitant and erratic course through them. Once inside he gave her full speed and aimed directly for the *Golden Sands*.

Coming up alongside, he stood off a few yards and shouted across. 'You holding?'

Jimmy was leaning casually on the rail. 'For now.'

'How many you got?'

'Forty-two.'

The wind had pushed the two boats apart. Tyler dropped the lifeboat back, then came back alongside. 'We can take thirty plus. I'll ferry them up to the tramp.'

He came in close and put Edwin Stephens and his nephew Dougie Tyler aboard. They went back into the deckhouse. To the passengers their sudden presence was a shock. They looked larger than life, alien, with their lank hair and spray-soaked faces and their oilskins and fat kapok lifejackets. Charlie Treneer and the Stephenses came back too to help marshal the passengers.

Edwin told the women and children to come forward. Most

of the children followed passively. The family from Bristol made their way forward. The boy was still clutching his model boat.

The woman in a yellow hat knelt down in front of her son. She was reaching into her basket. 'Hurry!' Charlie told her. She pulled out a jersey and began rucking it up over her son's head. 'He's going to get cold.' She then took out a box from the bag and unpacked an orange. 'Here, darling –'

Charlie leaned over and scooped up the boy.

'Give him to me!' she clawed at Charlie but he took her boy outside. 'Give him!' she cried out as he was handed across the gap. But she followed.

With the last child aboard, Edwin Stephens stood by the awning and said: 'Now, everyone else please, in a queue – women first!'

The Welsh couple, who had been sitting hand in hand, both stood up. He kissed her as she went forward.

Mrs Bryant felt faint. 'Nothing . . . it's nothing.'

Lady Rafferty helped her to her feet. Joe Stephens took her right arm.

Mrs Franks and the other women around her reluctantly left the Master and made their way out.

Lawrence Rose was carried forward, and then the men formed a queue. Birkin was propped up between the others. He shuffled forward with them. 'We home yet?'

'Yes,' said Travers.

The lifeboat was filling. In good conditions there was room for forty-five, but when he had counted thirty or so on board Tyler said, 'You two – then we'll come back for the rest.'

Parson Hooper and Major Franks were the last to step across. Jack freed the line that had been holding in the bow. Tyler opened the throttle and they were off, rising over the first swells and heading eastwards towards the *Hopelyn*.

*   *   *

As the boat filled, Anna had been pushed back further along the side deck. Now they were moving she made her way forward. People were standing shoulder to shoulder but she could see Jack at his post in the bows. He smiled at her and winked and watched as she pushed her way through – in her too-big 'Grace' jersey, her hair without its headscarf and her face flushed and freckled from the day's sun.

'Excuse me . . . excuse me . . .'

'Stay still, woman!' said Lady Rafferty.

Anna ignored her. She squeezed past Mrs Bryant who looked very white. Double was saying to her, 'All right, Missus, we're all right now.' The boy with the model boat had been forced to leave it on the *Golden Sands* and was sobbing. Beside him was the woman in a yellow hat, and her cheeks were running with tears. Edgar leaned against her, picking his nose. He gazed up at Anna as she passed.

When Anna reached Jack, she whispered: 'Oh, thank God! It was so terrible, the rocks, the noise –'

He reached down and took her hand. 'You're safe now.'

'It just came closer and closer, to swallow us like a wolf . . .'

The lifeboat pitched up over the swells. Each time the bows dropped, the spray washed over the passengers and they turned away. Anna held the straps of Jack's lifejacket for balance. To feel now the boat's speed beneath her brought out all the half-suppressed fear and she pressed her head to the damp canvas of his lifejacket and started sobbing. He put his arm over her shoulder. But they were already in under the lee of the *Hopelyn*. Jack climbed up on the foredeck and caught their line. The steamer's topsides were lowest just abaft the bridge and they had let down a ladder. It took some time to get all the passengers aboard. Jack was still on the foredeck and Anna stayed with him for as long as she could. She stood back and let the others go ahead of her. Then Jack leaned down and said, 'Quick!' And he squeezed her shoulder and she turned and saw him with the line in one hand and his face above the lifejacket and he was shouting up to the seamen at the rail. She hurried down the deck and up the ladder. She did not look back.

CHAPTER 32

〜◈〜

As the *Kenneth Lee* left the *Golden Sands* and headed towards the steamer, Joe Stephens had ducked out of the wind and lit a cigarette. He offered one to Dougie Tyler and they leaned on the gunwale and watched the lifeboat go. There were eight now left on board the *Golden Sands* – Dougie and Red, Joe and Charlie and the Garretts, Major Cameron and Edwin Stephens.

It had grown cooler. The sun had slipped behind the cloud and the sea had lost its pale-blue warmth. The wind came dashing across the water. The waves looked more dangerous without the sun.

Joe and Dougie were watching the lifeboat push out past the Curate. She moved into steeper seas and dropped into a trough. When she came out again the *Hopelyn* looked close.

Dougie said, 'They're clear now.'

'Yes.'

Dougie flicked away his cigarette and turned. Jimmy Garrett was back in the wheelhouse. His bald head was half-visible through the glass and he was looking out over the bows as if it were a normal afternoon. Dougie wondered whether he intended trying to save his boat. It was possible the *Kenneth Lee* could put a line aboard and take them in tow, now that the passengers were off. But it was doubtful they had the power – perhaps they could pull them downwind, but in amongst these rocks it would not be easy, and their priority was saving life and not property.

As Dougie watched him, Jimmy's head disappeared. His rock-like frame came bursting out of the wheelhouse door. He half-ran, half-limped. Only then did Dougie see the chain lying loose on the foredeck. The seas had worked the anchor loose. They were drifting again.

Jimmy picked up the chain and pulled. Dougie and Tacker converged on the chain and pulled too. The flukes of the anchor were dragging up the rock and it came too easily. They let the chain go and it slackened, but when they threw a turn round the post it did not hold. They pulled and let it drop but the anchor was now clear of the rock. Below them the ground was dropping away to thirty fathoms.

There was nothing now, nothing left. Down towards Maenmor the bed rose again but to a series of smaller rocks and reefs and there the water was boiling and surging with the swell and tide and there was no shelter.

The chain came flopping over the bows and its heavy links clanged on the deck. Then came the anchor itself, thudding against the side. When he heard it, Jimmy cried out, a deep animal sound that started in his chest and rose in pitch to a wail, then stopped abruptly. He let the chain go and hauled himself back to the wheelhouse. Tacker stepped forward to secure the chain.

They were already fifty yards below the Curate. Without the check of the anchor the boat felt freer as she slid downwind. She was now heading for Maenmor at a speed of nearly two knots.

*   *   *

248

The lifeboat was coming back. Tyler saw at once that the *Golden Sands* had broken away again and he took the direct route, close in to the Curate where the ebb tide was rushing over the rock. He came alongside the *Golden Sands*. Jack leaned forward and tried to pass a rope to Dougie but it was not easy with the seas as they were and the *Golden Sands*'s movements so erratic.

Tyler told him to leave the rope and he manoeuvred the lifeboat in, backed off, then dropped in again. Cameron stood on the gunwale. The two boats were together for an instant and he jumped. Jack and Croyden hauled him in. Tyler tried again. But the seas caught the *Golden Sands* and pushed her away.

They were drifting clear of the Curate's lee now. The seas were growing. Their tops were starting to break again. The anchor's weight was holding the boat into the wind as they drifted, but the pitch was increasing. They were shipping a good deal of water.

Tyler came in again and they managed to pull Charlie Treneer aboard but all the time the seas were rising. The first rocks around Maenmor were two hundred yards away and as they drew closer the tide began to do odd things with the water. In places it came welling up beside the *Golden Sands* in smooth bubble-like patches. Or funnelled through an unseen channel. Or rose in crests that broke over the sides.

It was just a knock – a jolt on the starboard quarter – and it spun the *Golden Sands* a little and then they were free. From the lifeboat, Tyler saw it and he was able to manoeuvre the lifeboat around the rock and come back in.

Then the *Golden Sands* struck again – harder this time. Dougie Tyler was thrown forward. He fell into the scuppers. His uncle brought the lifeboat in again and Red Stephens jumped across. Maenmor was now fifty yards astern. With the weight of water in her, the *Golden Sands*'s drift had slowed.

They pulled Joe Stephens aboard. Dougie went to get

Tacker but he was in the wheelhouse. Edwin told him, 'You go – I'll get they two!'

Dougie stepped onto the gunwale, waited for the lifeboat and jumped across. Tyler dropped the boat back again and they all watched the *Golden Sands*, waiting for Edwin to reappear with the Garretts. The sun fell through the cloud and they shielded their eyes and squinted. The shape of Maenmor rose in silhouette and the *Golden Sands* had gone into its shadow. She was three, four seas off the rock and in the troughs they could see only her funnel and the top of the deckhouse.

Rising on a high crest, they saw Edwin going towards the wheelhouse and Tacker stepping out, over the broken door. He shouted something to Edwin but then the back of the next wave rose between the two boats. The sun shone green through its rounded crest and all those on the lifeboat waited for the next to come and when it did they looked down on the *Golden Sands*. She was upside down.

The water was filling with debris. From the lifeboat they could see boards and boxes bouncing in the surf. Tyler brought her in as close as he dared.

'Astern!'

It was Double who spotted a figure just off the wreck's stern. The others saw him too. It was Jimmy. His bald head was bobbing in the water. He was being washed away from the boat.

Tyler pushed the lifeboat in and Jack leaned over the bows with a boathook.

'Five feet!' he shouted back to the helm.

Jimmy was being swept down by the tide. He was now well astern of his boat. Behind him was the gap between the two peaks of Maenmor and the sun was flooding through it, picking out the milky tops of the seas as they broke and poured into it.

Jack leaned out over the foredeck. He was still short of Jimmy but he swung the boathook forward. Jimmy was struggling in the water. He could not reach the hook. The tide was taking him away and Tyler dropped back. He came in again, close in under the rock. Jimmy was in the sun now and they got to about three yards from him and Jack extended the hook again. This time it fell within his grasp. It struck the water by his shoulder. But he made no move towards it.

'Take it!' shouted Jack.

The water around him was white and foamy.

'Take it!' repeated Jack.

Jimmy stared up at those on the lifeboat; he seemed to be scowling. The tide was dragging him towards the gap. He was caught by a sea and he rose with it as it broke and the spray engulfed him. Tyler slammed the lifeboat into reverse. They watched the gap. The wave was squeezing between the rocks and there was no sign of Jimmy. Briefly he resurfaced behind the crest. They could see his head and one arm raised against the rock and the following wave was breaking and the great bulk of the water was driving through the gap, roaring and echoing in the tunnel, and it filled the tunnel and he was gone.

Tyler brought the boat back up towards the *Golden Sands*. She was being shunted up against the rock with each wave, dropping back and dragging down again with a long scraping sound. A crack had opened up along her port bow and each time she rolled down the rock, it grew. She was starting to break up.

There was no sign of Edwin, but they spotted Tacker. He was in the water astern, struggling to keep a grip on the boat's rudder. The seas were rolling in over the upturned hull but Tacker was sheltered at the stern, managing to hang on.

Tyler nudged the bows up towards him. Jack moved into position to grab him but a larger wave came and threw the lifeboat out of position. When the wave pulled back again, Tacker was not there.

They spotted him some yards off. He managed to reach

the rudder again. Tyler came in. The bows of the lifeboat rode on up over the *Golden Sands*'s hull and Jack reached out with the boathook. Tacker lunged at it. He caught it – but he could not hang on. The lifeboat rolled off the *Golden Sands* and Tyler reversed out.

On board the lifeboat Tyler looked to Croyden and Croyden nodded. There was never really a question whether they would go in again. The stricken ship was lower down the rock and the seas were swamping her. He drove up over the hull to within inches of Tacker. This time he managed to grab at the life-lines and three pairs of hands caught his shoulders and arms. They heard the next wave breaking behind them and knew that Tyler would be pulling them out again. They hung on to Tacker and hauled him in over the side.

But Tyler did not reverse the lifeboat. The next wave broke and caught the stern and Tyler was unable to back off. The lifeboat dropped into the trough, onto her beam-end. The coming sea rolled her over, up against the *Golden Sands* and over the top. When she dropped back she fell deck-first into the rock. And then the next sea came in and turned to foam on the rock and the boats were driven up again, and that sea dropped back and the next rose and broke and shunted the two boats up against each other and against the rock and then the next sea broke behind that one, building slowly and breaking and behind it already was the next wave rising, and the next . . .

CHAPTER 33

'We're simply trying to establish cause, Mr Tyler.'
'– was just that the last time we went in, sir, that last time – we couldn't get off like we had before, he'd been putting us in and pulling us out of there and he –'

'Who, Mr Tyler?'

'Cox.'

'Coxswain Tyler – your uncle?'

'Yes, sir – been putting us in and bringing us out again like the sea was smooth as anything, sir. He could work that boat like his own feet even in they seas, even when we was just yards from the rock, I never seen nothing like it. I was never worried for an instant not until we was upside-down and then, well, was too late to worry then –'

'Could you explain to the inquest what occurred in the moments immediately preceding the capsize?'

'What?'

'Before you went over.'

'Well, he brought us in again right on top of the hull and

253

we managed to get Tacker aboard but you could hear the two boats against each other and the seas breaking all around and we was right on top of her but our stern was still in the water and there was still power, I suppose. There was one sea coming, much bigger'n the rest and we could see him with a nasty great top and all a' we looking in the water for Edwin, sir, and there was still no sign. Someone said they could see him aft of the *Sands* – and I was thinking we'll go back now, before that 'un comes in and then we'll come in again and if Edwin was in the water that was better for we to pick him up, better for him too, clear of the rock and I was thinking he'll pull us back out now and bring us in again, he'll pull us back now but that big sea was already breaking and he was a big 'un and we was still in there . . .'

'Was there no indication at the time why Coxswain Tyler was unable to reverse out of danger?'

'No, sir.'

'And when the boat went over, she did not manage to right herself, Mr Tyler?'

'No.'

'Even though she was designed to do so?'

'That's right, sir, she was a self-righter. But to tell 'ee the truth we never liked they self-righters – easier they come up, easier they go over in the first place. That's what we always said.'

'Did you see any other survivors?'

'Wasn't easy in that sea. I was on the rock but I couldn't get no higher and I was watching each of the swells, see if I be washed off again. Below me was the wrecks, both bottom-up and knocking against each other and there was all manner a' stuff in the water . . . I did see one other, in a lifejacket, couldn't see who it was – and he got up on the rock along from me and he was struggling to keep there and one big sea comes in and covers him but he's still there when it's gone and I call out to him and he waves up at me. Still couldn't see who it was – maybe it was Croy or Jack from the bows but then the next big sea comes in and he's gone. The boats was still bottom-up and they was mostly trapped inside, I suppose. She didn't start to break up for a good while –'

'How long, Mr Tyler?'

'Hard to say, really, but once they started to go they went quick. Soon there was everything in the surf and I saw bodies among it all but I couldn't count them and I couldn't see who each was, they was all mixed up and the tide was taking them off but I shouted, I was shouting, sir, and I never saw one move. Not one of they bodies moved the whole time, except for being moved by the seas, couldn't move on their own even though I was shouting. I was shouting and shouting, sir . . .'

The morning after the accident a muddy haze covered the town. The wind had eased but there was still a long swell that broke high and white round the cliffs of Pendhu. At the lifeboat station, the RNLI flag flew at half-mast. Many in the town drifted up there. They found themselves going there without even thinking why. It just seemed the natural place to be, closest to what was gone. They formed small groups above the slipway, on the bank beside it and at the entrance to the empty shed. It was as if they were waiting for something, for news. But there was no news. Twelve bodies had been recovered the previous evening. They laid them out on the quay. The pilchard driver *Guide Me* had gone out to the rocks that evening and the wind had eased and they picked up young Dougie Tyler, shivering and bloody but alive. The boat came in through the Gaps and by that time everyone knew. They had gathered to stand two or three deep on the Town Quay and the East Quay and along the front between them. They stood in silence, looking down on the deck of the *Guide Me* and the bodies laid out like fish upon it. The body of Jimmy Garrett was never found.

Many of those who came to the station the next day brought flowers and left them inside the open doors. They then went out to stand on the bank. Major Franks was inside with the Secretary and some of the crew who had not been available the day before. Those men did not say much but stood together in one corner of the shed while Major Franks and the Secretary sat at a table registering volunteers for an auxiliary crew. A relief lifeboat was already on its way from South Wales.

In the evening, the salvage crew found the stern section of the *Kenneth Lee*. They brought it into the harbour and placed it on the East Quay and all could see the short length of chain locked tight around the propeller. The chain was found to be the same gauge as that attached to the anchor of the *Golden Sands*.

The jury of the inquest returned a verdict of death from drowning by misadventure.

A month later, the Board of Trade inquiry concluded that the accident occurred 'from a tragic set of circumstances, any one of which was unlikely to have resulted in disaster but which combined in rapid and terrible succession to make it unavoidable'.

No one was satisfied with this conclusion. Not the families of those lost, nor the Lifeboat Committee, nor the coastguard. Nor the reporters who could find no one to blame and only managed to talk to one man willing to give a statement after the hearing. 'Just a ghastly, ghastly calamity,' explained Mr Bryant. 'But the inquiry was well briefed. All safety procedures had been observed and I suppose if there are lessons to be learned we should simply remember that on this earth of ours it is the elements that hold sway in the end . . .'

Mr Bryant went back to Birmingham immediately afterwards. He never returned to Polmayne.

The funerals all took place during the first week. On 19 September a memorial service was held at St Cuby's church.

For the third day in a row it was raining. A strong south-westerly was driving showers in across the bay. The water shortages were forgotten. Above the churchyard the wind tugged at the beech-tops and against a grey and shifting sky flowed streams of still-green leaves.

Inside the church, it was packed. Those who could not get in stood in hats and raincoats on the verges above the creek. They lined the path that led down from the lych-gate. They stood with their backs to the shiny-leaved camellias, beneath the dripping myrtle trees and magnolias. They had come from as far afield as Falmouth and Fowey and St Ives. They took off their hats in the rain and held them as the families passed.

The first four rows of the church had white name-cards spaced along them. Major Franks escorted the Lord Lieuten-ant to the front pew. Behind him were the District and Div-isional Inspectors of Lifeboats, the Chief Inspector and District Officers of Coastguards, the Secretary and Officers of the Polmayne Lifeboat Committee and two police constables. Captain Maddocks from Porth was there in his old naval uniform and beside him sat Captain Williams. Behind them were members of the launch crew and the LSA Company and their families and behind them fifteen rows reserved for the bereaved.

Toper Walsh had arrived long before the service. For two hours he had been sitting alone beneath the window of St Anthony and St Francis. The multi-coloured light fell on his bare head and on his shoulders. Since the accident and the loss of his only son, Double, Toper had hardly left his house.

In a dark suit, and still limping, Lawrence Rose came in with Mrs Cameron. She had taken the train down from New-bury. Despite her late husband's decade of Petrel racing, it was only the second time she had been to Polmayne.

The Tylers arrived at the same time as the Stephenses. A grim-faced silence hung between them. Many thought that the weight of shared grief would bring the two families together but the only ones who could have initiated a reconciliation were those who had died at sea.

Coxswain Tyler's widow had a place reserved in the front pews and she was taken up the aisle on the arm of the only survivor, her nephew Dougie Tyler.

Mrs Cuffe arrived on her own, in the best coat she had had dyed black for Whaler's funeral in July. She was joined by Annie Treneer and Frank and Agnes Treneer and Croyden's widow Maggie and other members of the family.

Tommy Treneer came last. He was helped down the steps by a sidesman. Under his arm was his old Coxswain's cap, and his three RNLI service medals hung from his jacket. At the font he shook off the assistance of the sidesman and meandered down the aisle. Everyone watched his progress. Two or three times he stopped and put a hand on a pew-end. He looked unsure where he was. In the end Major Franks stood and led him to his seat.

It was ten past eleven when the Bishop of Truro and Parson Hooper and the Methodist ministers came out of the vestry and took their places on the chancel steps. The congregation rustled to its feet. The Bishop held up his arms: '*I am the Resurrection and the Light.*'

After the first hymn, Major Franks read Psalm 139: '... *If I take the wings of the morning, and dwell in the uttermost parts of the sea; Even there shall thy hand lead me, and thy right hand shall hold me* ...'

Parson Hooper climbed slowly into the pulpit. He trembled as he began his address. He described the debt that he and many others felt towards those who had died: 'I for one had never understood, never really understood, the supreme Christian duty of lifeboatmen. It is gallantry beyond words – to go out into the merciless sea when all others are heading for home, to rescue from the jaws of death men and women who are often complete strangers.'

He bent his head and his hands gripped the rim of the pulpit. Some in the congregation thought he had finished and there was a creaking of pews as they shifted in their seats. But he looked up again. The ones sitting beneath him could see the tears in his eyes.

'I watched those men ... I watched them as they brought us aboard the ship. I watched their faces as they escorted us from one boat to the other. I watched them as they went back into the maelstrom to collect the others – and I honestly believe that had they known what was to befall them they would still have gone. They would not have hesitated for an instant. Let us always remember their sacrifice. We must never forget.'

The service ended with 'Eternal Father, Strong to Save'. Outside the church, the rain had eased. Mr Evans the schoolmaster had been standing on the steps beneath the tower conducting those unable to get in.

> *Who bidd'st the mighty ocean deep*
> *Its own appointed hour keep ...*

As the verses progressed, those who had been sheltering from the showers came forward and sang together and their rising voices joined with those inside the church to ring out across the river.

> *From rock and tempest, fire and foe,*
> *Protect them wheresoe'er they go ...*

The clouds thinned and a burst of vagrant sun swept over the church roof, across the water and up along the back of Pendhu Point and the just-ploughed fields of Ivor Dawkins.

> *And ever let there rise to thee*
> *Glad hymns of praise from land and sea.*

To one side stood Anna Abraham. She was alone. Her fair hair was spilling from a dark grey headscarf. Two days after the memorial service she gave up the lease of Ferryman's Cottage, took Whaler's repainted sea chest and left Polmayne for good.

In the weeks following the accident Parson Hooper proved himself again to be sound and resourceful. He visited the bereaved. He ensured that they were aware of the various funds available for them. He put the correct gloss on the version of events presented to reporters: 'No, at no time was there any panic on the *Golden Sands*. Everyone behaved with the utmost decorum . . .' It was he who arranged the memorial service, who with Major Franks launched the appeal, and who commissioned, with diocesan funds, two memorial crosses from Pascoe & Sons – one for the churchyard and one to be placed on the cliff above Hemlock Cove, overlooking the Main Cages. When the *Constantine* came in one evening and anchored in the bay, it was Hooper who escorted Captain Henriksen and his crew up to the cliff, who said a short prayer before the Captain knelt and laid the wreath of kaffir lilies and nerines that his wife and his men had made for the victims.

The days grew shorter. The last of the summer visitors left and around Armistice Day the pilchard fleet headed as usual up to Plymouth. The town withdrew into itself. The wound of the accident began to close up. Some people still came to the town out of curiosity, others to express their sympathy. But at the first mention of the *Kenneth Lee*, they were met with silence.

Parson Hooper found his days becoming emptier. He took his services and his own congregation after the accident was closer, more unified. But in the town his offers of help and support were accepted less and less often. On 20 November he was admitted to hospital with a case of 'nervous exhaustion'. After a week, he was sent to a nursing home in Newquay. Mrs Hooper took lodgings to be near him. Soon afterwards a removal van arrived at Polmayne's rectory and by Christmas a Reverend Perkins had arrived to replace him. It was he who was contacted by Pascoe & Sons to collect Hooper's last Tablet, which had been commissioned on 19 November. Perkins recognised the quotation from Isaiah:

And I will lay it waste; it shall not be pruned, nor digged;
but there shall come up briers and thorns;
I will also command the clouds that they rain no rain upon it.

All through that autumn the Golden Sands Hotel remained closed. In December the board on the front of the building was taken down. By May of the following year a new sign, smaller, had been erected at the gate: Pendhu Lodge Hotel.

In late October, Ralph Cameron's Petrel *Harmony* was towed a mile south of Pendhu Point and scuttled.

One afternoon in January 1937, Joseph Johns arrived back in Polmayne. In Australia he had heard of the loss of the lifeboat, and despite the success he was having there he was overcome by nostalgia for Cornwall. It was Joseph – with the help of his grandfather Boy – who bought the *Maria V*. The solicitors had some difficulty tracing Jack Sweeney's family, but when they did they were instructed to donate any proceeds from the sale of the boat to the lifeboat fund. By March 1937 the *Maria V* was at sea again, long-lining down at the Ray Pits, and Harry Hammels was crewing, laying out his cards to find out where the fish were.

In June, though, Hammels suddenly left Polmayne. He disappeared. Someone said he had joined a ship in Falmouth, headed for the Far East, another that he signed up as crew on a yacht in the Mediterranean.

The summer of 1937 was as busy as ever in Polmayne. The Pendhu Lodge Hotel was full. Tents filled Dalvin's field and in August Ivor Dawkins put aside another for visitors' use. Five new villas had been completed above the church. Another fourteen dwellings were completed and occupied at the Crates. At Pennance the water had risen high up the dam wall. At the head of the reservoir, in a few inches of clear water, could be seen the sodden ferns and the slate roof of St Pinnock's holy well. Most of the town now had access to mains water. Installation of the sewerage was also completed.

In the middle of June, Petrel racing began. The points series was raced for the Cameron Cup.

A new parking scheme had been set up on the Town Quay. White lines were painted on the cobbles right up to the end of Parliament Bench. When Toper Walsh saw a woman take her young son behind their car and undo his trousers, he shouted: 'And I'll come and piss in your bloody living room!'

On 1 September, up at the Crates, Tommy Treneer died. No one but Annie Treneer had seen him for months, and when they heard he had died many who did not know him that well were surprised because they thought he had been dead for years. It was almost exactly a year after the loss of the *Kenneth Lee.* A large crowd turned out for his funeral. His coffin was led to the chapel wrapped in the RNLI flag and topped by his old sou'wester.

'Polmayne'll never be the same without Tom,' said Toper.

'Never,' agreed Red Treneer.

'Eeee,' said Boy Johns.

EPILOGUE

~~~

O n a warm day in July 1972, a Morris Traveller drove
down into Polmayne. It passed the Crates and the
rectory, and came round on the new road above Pritchard's
Beach. By the Antalya Hotel was a large 'P' sign with an
arrow pointing to the space once occupied by the cottages of
Cooper's Yard. The half-timbered car came to a halt beneath
a creeper-hung cliff and an elderly woman climbed out.
Checking her reflection in the car window, she tied on a
pale-blue headscarf and headed out to the front.

It was the first time in thirty-six years that Anna had been
back. During that time she had remained living in the same
house in Hampstead. In 1942 she was officially widowed when
Maurice was killed in North Africa. After the war she let out
the basement to a Jewish composer from Budapest; the top
floor she converted for her sister Maria. She never remarried.
Every couple of years she exhibited her paintings in a gallery
in Cork Street. She spent two months each summer with
Maria in a cottage in Salcombe, and there she did something

that surprised even her: she learned to sail. She bought a small open boat named *Corinthia* and sometimes on calm days she sailed out past the bar and looked west into Cornwall. But in all those years she never wanted to go back.

A mild southerly was blowing in off Polmayne Bay. The Petrels were racing. On the Town Quay she watched a crowd of people queuing up to board a pleasure boat: *Polmayne Belle – Afternoon Cruise to Porth – Bar and Refreshments – Tea ashore.*

Beyond the quays she found the alley leading to Bethesda. Mrs Cuffe's rooms had long been converted into separate flats, each one with its own stable door. Ceramic name-plates were fixed above them: *Pendhu View*, *Bo'sun's Cottage*, *Forbes's Loft*. Above the steps to Jack's old rooms was one which read *Harbour View*.

That afternoon she walked up around Penpraze's yard to Ferryman's. Through the trees she heard the sound of shouting. She went no closer. She watched a man standing bare-chested in the shallows. Two children were sitting in a dinghy, splashing him with the paddles. At the slate-topped table was a woman in a floppy, wide-brimmed hat.

She took the ferry across the Glaze River and walked up through Priory Creek. As she climbed over the top, the Main Cages came into view one by one – the Curate, Maenmor and all its satellites. There, above Hemlock Cove she found the granite cross and the thirteen names beneath the inscription:

> *He sent from above. He took me.*
> *He drew me out of many waters.*
> (2 Sam. XXII 17)